The 1
A Tim and Mary Finn
Mystery
By Jeffrey Mechling

The Novel is a book fiction. The author has no affiliation with any state or Federal law Agencies or Federal Agencies

A ny names, characters, business, evets or localities' are similarly coincidental.

The Decoys

Published by the Good as Gone LLC
Los Angeles and Middleburg
April 1, 2020
Book Editing by
Bronywn Hem us

For Kathleen

Chapter 1

"WOULD YOU LIKE ME BETTER as a blonde?" The question by Mary Ann, Tim Hall's wife, caught Tim completely off guard. The two were returning from their weekly Saturday shopping trip and Tim was enjoying the drive home. It was a beautiful late November day with temperatures in the mid-sixties.

"Ah, sure, I guess so, I mean, I guess I would. Why? Are you thinking about dying your hair, Mary Ann?" Tim was being careful. In his experience, women would often ask one question while meaning something entirely different.

"Well, I was just thinking of making a change. Jane and I were discussing it over lunch the other day."

Special Agent Jane Dutton was one of Mary Ann's new friends at the Washington, DC-Northern Virginia regional FBI office. Mary Ann, or Special Agent Mary Ann Wilson-Hall as she was now officially known, had recently become an FBI-CIA liaison officer based at the CIA's headquarters. Mary Ann's new job required her to attend numerous meetings in downtown Washington, DC, where she'd made new friends that Tim did not know. This new development did not particularly bother Tim; on the contrary, he was happy that his wife was enjoying her new job and friends. Tim was just having a difficult time keeping track of all of these new people, and Jane Dutton was one of them. Mary Ann spoke of Jane constantly, yet Tim had never met her.

"Is Jane a blonde?" Tim decided that would be a safe question to ask.

"Yes, but she is not a natural blonde. She has those dark roots, which I think are very chic."

"Chic" was a word that Tim did not believe he had ever heard his wife say. The old Mary Ann, the one he'd met while she was working undercover, would have never used the word "chic."

"And how old is your friend Jane?"

"Oh, somewhere between thirty-five and fifty years old," Mary Ann said with a laugh as she grabbed Tim's hand and kissed it. "I don't know if I want to go through with it. I mean, it's a whole process and you have to keep doing it over and over because, after all, you don't want your roots to get too dark." She placed her head on Tim's shoulder.

Tim was somewhat relieved to hear Mary Ann say that she was not seriously considering going blonde, although he suddenly found that the prospect of Mary Ann changing hair color was beginning to turn him on. Tim's right hand moved off of the steering wheel and began to move across Mary Ann's silk blouse until it found her right breast.

"Mr. Hall," Mary Ann whispered in Tim's ear, "what do you exactly think you are doing?" She moved her hand between Tim's thighs.

"You know," Tim began, "a guy could have an accident behaving like this." But Tim really did not want Mary Ann to stop what she was doing.

"Well you certainly know how to ruin a moment, Agent Hall," Mary Ann teased as she pulled her hand away. "Besides," she continued, "we need to stop at the drug store."

The drug store that Tim and Mary Ann Hall used was located in the last strip mall at Leesburg's edge. The store sat on top of a small hill close to a number of big box stores. The place was a real pain in the ass to reach and Tim complained about the "two hard right-hand turns" he was required to make. Tim found a parking spot close by the door and both he and Mary proceeded to enter the store together. They walked toward the pharmacy area and Tim thought how the store seemed strangely quiet, especially for a Saturday morning.

"Tim, I don't like this one bit," Mary Ann said and Tim noticed that she had unholstered her Glock pistol and now held it against her thigh.

"You two, put your hands up and walk toward me," said a young white male. The young man was at the other end of

THE DECOYS

the building, about ninety feet away, Tim figured. They were still within range of the shotgun. Tim knew that Mary Ann had absolutely no intention of complying with the young man's request.

"FBI! Drop your weapon." Tim had never heard Mary Ann's voice sound so authoritative. Tim certainly would have dropped his weapon if he were the young man but, instead, the young man looked confused and tentative, almost as if he was waiting for something to happen. Next, the young man seemed to notice that Mary Ann had a gun, so he turned his shotgun directly at her—the last living act he committed.

Pop, pop, pop. Three pops, each followed by an ejected shell casing that made a tinkling sound as it reached the floor. Each bullet hit the young man square in the chest as both his arms flew back. The shotgun left the young man's hands and hit the floor.

Instinctively, Mary Ann began to turn left and then right to see if the area was clear.

"Tim? Would you check and see if the pharmacy is clear?"

By now, Tim Hall had unholstered his Glock 22 9mm pistol and begun to walk to the pharmacy counter. He carefully checked each aisle to make sure no one else was hiding in the store. Tim had no formal training in proper searching techniques and was a little surprised that Mary Ann had trusted him with such a task, but he supposed she had no choice. Tim could hear her speaking to someone; most likely someone she'd called on the FBI hotline.

As Tim arrived at the pharmacy counter, he heard voices and found three women huddled together on the floor. To their right was another woman on her stomach. She wore a white coat that was covered in blood from what appeared to be a gunshot wound in her back. The three women on the floor looked up at Tim but did not say a word. Tim sensed that there was another gunman in the room. He raised his Glock 9mm, held it with both hands, and pointed it in the general direction of the selves, where all of the medicine was stored.

"United States deputy marshal! Show yourself," Tim yelled. Although he was not sure if that was the correct command, he did not have to wait long to find out. Another skinny white male appeared holding a pistol against the head of a young woman.

"Dude, place your weapon down on the counter or else I will blow this fucking lady's head off," the skinny man said.

Tim's first inclination was to just shoot the man. After all, that had worked at the safe house, but this was a different situation. Tim was in a public place and he was now presenting himself as a deputy United States marshal, so he decided to try and act like one.

"That's not going to happen," Tim said, "but you can certainly leave," he continued. "I won't try to stop you."

Perhaps offering a suspect their freedom was not US marshal protocol, but Tim just wanted this guy to let the hostage go and leave. After that, the real cops could look for the guy. Tim really did not expect the gunman to take him up on his offer so he was surprised when the skinny man pushed the hostage toward him and started walking back toward the exit. As Tim was deciding whether or not to shoot the man when he heard Mary Ann once again shout, "FBI! Drop your weapon."

Two shots were exchanged. The one fired from the gunman's weapon was muffled while Mary Ann's made a lot more noise. Tim saw the gunman fall by the emergency exit and jumped over the counter.

"Are we clear in there?" Tim heard Mary Ann ask from the other room.

Tim turned around and saw that all four girls were now gone, leaving only the woman with the gunshot wound.

"Mary Ann, are you OK?" Tim asked.

"Yes, I'm fine," Mary Ann said as she entered the room.

Tim walked over to examine Mary Ann just to be sure that she was telling him the truth.

"What happened to the shot that guy fired at you?"

"It hit somewhere to my right. Did you notice that he had a silencer on that weapon? That was strange. You usually do not bring a silencer to a robbery unless you intend on shooting someone that—"

"That you don't want anyone to hear," Tim said, finishing Mary Ann's sentence.

"Well, this guy is dead, Tim," Mary Ann said as she examined the second gunman. Looks like I got him right below his nose."

"This one is still breathing," Tim said as he knelt down next to the woman in the white coat.

"Help should be here about now. I called this in over five minutes ago and—"

"Sherriff's department!" someone yelled from the front of the store. "Place any weapons down and place your hands behind your head!"

"Now this is the dangerous part," Tim said as he placed his Glock down and laced his fingers behind his head.

"Yeah, tell me about it," Mary Ann replied as she did the same. "Now comes the fun part."

Chapter 2

Tim leaned against his Mercedes 560, which was in the middle of a sea of flashing blue and red lights. There were at least twenty-five police vehicles of different sizes and types representing Loudoun County, the town of Leesburg, the Virginia State Police, and the Federal Bureau of Investigation. There were also four medic units, two fire engines, and some Loudoun County fire department officials. A medevac helicopter had landed across Route 15 in order to transport the wounded pharmacist to one of the local shock-trauma centers. Her condition appeared to be grave.

Mary Ann had notified the FBI that she'd been involved in a shooting and the FBI had apparently done the rest, calling both the Loudoun County sheriff's office and the Leesburg police. The FBI had also dispatched their own team of investigators and Tim began to notice an increasing number of familiar blue windbreakers with the letters FBI embossed on the back. Tim wondered if the local authorities were pissed off that Mary Ann had first called the FBI, but he was sure that was protocol for her. Robbing a pharmacy surely broke some sort of federal statute, but the use of a firearm in a robbery was definitely a local matter and there was a good chance that the locals were not happy that the FBI had invaded their crime scene.

"I understand that there is some beautiful property for sale across the Potomac River in Frederick County Maryland that would make an excellent location for a CIA safe house," said Lt. Paul Henderson of the Loudoun County Sheriff's Office as he approached. Paul Henderson was the Loudoun County federal law enforcement liaison officer and was responsible for the facilitation and cooperation of the various federal agencies. In other words, he was a kind of federal peacekeeper.

"You know, Tim, when your late wife Pam ran that safe house of yours on Lovettsville Road, I never heard a peep from you guys. Hardly knew you were even up there. Then you came along and now we have had at least three significant events, including the incident today, and—"

"Paul? Now calm down," Tim said. "First of all, there have only been two events at my safe house, not three, and about today—what did you expect my wife to do? Remember, she is a special agent with the FBI who happened, by chance, to interrupt a robbery. You're behaving like she's some kind of vigilante marauding across the county."

"You're right, Tim," Paul replied, appearing to cool down somewhat. "It's just that for a jurisdiction our size, we have very few shootings and the politicians like it that way, especially our new commonwealth attorney. She will not be too happy about today."

"Paul, the kid had a shotgun pointed directly at us and appeared intent on using it. He or the other guy had already shot that poor pharmacist."

"Yeah, about that, did your wife really need to shoot him?"

"What can I say, Paul, the guy took a shot at her."

A plainclothes Loudoun County deputy stepped out of the drugstore and called Paul over for a conversation. The deputy then went back inside while Paul walked back over to Tim.

"They are ready to take your statement now—and Tim, do me a favor and don't be a wise-ass."

"Never crossed my mind, Paul," Tim said as he patted Paul on the back and walked back into the drug store.

"They," as Paul Henderson had referred to them, were six investigators who had set up a makeshift interrogation room in the pharmacy waiting area since there'd been a disagreement over what police station the interviews should be conducted at. Apparently, it wasn't clear who had jurisdiction over the robbery and the shooting. The drug store itself was right over the town limits, however, since certain parts of the robbery had taken place in the town, it was decided that a detective from the Leesburg police should be allowed to participate in both Tim and Mary Ann's interview. A Virginia State Police investigator with jurisdiction over both the town and the county was there to mediate any disagreement. The last two investigators were FBI.

As Tim was being escorted to the rear of the drug store, he passed Mary Ann, who had apparently finished her interview. Someone had also supplied Mary Ann with an official FBI windbreaker, which Tim commented on as they passed.

"Hey, can I get one of those?" Tim said, referring to his wife's windbreaker.

"Please, no talking," the deputy admonished.

Tim just shrugged his shoulders at his wife and continued to the back of the store. He was next shown to a chair. In front of Tim, from left to right, sat two women, two men, another woman, and another man. They each introduced themselves and told Tim which department they represented. In the corner, there was also a woman taking notes. The investigator from the Virginia State Police was the first to speak.

"Good morning Mr. Hall. Once again, I'm Sergeant John Marshal and I am a senior investigator for the seventh division of the Virginia State Police. Just so you know, this session is being recorded."

The state police investigator next stated the time and date of the interrogation. He then began.

"For the record, would you state your full name?"

"Sure," Tim replied. "My full name is Robert Timothy Hall."

"And what is your occupation, Mr. Hall?"

"I am a case officer for the Central Intelligence Agency and a special United States deputy marshal for the United States Marshal Service." Tim's response appeared to have quite the effect on the panel, who began to write in their notepads.

"Thank you, Mr. Hall. Would you mind explaining your positions with the United States Marshal Service and the Central Intelligence Agency to our panel of investigators?"

"Sure. I manage a joint CIA and United States Marshal Service facility here in Northern Virginia and, because I often need to manage individuals under federal indictment, I

THE DECOYS

was appointed a special United States marshal by the United States attorney general.."

"Thank you, Mr. Hall, for that explanation. Now will you, for the record, tell us what occurred here this morning?"

"Well, my wife and I were finishing up our Saturday shopping and this drug store was our last stop. As we entered the store, my wife Mary Ann mentioned that she felt that the store was oddly quiet. At that point, a man appeared to the left of the pharmacy section and pointed what appeared to be a twelve-gauge shotgun at the two of us and demanded that we walk toward him. My wife next identified herself as an FBI agent and requested that the man put down his weapon and surrender. The man refused and pointed the shotgun directly at my wife. My wife then fired three shots which appeared to me to hit the suspect in the upper region of the chest area. The suspect fell while dropping his weapon. My wife then requested that I go to the pharmacy and continue our investigation while she went to check on the shooting victim. At the pharmacy counter, I observed that a woman who appeared to be a pharmacist was lying face-down on the floor. There were also three other women huddled in the corner, whom I thought to be employees of the store. However, I suspected that another suspect may be hiding in the back of the pharmacy, so I identified myself and the suspect then appeared holding what appeared to be a hostage. As I held the suspect at gunpoint, I told him that if he surrendered his hostage then I would let him leave. My wife then confronted the man and shots were exchanged between my wife and the suspect resulting in his death."

"Thank you, Mr. Hall. Now, are there any questions?" Sergeant Marshal asked but, before anyone could ask one, Bob Fredericks of the CIA appeared along with a lawyer from the United States Department of Justice.

"I'm sorry everyone, but that is all Mr. Hall will be saying at this time and I have an injunction signed by Federal Judge John McGinn of the Eastern District of Virginia. Mr. Hall is not available to answer any further questions due to issues related to national security."

"Now wait a goddamn minute," said one of the Loudoun County investigators. "You can't walk in here and interrupt our questioning. I don't care what injunction you have in your hand."

Bob Fredericks was unfazed by the man's objections and instead produced a cell phone and dialed a number. After conferring with someone, Bob Fredericks handed the phone to the investigator.

"Here, someone would like to speak with you, Detective."

The investigator, whose face was now turning beet red, grabbed the phone from Bob Fredericks.

"This is Bob Jenkins of the Loudoun County Sherriff's Office. Who in the hell is?" Bob Jenkins first stopped speaking and then immediately changed his tone of voice. "No sir, yes sir, right away sir." He then handed the cell phone back to Bob Fredericks and turned to address Tim Hall.

"Mr. Hall, you have my apologies. You are free to leave when you are ready."

"Let's go, Tim," Bob Fredericks said and the two walked out of the store and back to Tim's Mercedes, where they

THE DECOYS

found Mary Ann waiting there for them. There was now a crowd of people standing outside the yellow police tape, where it appeared some county officials were getting ready to give a press conference.

"You two, wait for me right here," Bob Fredericks told both Tim and Mary Ann. Neither had ever heard mild-mannered Bob speak to them like that before. They both watched as Bob marched over to a well-dressed woman and tapped her on the shoulder. When she turned, Bob handed her what looked to be another court order. He next said a few words to the woman, turned, and headed back to Tim and Mary Ann.

Just as he reached them, a black Chevy Suburban SUV pulled up. A well-dressed young man got out of the front seat and held the back door open for Tim and Mary Ann.

"I need to speak with you two," Bob said as he entered the SUV. "I will have someone drive your Mercedes back to Lovettsville Road while the three of us talk."

Tim and Mary Ann both entered the SUV. The vehicle contained bench seats that faced each other. Tim and Mary Ann sat together on one side while Bob sat opposite them. As the Suburban pulled out from the drug store parking lot, it all of a sudden occurred to Tim that he still had the keys to the Mercedes. As Tim began to reach for them, Bob Fredericks held up his right hand.

"Don't worry, Tim, we have a spare set of keys," Bob reassured him.

Of course you do, Tim thought to himself. After all, the agency owned the car.

Bob watched the local politicians gather for the press conference and gave the well-dressed woman a slight wave as they drove past. Once out on US 15 and heading north, Bob turned his attention back to Tim and Mary Ann.

"We need to talk."

Chapter 3

"I cannot express how happy I am that you two are still alive," Bob Fredericks said.

"Me too, Bob," Tim replied, "so why are we getting such an attitude from the local authorities?"

Bob hesitated for a moment and looked down at the floor of the Chevy Suburban as if he was perhaps hoping to find an answer there. He then raised his head and stared directly at Tim and Mary Ann.

"You two did not exactly interrupt a robbery this morning. Those two guys were professional assassins who were there to kill the two of you."

"OK, well that makes sense," said Mary Ann.

"Not to me, but I'm kind of the slow kid; would you mind explaining it?" Tim asked. "The whole setup doesn't make sense. It was Saturday morning and no one was in the store? How did they make that happen?"

"They had help," Bob Fredericks said. "Lots and lots of help. They've probably been watching you for a couple of weeks now, following your daily patterns."

"A couple of weeks? How long have you known about this, Bob?" Tim asked.

"I heard that there was something going on over a week ago but I did not think it had anything to do with you two until this morning."

"But why not just walk up to us and pop a cap in our butts?" Mary Ann asked.

"Well, they certainly didn't want to have it look like a hit job. That would have raised too many eyebrows. However, if the two of you were killed while preventing a robbery? Now that is true genius. You two would have been celebrated as heroes," Bob said.

"You are beginning to sound a little too enthusiastic about this plan to kill my wife and me, boss."

"Sorry, Tim, but you have to admit, it was a great plan."

"But why are they after us?" Mary Ann wanted to know.

"That is a little complicated to explain, Mary Ann," Bob replied, "but I think it is because of something Tim may have done while he was working in Columbia."

"You mean spying in Columbia," Mary Ann said.

"We don't really refer to what we do as spying, Mary Ann."

"OK, so Tim was working in Columbia. What's the big deal about that?"

"I was posing as a major drug dealer in the nineties, but it was a very successful operation," Tim said, sounding defensive.

"Yes, I recall you telling me all about that, Tim. That was the one where you killed all those people and, oh yes, you became a heroin addict."

THE DECOYS

Bob gave Tim a look while Tim stared down at the floor. A feeling of unease filled the SUV. Mary Ann, realizing that she had made a major faux pas, attempted to recover.

"But I'm sure Tim was only exaggerating."

"No, Tim has it about right, Mary Ann," Bob said as he reached into his briefcase and pulled out a file. "The State Department is administrating a program in Columbia to encourage farmers not to grow coca leaves, which, as you know, are used to manufacture cocaine. Since there would be significant opposition to this plan, a contract was signed to basically eliminate that opposition and Tim's name is on that contract—or, at least, we think it is."

"How in the hell did they get my name?"

"We gave it to them," Bob said.

"Would you like to explain, Bob?" Mary Ann asked.

"Someone from State called and asked if we knew the name of a man known as *'El Malvado Traficante de Drogas,'* or 'the Evil Drug Dealer,' and the agent he spoke with cross-referenced that name and found it was Tim Hall. After all, we did have it on file. So, you see, this was all just one big mistake. Some people still think Tim is the big drug dealer that he once pretended to be. But the good news is that they failed and maybe all we have to do now is to put out the word that Tim is not the person they think he is. That in itself may stop any future attempts."

"I kind of doubt that, Bob. Once there is a price on your head, it is hard to take it off."

"Why don't you just call someone over at the State Department and tell them to cancel the contract?" Mary Ann asked.

"That is a lot easier said than done. For one thing, there are legitimate people on the list that need to be taken out; plus, once a government contract is signed, you just cannot unsign it," Bob explained.

"Legitimate people on the list? Do you mean that the US government really plans to kill all the other people on that list?"

"The government does not kill people, Mary Ann. They just hire people to do it for them," Tim replied sarcastically.

"So, tell me, Bob, what is the story about the store employees?" Mary Ann asked.

"We believe all of the employees in the store were actors but I don't think we will get much out of them. The real employees were called and told that the store was closed because of a water leak. The only one who did not get the message was that poor pharmacist. We think that she was about to call the cops when she was shot in the back. The FBI called me after Mary Ann called them. That is when I figured out that this contract job on you was for real. Lucky for us, the assassins did not do a very good job this morning."

"I think that they shot the pharmacist just before we walked into the store," Mary Ann began. "That would have been an unexpected event and may have completely thrown off their timing. I believe Suspect Number Two was the shooter who was assigned to take us out as he had a silencer on his Glock. Suspect Number One was meant to be a distraction. While Tim and I were focused on Suspect Number One, Suspect Number Two was supposed to pop up someplace and take us out."

"You are probably right about that, Mary Ann. So, in a way, the pharmacist saved both of your lives. I can't tell you how many times I have witnessed similar tragic distractions."

"Yes, we call it providence, Bob, and without it I would have been dead a long time ago."

Chapter 4

By the time Bob Fredericks had finished explaining the events of the morning, the Chevy Suburban had arrived at the front door of the Lovettsville Road safe house. The first thing Tim noticed was that there was a lot more security present than there had been when he and Mary Ann had left that morning.

"As you can see, Tim, I have taken the liberty of bringing in some more security," Bob said as Tim surveyed the grounds. To Tim, it appeared that Bob had doubled it.

"Bob, would you join us for a late lunch or early dinner?" Mary Ann asked.

"That would be wonderful," Bob replied. "It will give me the opportunity to discuss what I need from you."

Tim had no clue what Bob Fredericks was talking about. The safe house had been keeping him busier than usual and Mary Ann certainly had enough to keep her busy.

The Mercedes 560 pulled into the driveway alongside them and parked by the entrance to the kitchen.

"I sure hope that the steaks and chops I picked up have not spoiled else we may have nothing to eat," Mary Ann yelled as she ran to unload the Mercedes.

"Tim, I got to admit, your wife is something else," Bob said.

THE DECOYS

Tim often heard comments like that about his wife from other men. Many seemed very envious of Tim's marriage and some could not figure out how Tim had been able to get such a woman. Tim did not know either but he'd often heard the same thing about his first wife, Pam, too. In all honesty, he did not know why certain women were attracted to him. Tim did not consider himself a particularly good-looking man and, for that matter, did not think that he was very charming either. On the other hand, although Mary Ann was beautiful, she could be a real pain in the ass. She was for some reason very competitive with Tim and often implied that the job of an FBI agent was much tougher than one of a CIA analyst. Tim had stopped comparing his job to other people's years ago and thought that it was silly to do so.

All said, Tim did love Mary Ann and had recently told her that no other woman had loved him as much as she did. Mary Ann had also promised to be nicer to Tim after they'd returned from Florida and Tim could see that she was trying her best to keep her word.

He was also concerned about how she would handle the shooting and killing of the two young men in the drug store that morning. During an argument over the summer when Mary Ann had questioned his manhood, Tim had told Mary Ann about the killings in Columbia while goading Mary Ann into admitting that she had never killed anyone. Of course, now she had killed and Tim felt even guiltier.

However, now that it had turned out that the men had been paid killers, Tim hoped that the entire experience would be easier for his wife to process. Hopefully, she'd be less sad about taking such young lives. The two assassins had been there for one reason only. Tim would still need to speak with Mary Ann about it after Bob left.

Tim and Bob entered the library and made drinks. Tim took Mary Ann's vodka tonic into the kitchen, where she was putting the groceries away with the help of a young female deputy marshal by the name of Janice. Mary Ann often made friends with the female deputy marshals that made up the security detail of the safe house.

"Do you need me to help with anything?" Tim asked as he handed Mary Ann her cocktail.

"No, honey, go and entertain Bob. I'll be right in after I start dinner. Janice has offered to help."

"That's great, honey, and thank you, Janice."

"Not a problem, Mr. Hall," Janice replied. Janice appeared to be the kind of woman who felt that perhaps Tim should be in the kitchen instead of Mary Ann. Tim suspected that perhaps Janice might have eyes for his wife, which, in some cases, would have turned Tim on, but not with Janice. Definitely a women's woman, Tim thought as he made his way back to the library.

"Do you think Bob likes spaghetti?" Mary Ann called after Tim.

"Yes, I'm sure that he does," Tim yelled back.

"I love spaghetti," Bob said without looking up from the coffee table book he was reading.

"I'm sure glad that is settled," Tim laughed as he made himself another drink.

"Janice has volunteered to finish making dinner for us," Mary Jane announced as she joined Bob and Tim in the library.

THE DECOYS

"I think Janice has eyes for you, honey," Tim said as he closed the two sliding doors that separated the library from the rest of the house.

"That would not surprise me at all," Mary Ann replied as she made herself another drink. "It seems like half the women in law enforcement are gay. That's no big deal, is it, Tim?" Mary Ann seemed to be baiting her husband but Tim knew better than to take it.

"I would not know anything about that, dear, and I do not feel qualified to discuss it," Tim said, hoping to put the issue to rest.

"So, Mary Ann, how did your interview with the FBI go this morning?" Bob asked.

"I have been meaning to ask you about that, Bob. I thought I was there to give a statement about the shooting but instead the entire interview felt like"—Mary Ann paused as if considering her words—"well, it felt like an interview for a job."

"You mean to tell me that you did not have to face a tribunal of Northern Virginia law enforcement like I did?" Tim wanted to know.

"No, honey, not exactly. Everyone interviewing me was an FBI agent."

"So, Bob?" Tim said. "Do you want to tell us what this is all about?"

"I need you two to fly out to San Francisco and start an investigation."

"OK, got it, Bob," Tim said. "Now tell us what you want to investigate."

"That is the thing, Tim. I can't tell you or Mary Ann about the investigation because of the secrecy involved. In fact, less than ten people are aware of the investigation you will be starting."

"OK, so you want me and Mary Ann to start an investigation to find out what?"

"I can't tell you that, Tim. At least, not right now."

"OK, sure, no problem, but what reason do we give for our visit to the San Francisco FBI office?"

"Officially, you are being sent to San Francisco to investigate a man."

"And who would this man be?" Tim asked.

"Bernard Haskell. Do you know him?"

"Barnyard Haskell!" Tim exclaimed. "I thought he retired long ago."

"Nope, still on the payroll. As a matter of fact, he was featured in a *New York Times* article earlier this year about the homeless living on the streets of Oakland and Berkeley. Bernard lives in a camper mounted on a pickup truck." Bob handed an iPad to Tim with the article. Tim in turn handed the iPad to Mary Ann, who started to read.

"How did that go over at Langley?"

"Well, almost no one remembers Bernard, or 'Barnyard' as you like to call him, so no, I was not called into the director's office demanding to know why one of our agents was featured in a *New York Times* article," Bob laughed.

"OK, I'll bite. Why do you call him 'Barnyard'?" Mary Ann wanted to know.

"Because he smelled like a barnyard," Tim answered. "We worked together in Central America and after about a

THE DECOYS

week of no showers, you could not be in the same room with him. Actually, it was Rebec..." Tim stopped short of saying his late partner's name but Mary Ann picked right up on it.

"So, it was your former partner and the woman you were having an affair with—Rebecca Scott," Mary Ann said matter-of-factly. "Honey, I know some women never want to hear the names of their husband's former lovers, but I'm not like other women."

Mary Ann was certainly right about that. She was nothing like any woman Tim had ever met.

"You're right, Mary Ann. Yes, Rebecca Scott gave him the name and at the time everyone felt that it was pretty funny—but, in retrospect, I guess it wasn't."

"All I can say is that Central America sounds like a real party back in the 1980s," Bob commented. "I have never personally met the man so you will have to give me a report on his personal hygiene."

"Well, I'm all for it," Mary Ann exclaimed, sounding truly excited. "Are we going undercover?"

My God, Tim thought. Working undercover was becoming an addiction for his wife. Tim, on the other hand, hated it. To him, it meant constant anxiety and having to worry about getting found out, but Mary Ann really seemed to find it exhilarating.

"No, I'm afraid not this time, Mary Ann. This time it is important that you are your true self."

"Thank God for small favors," Tim said under his breath. He could see it now: the Smiths from Ohio vacationing in Northern California.

"OK, Bob, but what's the angle?" Tim asked.

"California is currently a wreck. The homeless population is out of control, the largest utility in the state is unreliable, and there are at least four separate bush fires."

"And you think that is part of some conspiracy?" Tim asked. "Sounds like a normal year to me."

"Ordinarily I would agree, but we are coming into an election year and how California votes is going to have huge ramifications."

"Bob, California is going to vote Democrat, just like always."

"True," Bob replied. "But the number that vote Democrat versus Republican is critical this year. If the United States is to ever move toward a popular voting system, we need to know if anyone is working the system to make that happen. Or, at least, that is your cover."

"What is Bernard working on?"

"I can't tell you that," Bob said once again.

"So, we're going?" Mary Ann exclaimed. "Wonderful, I have never really been to California—unless Twentynine Palms counts.

"Yes, it does, and what were you doing at the Twentynine Palms Marine Corps base?" Tim wanted to know.

"I can't tell you," Mary Ann responded, "but it was very hot out there."

"So, you were working undercover in Las Vegas but never made it to California?"

"Well, I can't swear to it, but I did spend a lot of time in the desert, so I guess it is possible that we crossed the border at some point," Mary Ann speculated.

"Can we get back to the subject of Agent Haskell?" Bob wanted to know.

"Yeah, sure, Bob," Tim answered, although he was still not sure if his wife was telling the truth about never going to California.

"OK then. I need you two to go out and meet with the local FBI in San Francisco and then go and interview Bernard in Oakland. See where it all leads and if anyone tells you anything. I will be especially interested if anyone asks you or Mary Ann to do anything. Spend maybe a couple of weeks and, hopefully, something will turn up. Oh, and by the way, you both are now members of the Conspiracy Task Force."

"Great, Bob. Question: who's going to mind the store here while we're gone?" Tim asked while his hand made a circle motion, indicating that he was speaking about the safe house.

"Got it covered," Bob said and began to dial a number on his iPhone. "Wait until you meet Tim and Mary Ann number two."

There was a knock on the front door that Tim jumped to his feet to answer, but Bob held up his hand. "Let me get it, Tim," he said as he walked out of the library.

"What in the hell is he up to now?" Tim said to Mary Ann, but he did not have to wait long to find out. In walked a man and a woman who very much resembled Tim and Mary Ann. No, they were not exact doubles, but they would certainly pass.

"Tim and Mary Ann Hall, I would like you to meet Jim and Ann Marie Halfway. Jim and Ann Marie are married

United States deputy marshals and I have asked them to assume your roles here."

"You mean these two are our body doubles?" Mary Ann asked, ignoring Jim and Ann Marie.

"No, not exactly," Bob countered. "While you are gone, I do not want to make it obvious that you are gone. Jim and Ann Marie will not be assuming your identities, just your roles."

"Jim and Ann Marie? Did Bob tell you that someone tried to kill us this morning?" Tim asked.

"Oh, don't listen to my husband, Jim and Ann Marie," Mary Ann said, stepping into her role of hostess. "Would you like to stay for dinner? We are having spaghetti."

Chapter 5

It was almost 11 PM when Bob Fredericks along with Jim and Anna Marie Halfway left the safe house. Once it had been decided that Tim and Mary Ann would be traveling to the West Coast for a number of days, Tim gave the two deputy US marshals a briefing on the operation of the safe house in addition to a tour of the grounds. Once again, it was explained to Jim and Anna Marie that they should not try to impersonate Tim and Mary Ann Hall but instead just continue their daily activities, such as making trips to the store. In reality, Jim and Ann Marie Halfway were supposed to act as decoys and, if someone did happen to try to take out the decoy Tim and Mary Ann, then they were prepared for that. The fact that these two deputy United States marshals would be risking their lives made Tim uncomfortable, but each assured him that this was part of their jobs and that they had both done this kind of work before.

Mary Ann, on the other hand, was much more comfortable with the arrangements and went as far as showing Anna Marie her current wardrobe. She also gave Anna Marie permission to wear any of her clothing.

"This is the kind of stuff you sign up for when you take this job," Mary Ann told Tim, referring to some universal "cop code" that Tim was apparently unaware of.

The thing that really bugged Tim though was the fact that Bob Fredericks appeared to be doing everything in his power to get Tim and Mary Ann out of town, including making up some lame assignment in the Bay Area of California—and all this even after Bob had made such of point of trying to convince him and Mary Ann that whoever had been hired to take them out would most likely not try a second time. If that was really true, then why hire a phony Tim and Mary Ann to act as decoys?

"I think it is sweet that Bob is going out of his way to protect us and it just shows how valuable of an asset you are," Mary Ann stated as she began to look through her closet for clothes to pack for the West Coast.

"There was a time when agents were expected to take care of their own problems, including assassins, but now they bring in Ozzie and Harriet," Tim said, referring to a very old TV show.

"Ozzie is a very funny name," remarked Mary Ann. "Are they friends of yours?"

"Yes, in a strange sort of way," Tim responded, not really wanting to explain who Ozzie and Harriet Nelson were.

"So, is it true that San Francisco gets cold while the rest of the Bay Area does not?" Mary Ann asked.

"Sometimes, during the summer, it is like twenty degrees colder in San Francisco than it is over in Oakland, but right now the temperatures are about the same in both cities," Tim told Mary Ann.

"Are you excited about going home?"

THE DECOYS

"My home is here in Northern Virginia now, Mary Ann. I have only been back a couple of times. Once was to bury my mother."

"I don't think I have ever asked you about your family, Tim." Mary Ann was now lying down next to him. "What were they like?"

"That is a good question, honey, but, to be honest, I don't really know. They were both school teachers and I never really spent much time with either of them. My grandmother raised me until I was in high school, and then she died. However, by that time, I was pretty much on my own. I was accepted to UC at Berkeley and I rarely came home while I was there. After that, I was recruited by the CIA and sent east for training. I never really returned. At least, not for any length of time."

"Did Pam ever meet them?" Mary Ann asked, referring to Tim's first wife.

"Yeah, she did. She insisted that I take her home to meet them. So I do, and we end up taking them out and having a rather odd dinner. My parents hardly ever said a word to each other, or to me for that matter, so there the four of us are, just eating in silence. My parents knew that I was working for the agency and were not happy about it. So, there is Pam, and she is asking my parents a hundred questions. Meanwhile, my parents are just giving one-word answers until Pam asks if they are proud that their son is working for the CIA. So my mother, who is this lifelong Democrat, says, 'No, Pam, we are actually very ashamed of what our son is currently involved with.'"

"Oh my God, Tim! What did Pam do?"

"Pam threw her drink in my mother's face, got up, and left. You should have seen the expression on both of my parents' faces. They were speechless," Tim said with a chuckle.

"And what did you do?"

"I just thanked them for dinner and followed Pam out of the restaurant."

"Weren't you mad at Pam?"

"No, I was thankful. Up until then, no one had ever defended me, least of all my parents. It was actually nice to have found someone who would."

"Tim? I know this is a funny question, but did you ever think that your parents were not really your parents?"

Tim sat by Mary Ann in silence for a minute until he rolled over and kissed her.

"Yes, it had occurred to me and it also occurred to Pam. I had an aunt who moved to San Francisco. The gossip in Fort Bragg was that Aunt Louise, my mom's sister, was my real mother and that she dumped me on the people I grew up with. That would explain why they did not appear to like me very much, but what could I do? Knowing would have just complicated things further."

"You know that I will always defend you, Tim," Mary Ann said as she pulled Tim down on the bed so they were now facing each other. "You know that, don't you?"

"Of course I do, Mary Ann, but remember I fell in love with you the very first time I met you. You had me then and you still have me now."

Mary Ann pulled Tim's t-shirt off and then removed hers.

"Let's try to continue where we left off this morning," Mary Ann whispered as Tim placed his head between her two breasts. Tim next slowly moved his hand down Mary Ann's back and across her buttocks. Mary Ann held Tim's head tightly between her breasts and he could hear her heart beginning to beat faster. Tim's hand was now between Mary Ann's legs and he could tell that she was ready for him. Tim started to lower his head but Mary Ann stopped him.

"Honey, I'm ready now," Mary Ann told him as she climbed on top and inserted his member inside her vagina. This act made Tim think of an old joke about the definition of a nice girl, which almost made him laugh out loud.

"If you don't shut up, I will fix that," Mary Ann told him softly and the thought of being subdued by his wife made Tim explode inside Mary Ann within only forty-five seconds.

"Good God, honey, did I push some kind of cum button?" Mary Ann laughed as she rolled off of Tim.

"I'm sorry, babe," Tim said, beginning to feel guilty for not lasting longer.

"Not a problem, Timmy," she said as she placed her head on his shoulder. "It has been a very long day; however, I am pleased that I still do it for you."

"You will always do it for me, Mary Ann," Tim said, but his wife had already fallen asleep. He soon followed.

Chapter 6

Morning came and Tim woke to find himself alone in bed.

"Mary Ann? What are you up to?"

"I'm packing. You do remember that Bob wanted us on the black flight leaving Dulles this afternoon?"

Tim did remember but still could not believe that he'd allowed Bob Fredericks to talk him into taking a meaningless assignment on the West Coast. At least, that was how Tim viewed it. The details of the job had been discussed so quickly the previous evening that Tim needed a few minutes to recall the events.

First Mary Ann and Tim would take a so-called "black flight" out of Washington Dulles Airport at 5 PM that afternoon. A black flight was a type of secret CIA charter plane used to transport agency personnel to various locations around the world. These flights were secret and appeared on no airport manifests; at least, not the ones that anyone could see. The planes were often regular Boeing 737s, yet they showed no markings and were usually all white. The seats in these planes were also better than your average United Airlines flight, with plenty of legroom. The flight crew members all wore uniforms and in that way they were no different from the crew members of any other commercial

THE DECOYS

flight. Tim guessed that the one he and Mary Ann were taking was bound for locations on the Asian continent and was only stopping in San Francisco to refuel.

The next morning, Tim and Mary Ann were scheduled to meet with agents at the San Francisco FBI field office. Tim had no clue what was going to happen there except that he'd have to pretend to be investigating Bernard Haskell. Afterward, Tim, Mary Ann, and whoever else would drive over to Oakland and try to track down Tim's former colleague, Bernard Haskell, otherwise known as Barnyard Haskell, and interview him on the subject of conspiracies. This was where Tim lost track of the point of the assignment. Did Bernard know what the secret operation was?

"What in the hell are we supposed to do after we interview Barnyard?" Tim yelled, hoping that Mary Ann could provide some kind of answer.

Mary Ann appeared from the walk-in closet holding a gold satin blouse with a pencil skirt.

"Does this look professional enough for you, honey?"

"It does for me, but isn't it a bit outrageous for the FBI?"

"Maybe for around here in DC, but not for San Francisco—or, at least, I hope not, since this is what I plan to wear," Mary Ann replied.

"So, did you hear me ask about the assignment?"

"You mean about what we're supposed to do once we interview your friend Barnyard? Yes, I heard it, but I have no answer for you. I imagine we will just have to see where it leads."

"But what if it leads nowhere?" Tim was beginning to sound anxious.

"Honey, this is how investigations work. You ask questions and try to find leads. Sometimes the leads go nowhere."

Tim understood Mary Ann's point. Tim's career as a CIA agent had always been task-orientated: Tim was given an assignment and expected to carry it out successfully, even if the task was just to create confusion and doubt (which the CIA was very good at). That was very different to an investigation. *Maybe I should just let Mary Ann take the lead here*, he thought. That way, she could do all of the worrying; Tim would just be along for the ride.

"Did you find anything for me to wear?" Tim asked Mary Ann, hoping to change the subject.

"Did I ever!" Mary Ann now sounded excited. "This is a killer suit."

Mary Ann disappeared into the closet and reappeared with a suit, which she laid on the bed.

"Look at this," Mary Ann exclaimed. "It's an Armani!"

It certainly was an Armani suit: a beautiful gray one. It had been a gift from Tim's late wife Pam, given to him the year before the ill-fated trip to China. Tim had never worn it and had totally forgotten about it, yet here it was, laid out before him.

"It's a beautiful suit, Tim, and you should wear it," Mary Ann said, recognizing that Tim's reluctance was due to his history with his ex-wife.

"Pam always wanted me to dress better and I guess this was her last attempt," Tim speculated. "Perhaps she planned to bury me in this suit."

"Don't be silly, Tim. It is an excellent suit and you'll look great in it. You can't dress in Dockers for the rest of your life."

THE DECOYS

Tim really did not understand why he could not dress in Dockers for the rest of his life. After all, the world was now dressing "casual" and "casual" should be Dockers' middle name. That said, he couldn't think of a reason not to wear the Armani suit; he could wear it with one of his cheap black cotton tee-shirts—the ones that Walmart sold for three for ten dollars.

"Yes, go ahead and lay out the Armani, Mary Ann. I will wear it on the airplane."

"About that, Tim: do we have to do anything? Call and confirm?"

"Nope, just show up at the hangar. Everything should be all set. Otherwise, we come back home."

"Come down and have something to eat, Tim. Do you need me to help you pack?"

"No, I can handle it, Mom."

Mary Ann walked out of the room and downstairs without saying another word. Tim could tell that he was pissing her off and decided to try and summon some enthusiasm over their trip to the West Coast. Mary Ann, after all, had never been to the Bay Area and Tim began to think that it might be fun showing her around. Tim found his iPhone on his bedside table and dialed a number. A woman picked up after one ring.

"Joan Davis," said the voice at the other end.

"Joanie? Tim Hall here. My wife and I have a business trip scheduled for San Francisco this afternoon. Where do you have us booked to stay?"

Tim could hear Joanie pound her computer keyboard, which indicated to Tim that she was not having a good day.

"We have you booked at the Marriott Union Square for fourteen days, Mr. Hall," Joanie replied.

"Can you book us the Fairmount on Mason Street?"

"Yes, but that rate exceeds the government per diem by seventy-five dollars a day," Joanie responded dryly.

"Go ahead and book it, Joanie. I will make up the difference," Tim replied. "Also, do we have a car booked?"

"My information was that you would be supplied transportation by the FBI."

"Perhaps, but book us a car at Hertz. Something that looks like a police car."

"OK, Mr. Hall, but you will be responsible for the approval of your travel voucher."

"Yep, I will take care of it, Joanie. And Joanie?"

"Yes, Agent Hall?"

"Have a delightful day."

Joan Davis hung up without responding and Tim wondered if he had unintentionally insulted the manager of the CIA travel desk. Tim imagined that Bob would say something to him later.

By the time Tim had packed and headed downstairs, it was almost time for lunch. Mary Ann was seated at the kitchen table, typing something on her laptop. Tim stopped and planted a kiss on the top of her head.

"I'm sorry I'm acting like such an asshole, honey. There is just something about this whole trip that does not feel right; however, the only way we will know is to go out there and find out."

Mary Ann reached her right hand behind her back and found Tim's left hand. She then turned around and kissed it.

"You're not mad that I found the suit your late wife bought for you? I mean, if it really bothers you then don't bring it."

"It has nothing to do with that whatsoever," Tim said, trying to reassure Mary Ann. "This has more to do with what they are really trying to have us do out on the West Coast."

"Tim, we won't know until we go and find out, now will we?"

"Yes, I suppose you're right, Mary Ann, and I promise to shut up about it."

"I really doubt that will happen, Timmy, but do me a favor and try," Mary Ann said as she kissed him.

At 3 PM, the agency sent an SUV to take Tim and Mary Ann to Washington Dulles International Airport. Earlier, Tim had imagined that he would just drive the Mercedes S550 and park at the hangar. That had been the plan until Bob Fredericks called at 1 PM and told Tim that it would be a good idea to let Jim and Ann Marie Halfway use the Mercedes while Tim and Mary Ann were away. Tim did not bother to argue and even agreed that the plan made sense. What was troubling him however was the thought that a group of assassins was still out there, intent on killing him and his wife. The notion that the group who'd set out to murder Tim and Mary Ann would just go away after one unsuccessful attempt was silly. The mystery to Tim now was the question of who exactly was behind this plot and, more importantly, why. He also no longer believed that this was all because the Department of State had misidentified Tim as an international drug dealer. No, this went much deeper.

"Will we have any problem bringing firearms onto the black flight?" Mary Ann asked.

"No, not unless you plan on hijacking the plane," Tim answered while realizing that was an awful joke. "As a matter of fact, I plan on remaining armed during our entire visit to the West Coast," he continued.

"I'm not sure how that will fly with the local FBI," Mary Ann countered. "They may not buy into the whole special deputy United States marshal bit—you'll be a long way from your secure assignment site, after all."

"That's not a problem. I have a license to carry in the state of California as a private investigator."

"A private investigator?" Mary Ann seemed surprised. "Since when?"

"I have had a license since the 1990s and it has been renewed."

"But you told me that you had not been back since your parents passed away."

"I meant Fort Bragg. I have not been back to Fort Bragg since my parents died, however, I have been to California lots of times."

"You never cease to amaze me, Tim," Mary Ann said as she placed her arms around her husband's neck and kissed him.

"Mary Ann, those people who tried to kill us yesterday are still out there and, despite what Bob says, I think that they will try again. Although we are remaining in the United States, California is in some ways its own country. We will be representing the United States government; however, that won't impress many Californians."

THE DECOYS

"I really don't understand what you are trying to say, honey," Mary Ann said, now looking concerned.

"What I'm saying, Mary Ann, is to be careful. Don't trust anyone we happen to meet. You and I have somehow become involved in a messy conspiracy and the other side is playing for keeps."

"Well it would help, Tim, if you told me what in the hell is going on," Mary Ann said as she looked at Tim.

"Sure, honey. I will tell you as soon as I figure that out."

"Alpha Two to Alpha One" It was Janice on the safe house radio.

"Alpha Two, go ahead," Mary Ann responded.

"Alpha One, your ride to the airport has arrived."

"Ten-four," Mary Ann responded.

"You know, I am the only one who is supposed to use that radio," Tim said jokingly.

"Screw you," Mary Ann responded. "We have a plane to catch."

Chapter 7

Tim and Mary Ann left the safe house and were met by Deputy Marshal Janice and a young man in a dark suit and sunglasses. They were both standing in front of a black SUV.

"Is everything good to go, Janice?"

"Yes sir, Agent Hall. I have my orders."

"And you will help Deputy Marshals Jim and Anna Marie Halfway?" Mary Ann asked.

"Yes ma'am, Special Agent Hall," Janice replied.

"Then we will leave things in your capable hands," Tim responded as he held the SUV door open for Mary Ann.

After Tim checked that both of their bags had been loaded, he walked around and entered the SUV from the other side.

"You look wonderful in your suit, Tim," Mary Ann said as he settled down next to her.

"Check this out, honey," Tim said as he opened his suit jacket to reveal a classic-looking shoulder holster.

"Wow, just like Kevin Costner in *The Untouchables*," Mary Ann remarked.

"Yep, even looks good over a ten-dollar tee-shirt from Walmart."

Mary Ann laughed as she picked up and opened a folder that outlined the details of their trip to San Francisco. Tim meanwhile watched the safe house disappear as the SUV descended the steep driveway and turned onto Lovettsville Road and then onto Route 15. Tim purposely kept the conversation short since he did not want the young man driving the SUV to overhear any of their conversation. Tim hated to feel paranoid, but he really felt that the only person he could trust at the moment was Mary Ann. Even Bob Fredericks was suspect. If anyone had the ability to kill him and Mary Ann, Bob was the guy. After all, he had all of the codes to the safe house. No, Bob could not be ruled out, though Tim did not really feel that Bob had anything to do with the assassination attempt.

The SUV arrived at Dulles International Airport a little over one hour later. The agency driver made his way through various air cargo warehouses until they arrived at a gate. Two armed men appeared and the SUV driver got out of the vehicle and produced a paper from his coat pocket. The presence of two men armed with machine guns made Tim nervous enough to place his right hand inside his suit jacket, but he then felt Mary Ann's hand on his elbow.

"I think it's OK, Timmy," she said softly. "If these two were going to harm us, they would have done so already."

Tim relaxed somewhat as the gate began to open and the young man from the agency got back in the SUV.

"For a minute I thought we might have trouble with those two guys, since I have never seen them before," the young man remarked as he removed some type of automatic weapon from the inside of his jacket and laid it on the passenger seat.

"Security has been insane around here lately," he said and continued to drive. The SUV was now on actual airport tarmac and Tim could see that they were heading to a different airplane hangar than the one he was familiar with, though this one did have the familiar white Boeing 737 parked out front. Tim looked at his watch. It was exactly 4:30 PM.

The young man parked the SUV in a spot that read *Official Vehicles Only*. Two other security guards appeared from inside the hangar and grabbed Tim and Mary Ann's bags.

"Have a safe trip," the young man driving the SUV said as he returned to his vehicle. Tim and Mary Ann both thanked him and followed the new security guards inside the hangar. There they found twenty or so men and women sitting in four rows of chairs—it was just like a regular airport terminal, Tim thought. There were even a couple of families with children.

"Tim Hall, you old dog. I thought that you had hung it all up by now," said a fat man with a white beard almost like the beard Santa Claus would wear. "Do you have some papers for me to see?"

"Sure, Wally," Tim replied, not bothering to introduce this new man to Mary Ann.

"And is this the little woman?"

"She is, but I would not call her that to her face."

"And you two are just going to San Fran?" the man asked, looking at Mary Ann as if he was examining her.

"That's as far as we are going," Tim said with a smile.

"Then have a nice trip," Wally said as he turned and walked away.

"Do you want to tell me that that was all about?" Mary Ann asked.

"Find a seat and I will tell you," Tim said as Wally disappeared through a door.

"So, do you want to tell me who that was and what it was all about?" Mary Ann exclaimed. "I was about to shove that guy's clipboard up his butt. Little woman—my God!"

"Cool down, Mary Ann. That guy's name is Wally Walker and he is the customs officer. What I mean is, he works for the CIA but he reports to the United States Customs Service. Unfortunately, CIA personnel are not immune from contraband checks, even though we do not have to clear the traditional customs authorities. Wally can make your life hell and you don't want to get on the wrong side of him."

"Well if he treats me like that on the return trip, I swear I will shove that clipboard up where the sun don't shine," Mary Ann reiterated.

"Ladies and gentlemen," a voice from an internal speaker system announced. "We will begin to board in just a few minutes. Please have your orders out and ready for examination."

"Let's try to get on board, honey. I will feel a whole lot better once we get in the air," Tim said, remembering suddenly that he really hated to fly.

"Where do we sit?" Mary Ann asked.

"Well, it is open seating, like they do on Southwest Air, but you'll see that it is all a little different."

It certainly was different. The Boeing 737 seating configuration allowed for a good amount of legroom, and there were tables set up where groups could meet if need be. Tim and Mary Ann found seats toward the front of the airplane. A flight attendant came by and offered them beverages. Soft drinks were free, alcohol was not.

"Glad to see that some things have not changed," Mary Ann said.

Next, the flight attendant stood up front and gave the usual safety speech. Ten minutes later, the black flight was in the air and headed west.

"That was fast," Mary Ann commented as the airplane began to gain altitude.

"Yes, it was," Tim replied, "and I am not sure why these flights get to bypass the departure line and take right off, but they always seem to do so. I guess it has something to do with national security or something."

"Yes, or something," Mary Ann replied. "I think I am going to take a nap. I was up pretty early."

"You may as well, babe, it's a very long flight."

Tim did not think he would be able to fall asleep, but he soon found himself drifting off. Perhaps it was the effect of the Xanax he'd popped in his mouth before they boarded the airplane, but Tim just could not shake the feeling of dread he had about the trip to the Bay Area. He always enjoyed San Francisco, so what was so different now?

"Ladies and gentlemen, we will be making a short stop at the San Francisco International Airport in order to refuel. Please remain in your seats during this short layover."

THE DECOYS

Tim opened his eyes and saw that Mary Ann was already awake.

"Did you get any sleep, babe?" Tim asked.

"Oh, about an hour, but you? You passed right out."

"Yeah, I passed right out," Tim responded. "So, what have you been doing for the last three hours?"

"Oh, I just read stuff on my iPhone. Do you know something, Tim? Our nation's capital is truly a screwed-up place."

Mary Ann was interrupted by the flight attendant before she could elaborate any more on the state of the District of Columbia.

"Mr. and Ms. Hall? You will be the only passengers to disembark in San Francisco so, if you would, please exit the plane as soon as we reach the gate. We really don't want the other passengers to get off. It will only cause confusion."

"Well, confusion is our middle name, but we will do anything to help," Tim replied.

The flight attendant gave Tim a half-smile, which indicated that she'd got the joke but did not think it was particularly funny.

"Don't worry, honey, not all of the girls are going to find you charming," Mary Ann said.

"Just as long as you do, babe; that is all I ask."

Once the airplane landed, it taxied for twenty minutes until it found an available terminal gate. Other passengers saw Tim and Mary Ann collect their things and head for the door.

"Is it all right if we get off the plane for a while?" Tim overheard another passenger ask the flight attendant. He did not wait around to hear an answer. There were two attendants standing guard at the jet bridge, making sure no passengers wanted out.

"Thanks for flying No-Name Air," Tim said as he walked past. One of the flight attendants actually laughed. Mary Ann meanwhile grabbed Tim's hand and pulled him along. They both walked up the rather long passageway and then out into the terminal. Waiting for them were a young man and woman, both wearing FBI Identifications.

"Agent Hall?" said the woman.

Tim looked up to see that she was addressing Mary Ann.

"Yes," Mary Ann responded, looking directly at the two agents.

"I'm Special Agent Cindy Andrews and this is Special Agent Matthew Boykins. We are here to drive you and your husband to your hotel."

"That is OK, Cindy," Tim said. "We have our own transportation, but you can drop us off at Hertz if you want to."

Both young agents looked confused at Tim's announcement.

"But our orders were to bring you into the city," Agent Cindy protested.

Mary Ann also seemed confused.

"Excuse me, Cindy, but I need to have a conference with my husband," Mary Ann said as she pulled Tim over to a corner.

"Tim, we have only been here for five minutes and you are already embarrassing me. Now, what the hell is going on?"

"Mary Ann, I am pretty sure that another attempt will be made on our lives in the next twenty-four hours and I can't in good conscience place our lives in the hands of these two kids."

Mary Ann looked directly at Tim for twenty seconds without saying a word. She then returned to Special Agents Cindy and Matthew.

"Cindy, my husband is an agent with the CIA and, unbeknownst to me, he has made other plans. Would you please drive us over to the rental car area?"

"Sure, Agent Hall, but would you mind explaining that to my boss, Supervising Agent Carol Russo?"

"Not a problem, Cindy. By the way, I have seen you before, haven't I?" Mary Ann asked.

"You have, Agent Hall. I took your workshop at Quantico: 'Expectations for Women FBI Agents.'"

"And has that worked out for you?"

"It sure has," Agent Cindy replied. "I would love to speak with you about it."

"And I would be happy to listen."

"Excuse me," said Agent Matthew Boykins, "but I have my boss on the phone, Carol Russo."

Tim watched Mary Ann take the phone.

"Carol? Hi, Mary Ann Hall here. First of all, thank you for sending your two agents to meet me, however, my husband has arranged a surprise."

Tim watched Mary Ann's facial expressions in order to read what Agent Russo was saying.

"Yes, yes, yes. Tim is from the area and knows his way around. OK, well thank you, Carol, and we both look forward to meeting you."

Mary Ann handed the iPhone back to Agent Matthew and walked back over to Tim.

"Boy, Carol Russo sounds like a real piece of work. She had apparently arranged an entire itinerary for us but I have everything straightened out now—or, at least, I think I have."

"Well, thank you, honey. I really did not expect a reception committee or else I would have given you a heads-up. I also changed our hotel but please, don't tell the kids. The fact that the word is out about us driving ourselves is bad enough," Tim said.

"And you really feel that there is a credible threat to our lives?" Mary Ann asked.

"Yes," Tim said. "Whoever is out to get us is not going to be fooled by Jim and Ann Marie Halfway. You and I have to believe that around every corner, someone will be waiting to kill us."

Chapter 8

Tim and Mary Ann rented a brand-new black Ford Taurus from Hertz. As Mary Ann filled out the paperwork, Tim noticed that FBI Agents Andrews and Boykins were still parked on Airport Blvd. The two agents were parked just far away enough that one would not see them unless one was looking.

"It looks like our new friends are planning on tailing us," Tim said as Mary Ann walked back with the rental car paperwork.

"I expected that they would. Do you think you can lose them?"

"Pretty sure I can," Tim said.

"But do we want to lose them?" Mary Ann asked.

"I really doubt that these two are involved in any conspiracy, or at least not knowingly involved, but we cannot risk them revealing our new location. Therefore, we will need to lose them."

"Well, this should be fascinating to watch," Mary Ann joked.

Mary Ann and Tim slowly exited the rental car parking lot and drove on to California Route 101.

"Which interstate highway is this?" Mary Ann wanted to know.

"It's not really an interstate, it is California 101, better known as the 101. It is a road that runs from north to south through the state."

"Well it looks like an interstate."

"California used to have the best roads in the United States but not so much anymore," Tim said as he checked the rearview mirror. "Yep, they are still back there."

"Well, you have not done much to lose them yet. You are only driving fifty miles per hour," Mary Ann said.

"There is a method to my madness," Tim said as he sped up.

Tim appeared to pass exit 429C but then made a sharp right turn and almost collided with a taxi cab. They were now on Bayshore Blvd. Tim next took a quick right on to Crane St. and then another right on to Paul Avenue. There was a traffic signal on Paul Avenue and Third Street which Tim went through. They were now on Third Street.

"And it looks like they are still tailing," Mary Ann said, now laughing. "You do know what you are doing, don't you, Dad?"

Tim suddenly made a sharp right on to Palou Ave and then a left on Ingalls Street. Mary turned to see that Agents Andrews and Boykins' vehicle had come to a stop.

"Tim? It looks like they have stopped following us."

"Not a lot of cops like coming up here," Tim answered.

"Where exactly are we?"

"In a place called Hunters Point"

"Well, it sure looks a little scary."

"Yeah, well we will not be here very long," Tim said as he turned left on to Evans St. and then right back on Third St.

"Do you see them now?" Tim asked

"No, it looks like you lost them," Mary Ann replied. "So what was the point of driving through that particular neighborhood?"

"Hunters Point has a reputation of being the most dangerous neighborhood in San Francisco and it is easy to get turned around up there. Special Agents Andrews and Boykins most likely needed to stop and ask someone for advice on how to proceed. Meanwhile, we'll head on and they'll most likely head to Union Square."

"But we are headed to—"

"Nob Hill."

"Seems like I've heard of that," Mary Ann said.

"Yes," replied Tim, "everyone has."

Tim remained on Third Street until it became Kearney St. He then made a left on Pine St. and then a right on Mason Street toward the Fairmount Hotel.

"Oh my God, Tim, this place is beautiful," Mary Ann exclaimed.

"Wait until you see the room, babe, it will truly knock your socks off."

Tim could tell that Mary Ann was truly impressed with his choice of hotel. While Tim checked in, Mary Ann wandered around the lobby, eyeballing the various retail stores.

"We are all checked in now, Mary Ann. I have gone ahead and ordered dinner for the two of us in the room."

"God, Tim, isn't it too late?"

"Did you set your watch back?"

"No, but I have been using my iPhone and it is only nine. It feels like midnight."

"Well, it's midnight as far as your body clock is concerned. Come, let's have a drink while we are waiting for dinner."

Tim was able to find a booth so Mary Ann could have her back to the wall. Tim sat next to her.

"Tim, can we afford this?" Mary Ann asked. Tim found this a strange question since his wife had never asked about his finances. Finances were one of the areas that they kept separate in their marriage.

"Mary Ann, you and I don't pay a mortgage or rent, while much of the food we eat is on the safe house expenses. I had almost five hundred thousand dollars in the bank when I met you. I am paid one hundred and fifty thousand dollars per year, not including danger pay. And, on top of that, Pam had a life insurance policy of a million dollars with double indemnity, which means—"

"You were paid two million dollars," Mary Ann said, finishing Tim's sentence. "I guess that is why you never ask me for any household money."

"I figured a lot of your money goes to supporting the girls," Tim said.

"Yes, it does," Mary Ann replied.

"So, do you need any money, Mary Ann?"

"Why do you ask, Tim?"

"I'm just wondering if you need any help supporting your daughters. I'm ready to help if you need any."

"Dennis would have a shit fit if he found out your money was going to help support the girls," Mary Ann said, referring to her ex-husband.

THE DECOYS

"Well, first of all, I don't really care what Dennis thinks, but, second, it is not my money. It is our money."

"I have a lot of credit card debt, Tim."

"How much?"

"Oh, I don't know. Fifteen to twenty thousand I guess."

"OK, well that's not too bad. We will take care of that when we get back home"

"I also pay half of Dennis's mortgage."

"And how much is that?"

"Five hundred and eighty-seven dollars a month."

"Wow, that's a fortune," Tim said, almost laughing. "I'm not sure if you can rent an apartment in Northern Virginia for that amount of money."

"What can I say," Mary Ann replied. "It is Ohio."

"So how did you manage to pay all of that while you were undercover?"

"My entire paycheck plus anything else went to my dad and he made the payments on everything. I have a bank account in both of our names and whatever is left in there every month is what I have to live on."

"And how much is that?"

"Not a lot, which is why I use the credit cards."

"Do you mind if I ask how much you make a year, Mary Ann?"

"One hundred and thirty thousand dollars per year plus night differential."

"You mean you do not receive danger pay for hanging out with that psychopath Toby? What, how long's it been—a year?"

"Almost two, and no, you have to be stationed out of the country in order to receive danger pay."

"Mr. and Ms. Hall?" the waitress interrupted, "Your dinner is ready in your room. Would you like me to take your drinks upstairs?"

"No, we will take them," Tim replied. As the waitress walked away, Tim got to his feet and then held out his hand to his wife.

"Mary Ann, you no longer need to worry about money. Just give me your credit card statements. I will take care of them from now on."

Mary Ann placed her head on Tim's shoulder as the two of them walked toward the elevator.

"That would be great, Tim, as long as you don't mind."

"Not at all, honey; that is, after all, part of my job: to fix things."

It did not make sense to Tim that his wife had sent her father almost three hundred thousand dollars over the last twenty-four months and was still over twenty thousand dollars in credit card debt. It seemed to Tim that Mary Ann's dad was taking a cut from the payment, but why?

Tim and Mary Ann's room at the Fairmount Hotel was beyond perfect. The dinner table was set next to a picture window that overlooked the city's skyline. There was also an outdoor patio but the night was much too cold for them to consider eating outdoors.

Tim had ordered a combination of lobster and sirloin steak, figuring that his wife would like at least one of the two. She ended up eating both. Tim also ordered a bottle of Dom Perignon 2009 champagne.

"You are spoiling me, honey, and I am a public servant. How would this all look to the inspector general?" Mary Ann asked.

"Oh, I imagine it would look very suspicious if you could not demonstrate where the money came from," Tim said.

"Do you ever feel guilty about having more money than the average United States government employee?"

"In the 1980s," Tim began, "Pam and I lived in a lousy apartment in a shitty part of Falls Church Virginia."

"Is there a shitty part of Falls Church?" Mary Ann asked.

"Do you know where Seven Corners is?"

"Yes, that is where one of our employees was shot by the DC sniper."

"I rest my case," Tim replied. "But the point is that Pam and I were making twenty-two thousand dollars apiece, which was not great even in the 1980s, and it took us—or, rather, me—over forty years to reach the point where I was not living from paycheck to paycheck."

Tim knew that he was beginning to ramble so he decided wisely to stop talking and look out the window instead.

"Timmy, you should take your suit off and hang it up. You know, so it doesn't get messed up. Do you need any help?"

Tim nodded.

"OK, then stand up and let me help you. Now, first, turn around and face the wall."

Tim complied with Mary Ann's request.

"Now take off your jacket and hand it to me without turning around."

Tim again complied.

"Now, take off your belt and let your pants fall to the floor."

Tim once again did as he was told.

"Now place your hands behind your back."

Tim did and Mary Ann placed her handcuffs on his wrists.

"I always have wondered why guys like you marry woman cops. Must be some kind of fantasy playing out, don't you think?"

"I wouldn't know," Tim said, "but—"

"Shut the fuck up, dude, did I tell you to speak?"

Mary Ann pulled Tim's boxer shorts off and grabbed hold of his penis. Tim had not been this hard for as long as he could remember. Mary Ann turned Tim around and pushed him on to the bed. The pain of him landing on the steel cuffs did not go unnoticed, but Tim kept quiet.

At some point, Mary Ann had removed all of her clothing and was now completely naked. She climbed on top of Tim with her back to him and inserted his penis inside of her. She next began to move up and down, but very slowly. Tim was having no trouble remaining hard and this time would not prematurely ejaculate as he had the other night. As Tim watched Mary Ann's butt move down, he was momentarily distracted by a siren going past the hotel. *A big city—nothing unusual*, he thought to himself. Mary Ann quickly turned and faced Tim and began to move faster.

"Timmy, I want to cum the same time that you do. Can you make that happen?"

Tim really did not have a chance to answer as Mary Ann now moved even faster. He could no longer hold out any longer and came inside of her. Mary Ann was now all over Tim, telling him how much he turned her on. She then reached around Tim's back and removed her handcuffs. That was a big relief.

"I have always wanted to do that to a guy," Mary Ann whispered in Tim's ear, "but no guy would ever let me. I was the person who always had to be tied up, but you are so different, Tim, which is why I love you so much."

Tim heard two more sirens heading down the Mason Street hill, their air horns blaring. Definitely fire engines. That was at least the fifth one.

"Mary Ann? Did we bring one of the Motorola radios? The ones that I programmed with the San Francisco public safety frequencies?"

"You mean you would rather listen to a police radio than make love to me?" Mary Ann sounded disappointed.

"Let's just find out what is going on," Tim said to reassure her, "then we can play around some more if you want."

"I do want. I have some other things to try," Mary Ann said as she gave the radio to Tim.

The Motorola radio that Tim had bought with him was similar to a regular police scanner except that it was programmed to receive just about anything going over the air, including the encrypted channels now used by all the federal agencies. It did not take long for Tim to hear something.

"Battalion One to Engine Thirteen, do you have a situation report?"

"Engine Thirteen to Battalion One, the entire fourth floor is filled with smoke. We are making our way down the hallway. We have multiple victims. We are going to need multiple crews."

"Message received, Engine Thirteen. Union Square Command to San Francisco Fire Dispatch. We need a third alarm."

Tim got up and grabbed his boxer shorts, a pair of blue jeans, and a t-shirt. Mary Ann had come out of her erotic state and was also getting dressed. The two opened the door to the hotel patio and went outside. The night air was now full of sirens that seemed to come from all directions.

"Union Square is right over there," Tim said. Although the night was full of fog from the bay, Tim could make out some smoke. Tim's radio continued to broadcast condition reports from the scene that told of several victims suffering from smoke inhalation. Tim also heard someone mention the possibility of an explosion but nothing else.

"Union Square, Tim? Weren't we scheduled to stay in Union Square?"

"We were, Mary Ann, and I'm afraid that whatever happened down there tonight was meant for you and me."

Chapter 9

"I think we need to go down to Union Square right now," Tim said as he walked back into the room.

"I'm ready to go when you are," Mary Ann replied as she affixed her holster to her hip.

"Let me bring the radio so we can follow what is going on," Tim remarked.

"Sure, but keep it low. We don't want to attract any undue attention,"

Tim picked up the Motorola radio, which was now very active. He turned off the fire and police frequencies and the radio was suddenly quiet.

"I have never monitored the FBI radio frequencies, Mary Ann. What do you usually hear?"

"I'm afraid not a lot. We don't ramble on like the regular cops do."

"Alpha One to Charlie Two." It was the voice of a woman on one of the FBI radio channels.

"That might be the FBI," Mary Ann said.

"Charlie Two, go ahead." It was the voice of another woman.

"Do we have a status report, Charlie Two?"

"Alpha One, the best we can tell at this time is that an explosion occurred on the fourth floor of the hotel. We have one victim transported to San Francisco General. Their prognosis is poor."

"Ten-Four, Charlie Two."

The Motorola radio was again silent.

"I'm afraid that is about as much as we are going to hear, Tim, and I am surprised we heard that much. We use cell phones a lot more these days."

"Yeah, I get that now," Tim replied as he turned down the radio and placed it in his pocket.

He was dressed now and held the door open for Mary Ann. The couple proceeded down the hallway to the elevators and then to the lobby. Outside the hotel was a taxi cab.

"Hi," Tim said to the driver. "Can you take us down to Union Square?"

"Oh man, I don't know," said the driver. "There is a fire or something going on down there. There are a bunch of fire engines and police cars and—"

"Please get us as close as you can," Mary Ann interrupted as she pressed her FBI ID against the plexiglass that separated the driver from the passengers.

"OK lady, I'll do my best."

The taxi driver was correct: the area was a mess. Traffic was backed up on Mason Street and was not moving.

"It's only a couple of blocks from here," Tim said. "We may as well get out and walk."

Tim reached in his pocket and pulled out his wallet in order to pay the cab fare.

"No, dude, cops ride for free," said the driver.

Tim did not bother to argue and followed Mary Ann into the crowd of onlookers. As they rounded the corner on

Geary Street, they both saw that the police had blocked off the area and were not letting anyone pass.

"Do you have your ID with you, Tim?"

"I have the deputy marshal badge,"

"OK, but let me do the talking," Mary Ann said as she began to shove her way through the crowd.

Mary Ann saw a San Francisco police sergeant standing in the middle of the barricade and decided to approach him.

"Sergeant? My name is Mary Ann Wilson-Hall and this is my colleague United States Deputy Marshal Tim Hall. We would like access to the area in front of the crime scene." Mary Ann said as she shoved her FBI ID in the cop's face.

The police sergeant examined both IDs and handed them back to Mary Ann and Tim.

"I'm sorry, Agent Hall, but I have orders not to allow anyone access. Also, I have not seen either of you around here before."

"We just got in from DC this evening," Tim volunteered.

"That's even more a reason not to give you access," the police sergeant replied. "Do you have any local FBI contacts?"

"Yes, Carol Russo and Cindy Andrews," Mary Ann replied.

The names Carol Russo and Cindy Andrews seemed to elicit a humorous response from the sergeant and another police officer standing next to him.

"No, I have not seen Carol around tonight, or any night for that matter. Not sure about Cindy Andrews," the sergeant said. He turned around to see if any of the other officers knew of her.

"Yes, she is that cute redhead, and yes, I have seen her tonight. Over by the hotel," said a woman behind him.

"OK, let me see if I can find her," the sergeant said as he began communicating on his portable radio.

After a minute of back and forth over the police radio channel, the sergeant turned and waved both Tim and Mary Ann forward.

"Yes, if you stay here, Agent Hall, Special Agent Andrews will be here directly." The police sergeant's attitude seemed to soften as he allowed both Mary Ann and Tim behind the barricade.

"I have never had any problem getting through a police barricade in any city I have ever been to," Mary Ann complained when she and Tim were out of earshot of the police sergeant.

"Well, like I said, it is San Francisco, and—"

"There you two are!" It was the voice of FBI Special Agent Cindy Andrews interrupting Tim. Tim took a good look at her and had to agree with the police officer from earlier; Cindy Andrews was a cutie.

"John, these two are with me," Cindy said to the police sergeant who no longer seemed to care whether Tim and Mary Ann were allowed past his barricade. Tim figured that the cop had just wanted to bust some FBI balls. Typical.

"Why did you two work so hard to lose us at the airport?" Special Agent Cindy asked.

"Cindy, my husband and I have it on good authority that we have been targeted for assassination and that is all I can tell you at the present time."

"Well, I was afraid that you two may have—I mean, were involved."

"You were afraid that my wife and I were possible victims of this explosion? So, why did you think that, Cindy?"

"If you don't mind, I'll ask the questions, Mr. Hall," Special Agent Cindy Andrews said, trying to assert herself.

"Sure, no problem, Special Agent Andrews. What would you like to ask us?"

Tim's question seemed to leave Special Agent Cindy Andrews at a loss for words, so she turned her attention back to Mary Ann.

"Special Agent Hall, I would appreciate it if you could control your husband."

"Why, is he under arrest?" Mary Ann responded.

"Well no, not exactly, but my boss would like me to take you in as material witnesses, so if you would, Mr. Hall, I—"

Special Agent Cindy Andrews turned to see that Tim had disappeared.

"What the hell," Special Agent Cindy Andrews said as she made almost a 180-degree turn, but could not find Tim in the crowd. She then turned back to Mary Ann, only to see that she had also disappeared.

"Look at her, Mary Ann, she looks like she's lost her dog," Tim said as he and Mary Ann observed Special Agent Cindy Andrews from the shadows of the opposite corner.

"So, what do we do now, babe?" Mary Ann wanted to know.

"We go back to the hotel, honey, and continue what we were doing."

"Really? Are you still up for that?"

"Sure, if you are, but—" Tim felt his iPhone vibrate. It was Bob Fredericks calling.

"Bob, Mary Ann and I are close to taking the Red Eye flight back to Dulles tonight," Tim said, referring to the overnight commercial airline.

"Just tell me that you two are OK," Bob replied.

"Yes, we are OK but only because we switched hotels at the last minute."

"Tim, I'm beginning to wonder if I was wrong to tell you that you are on some hit list because of Colombia."

"What do you mean by that, Bob?"

"What I mean, Tim, is that you are on a hit list because someone does not want you in San Francisco poking around. Maybe someone does not want you speaking with Bernard Haskell."

"Bob, I thought one of the reasons you sent us out here was to keep us safe?"

"Tim, you know that you are never one-hundred-percent safe. No one is."

"Thank you, Bob. Great advice."

"Tim, the San Fran FBI called and they are freaking out. Have you contacted them?"

"We did, but the young woman we met wanted to arrest and hold us as material witnesses. That's not what I signed up for, Bob."

"Yes, I understand that, Tim. Let me call and straighten that out."

"Yes, please do that, Bob, and tell them that we have no interest in meeting with them."

"Tim, let me handle this. Now, do you have a place to stay?"

"We do, Bob, but, to be honest, I'm afraid to tell you where."

"I understand that, Tim, but do not under any circumstances return to DC or Northern Virginia until I give you the OK. It is not safe here."

"Yes, Bob, apparently there is no place safe for us to stay."

"And Tim, just so you know, I had nothing to do with this."

"Never crossed my mind, Bob," Tim replied and ended the call.

"You don't think Bob Fredericks had anything to do with these attempted murders, do you, Tim?" Mary Ann wanted to know.

"I really hope not, Mary Ann. I really do, but everything now is screwed up."

Tim and Mary Ann Hall walked directly through the police barricade, right past the police officers that had given them such a hard time about getting in, and took a cab back to the Fairmount Hotel.

Back in the hotel room, Tim and Mary Ann removed their clothing, got into bed, and embraced. They quickly fell asleep in one another's arms.

Chapter 10

At 9 AM the next morning, Tim woke to find that his iPhone was vibrating on the bedside table. He picked it up and saw that it was Bob Fredericks calling once again. Tim's first inclination was not to answer the call and return to dreamland, yet, as he recalled the events of the previous night, he reconsidered.

"Good morning, Bob. Mary Ann and I have lived to face another day."

"I wish I could tell you that I have solved all of your problems, Tim, but," Bob said, and Tim detected that Bob was truly down in the dumps.

"Bob, Mary Ann and I know that all of this is not your fault," Tim said. After a night's sleep, Tim believed that there was no reason to be mad at Bob.

"Listen, Tim, I have Carol Russo on the phone and she would like to speak with you."

"I have kind of had it with the FBI, if you know what I mean, Bob."

"Yes, I know, Tim, but Carol is a friend of mine and she really feels bad about your reception last night. Please just hear her out."

Tim heard the phone click a couple of times as if it was being transferred. Next, the voice of a woman came on.

THE DECOYS

"Tim? Tim Hall?" the woman asked.

"This is Tim Hall of the Central Intelligent Agency. Who am I speaking with?"

"Oh, this is Special Agent Carol Russo and I am calling to—"

"Yes, Carol, this is Tim Hall," Tim said, deciding to quit teasing Carol Russo, "what can I do for you this morning?"

"Tim—may I call you Tim?" Carol asked, sounding very tentative.

"Sure, Carol. So, what's up?"

"Tim, I just wanted to apologize for last night. Special Agent Cindy Andrews should have never suggested that you and your wife were being arrested as material witnesses. She was out of line and I am considering suspending her for a week."

"Carol, I don't think that will be necessary; at least, don't do it on our account," Tim said. He really did not want to get the young agent in any trouble.

"That's very kind of you, Tim. Look, I really would like to get together with you and your wife later this morning but you don't need to come all the way over here."

"That's nice of you, Carol, but Mary Ann and I are only a couple of blocks away. We are staying at the Fairmount."

"Oh, I just love the Fairmount," Carol Russo exclaimed. "They have a wonderful tea room."

"Yes, they do, would you like to meet there for lunch? Say, about one PM?"

"Thank you, Tim, that would be wonderful."

"Tell her to bring that brat of an FBI agent with her. You may have forgiven her, but I have not," said the voice of Mary Ann from under a pillow.

"Carol, my wife would like to request the presence of Special Agent Andrews," Tim said.

"Not a problem, Tim. She will be there. Now let me give you back to Bob."

"Thank you, Carol," Tim said, but Carol had already switched the call back to Bob Fredericks.

"Bob? How are the phony Tim and Mary Ann getting along?"

"They seem to be settling in very well Tim. Please don't worry, they can take care of themselves."

It made Tim sick to think that a man and woman would sacrifice their lives acting as decoys for them.

"Tim, I interviewed Jim and Ann Marie myself and they assured me that they could handle the assignment."

"OK, Bob, let me go ahead and meet your FBI friend."

"Carol Russo is a good person, Tim," Bob said. "She would not double-cross you. I will call you back if I have any more news about the various groups that are trying to kill you."

"Yes, Bob, and thank you. Once again we both know you are doing your best."

Tim hung up the phone and walked over to the door to the patio. It was a beautiful and sunny San Francisco morning.

"Wow, you sure have changed your tune about Bob Fredericks since last night. I thought you were about ready to retire and fly home."

THE DECOYS

"Yeah, I know, but now I am feeling sorry for him."

"Tim? I hate to say this, but Bob Fredericks seems to be the common denominator in all this. If I was leading an investigation, he would be my prime suspect. You don't think it is possible that he is involved?"

"Believe me, the same thing has crossed my mind. I mean, it is almost a little too obvious. If I had not decided to change our hotel room..."

"I just hope we are ignoring the obvious because we consider Bob our friend. So, what do we have planned for today?"

"You and I will be meeting Special Agent Caroline Russo at High Tea around one PM," Tim said.

"I am not overly sophisticated but I believe that high tea traditionally occurs a little later in the day."

"It does, but this is also America! We do any damn thing we want," Tim said as he jumped on the bed and on to Mary Ann. "Including making love with your wife, no matter what the time of day," Tim said as he kissed her.

"Well, if you say so, Mr. Hall," Mary Ann said as she wrapped her legs around Tim.

The two then remained in bed until noon.

Carol Russo looked nothing like either Tim or Mary Ann had imagined. She had long dark brown hair that reached beyond her shoulders. She wore a pair of dark slacks and an even darker sweater accented by a Hermes scarf. She appeared to be in her mid-forties. Tim would later say to Mary Ann that Carol reminded him of the author Ann Rice.

Carol Russo identified Tim and Mary Ann immediately as she entered the room and walked directly to their table.

She was followed by Special Agent Cindy Andrews, who appeared to have her eyes fixed to the ground. They were both at Tim and Mary Ann's table before Tim could get out of his seat.

"Tim, Mary Ann? Carol Russo," Carol said as she extended her hand. "I have brought this one with me so you can say what you need to say to her right now. She will not be staying since she has a long list of things to accomplish today."

Tim felt bad and really had nothing to say; however, Mary Ann had plenty.

"Agent Andrews. The man sitting to my right has done more for our country than you could ever hope to but last night you treated him like some organized crime boss. Arrested as a material witness? That is how we treat the bad guys, Andrews, not the good ones. I was on the phone this morning to Sam Rockwell, who is the special agent in charge of human resources. I was asking him if we had any openings in Bismarck, North Dakota because I think that would be a great location for you to learn how to be an FBI agent—however, Tim here told me that I was being too hard on you. Do you think I am being too hard?"

"No, ma'am," Special Agent Cindy said.

"So, what are you waiting for? Apologize to my husband." Mary Ann now seemed really mad.

"Agent Hall, I'm sorry, but yesterday was very stressful and—"

"Special Agent Andrews, I would quit while you are ahead," Carol Russo said, interrupting her young agent. "Now go and finish what I told you to do today."

"Yes, ma'am." And with that, Special Agent Cindy Andrews turned and quickly walked out of the room.

"Nice speech, Mary Ann, except a guy named Mick Vick is running HR these days," Carol Russo said with a laugh.

"Yes, I know, but that was the only name I could come up with," Mary Ann confessed. "Actually, I believe Sam Rockwell retired."

"Yes, ten years ago," Carol Russo said, and both she and Mary Ann started to laugh.

"That was almost the same lecture I received over twenty years ago," Carol said.

"That was the exact same lecture I received after I arrested some ambassador," Mary Ann said.

"So, I did not really receive an apology," Tim asked. "Instead, this was just an opportunity for you to haze your new agent?"

"Well, it was something like that, honey," Mary Ann said. "It's just a way to keep the kids in line."

"So," Carol Russo began, "now that we have officially met, what brings you out to the City by the Bay?"

"Well, we were under the impression that we had been sent out here to help you, Carol," Mary Ann said, and Tim saw a confused look come over Carol Russo's face.

"Help me? Help me do what exactly?" Carol asked.

Now Mary Ann seemed confused and looked at Tim for help.

"Carol, I think that I can help explain. Three days ago, there was an attempt on our lives, which was dressed up to look as though Mary Ann and I had walked in on a robbery. Our mutual friend Bob Fredericks over-reacted and sent me and Mary Ann out here to basically get us out of DC; however, Bob also wanted us to speak with Barnard Haskell. Apparently he feels that Barnard is sitting on some information. Information that is pertinent to something. Something that no one wants to talk about. We also think that the hotel explosion in Union Square last night was intended for us."

Carol Russo began to laugh and then placed her head in both of her hands. She then came up and looked at Tim.

"Yes our friend Bob Fredericks called me the other day and asked if I could help two of his people investigate Bernard who is a person we have been aware of for a number of years and I'm here to tell you that Bernard Haskell is a harmless old man. He is an advocate for the homeless and he does make a lot of noise. Does that sound about right?"

"Yes, I guess it does," replied Tim. "What about the Conspiracy Task Force?"

"Yes, I am operating the Conspiracy Task Force along with six other unrelated task forces. Exactly how many agents do you think I have, Tim?"

"I don't know, fifty?" Tim guessed.

"How about twenty? And most of them are working on the important stuff—bank robberies, kidnappings, and terrorism. We do check out anything that we feel is unusual but none of that has panned out so far and none has anything to do with Bernard. What I mean is that this is not like *The X-Files*," Carol said, referring to the old TV show.

"I'm very sorry, Carol, because I feel my wife and I have wasted your time this morning; however, that said, I really do think that Mary Ann and I should drive over to Oakland and interview Bernard Haskell if that is OK with you."

THE DECOYS

"Well, you do know that we have a resident agent office that covers Oakland and Berkeley, but I'm sure that they will not have a problem with it," Carol said.

"What about that explosion at the hotel last night, Carol? My husband thinks that was meant for us," Mary Ann said.

"I admit that it was very suspicious at first," Carol said, "but, as it turned out, the victim was a known drug dealer and we now feel that it was all intended for him. That should be good news, Mary Ann. I certainly would not want to be the target of some international hit squad."

"So, about Bernard, is it OK if Mary Ann and I go out there, say, tomorrow?"

"Sure, but why don't I send one of my agents with you?" Carol said. "Just to be safe."

Chapter 11

"So, do you feel Carol Russo was lying to us about the explosion at the hotel?" was the first thing Mary Ann asked as she and Tim rode the elevator back to their room.

"I don't know, Mary Ann. We cannot really prove that it was our room with the bomb. All we know was that we had a reservation at that hotel."

"Yeah, but the victim was an international drug dealer, and it just so happens that you are on a hit list because someone thinks you are an international drug dealer."

"Well, it is possible that Carol Russo expected us to be in that room last night and not having tea with her this afternoon. Why does she feel she needs to be a mother hen and send an agent with us to interview Bernard?"

The elevator door opened and Tim cautiously stepped out, looking both ways. Mary Ann followed.

"Tim, we cannot continue to live this way. Constantly looking over our shoulders."

"Oh, I agree wholeheartedly Mary Ann, and we will fix that," Tim said as he approached the hotel room. He had placed a small device on the inside of the door that was programmed to send a message to his iPhone if anyone opened the hotel room door while they were gone. In addition, Tim had also mounted a small camera in the upper corner of the

THE DECOYS

room. A quick check revealed that no one had opened the door or entered the room.

"Oh, that's just great," Mary Ann said. "I can just imagine us checking the camera for the rest of our lives."

"Like I said, darling, I will fix it," Tim said as he grabbed Mary Ann around her waist and pulled her close to him.

"So, what do we do now, Mr. Hall?" Mary Ann asked.

"Well, I'm thinking that you and I should go out for dinner. Would you like to do the tourist thing and go down to Fisherman's Wharf and look at the sea lions?" Tim asked.

"Sea lions? You mean like the sea lions in a zoo?"

"Yep, like the sea lions in a zoo except these sea lions live in the ocean. They are protected and can almost go anywhere they like."

"Well, that sounds fun," Mary Ann replied. "Then what do we do?"

"Oh, there is a decent place up the Embarcadero by Pier Seven where we can watch the container ships come and go."

"And then what?" Mary Ann asked.

"Then we come back here and make wild and passionate love."

"Provided no one tries to kill us first."

"They would not dare," Tim said as he kissed her.

"OK, then give me ten minutes," Mary Ann said.

As Tim and Mary Ann left the Fairmount, Tim noticed a cable car that was, for a change, not packed with people.

"Shall we?" Tim asked but Mary Ann was already ahead of him. Tim hopped on and sat on the bench while Mary Ann insisted on hanging over the side.

"I've always wanted to do this, ever since I saw my first Rice-A-Roni commercial," Mary Ann yelled over the sound of the bell. The Powell-Mason line took the two within a block or so of Fisherman's Wharf.

"So where are these sea lions you told me about?" Mary Ann asked.

"Just listen, you will hear them soon enough," Tim said, and he was right.

"Why are they here?" Mary Ann asked.

"They began to show up down here after the 1989 earthquake—the one that took down the top level of the Oakland Bay Bridge."

Yeah, I remember—my dad was watching a World Series game between the Oakland A's and the San Francisco Giants when that all happened. I was a Girl Scout back in those days and we organized some collection or something for the victims."

"You were a Girl Scout?"

"Sure was. It was a blast. I tried to get Molly and Amy to join but they told me that it was very uncool."

"Listen, Mary Ann," Tim said as he pointed to his left.

Mary Ann also heard the sound of the sea lions barking and ran ahead and stopped at the railing.

"Gosh, honey, there must be at least fifty of them," Mary Ann said as she first saw the sea lions lounging on the floating docks.

"I read someplace that November is the month when most of them come back," Tim said.

"What about the people who own these floating docks? Are they still able to use them?"

THE DECOYS

"They can if they are able to maneuver around the sea lions,"

"Do you mean the sea lions get special preference?"

"The sea lions have pretty much taken over the place,"

"Well, good for the sea lions," Mary Ann exclaimed.

It was now sunset. Tim and Mary Ann returned to the Embarcadero and proceeded to walk toward Pier 7. The street was filled with tourists and street performers. As they approached a man covered in silver paint pretending to be a statue, another man sprang up from behind a bush and yelled, "I got you!" Mary Ann reacted by taking the palm of her right hand and slamming it into the man's solar plexus. This resulted in the prankster doubling over and dropping to his knees. Another man, who appeared to be the prankster's friend, screamed at Mary Ann, "Hey man! My friend was only playing around. What is your deal?"

"Maybe your friend should not go around scaring women half to death," Mary Ann shot back.

Two women who had witnessed the action began to applaud Mary Ann. Meanwhile, Tim glanced over and saw two San Francisco beat cops standing by the public restrooms. They both appeared to be smiling.

"Looks like you have struck a blow for the sisterhood," Tim commented as they continued to walk down the Embarcadero.

"Tim, I may not show it, but I'm a nervous wreck. I'm half expecting someone to walk up to us and open fire," Mary Ann said and Tim could tell that his wife was still upset.

"I should have warned you, Mary Ann, that there are all kinds of jokers around here who are always screwing with the tourists. As a matter of fact, one of these guys did the same to me several years ago and I almost keeled over from a heart attack."

"Well those two cops standing by the restrooms should have done something."

"I was afraid they might arrest you for assault. Like I said Mary Ann, San Francisco is a different kind of city."

"Yes, I am beginning to see that, and I'm not sure how much I like it," Mary Ann said, appearing to calm down.

"Oh, we have not even scratched the surface yet," Tim replied as they arrived at their destination.

The Waterfront Restaurant was an old longshoreman's bar that had been converted into an upscale restaurant in the late 1960s. The food was decent but the main attraction was the restaurant's proximity to the San Francisco Bay's shipping lanes. The diners received a very close look at some of the largest container ships in the world. The waiting staff even made announcements to the crowd when an especially large ship passed by.

"Where do all these ships dock?" Mary Ann wanted to know.

"In Oakland," Tim replied. "From there, the containers are placed on rail cars or trucks. Container shipping really changed the shipping industry."

"Yes, I know," replied Mary Ann. "If you recall, I was locked up in one back in Baltimore."

"You know, I was never sure whether you were actually locked in that container," Tim said as he took a sip of his martini.

THE DECOYS

"Oh, I was locked in all right. Toby and Sebastian had become convinced that I was working undercover for somebody and needed to keep me on ice," Mary Ann said while she watched the container ship pass by. "To be honest, I was pretty scared."

"But you never seem traumatized by that kind of thing,"

"Looks can be deceiving," Mary Ann said as she held Tim's hand.

Realizing that he had ventured down a road with his wife that he perhaps should not have, Tim tried to change the subject.

"So, now that these big ships are able to pass through the Panama Canal, many of them are now traveling to other ports like Norfolk and New Orleans."

"Is there no subject my husband is not an expert on?" Mary Ann teased.

Before Tim could answer, their dinner arrived. Tim and Mary Ann had both ordered fish and they were pleasantly surprised by how good the meal was. Tim told Mary Ann that it was probably impossible to find truly bad food in San Francisco and went on to say that, in his opinion, most new food trends originated in the city.

"I cannot think of a better city for food except for maybe New Orleans," Tim said as he finished his third martini.

Mary Ann was pleased that she and Tim were having a night out and not worrying about being murdered. After dinner, they hailed a taxi cab outside the restaurant to take them back to the hotel. Tim suggested that they take a ride first and asked the cab driver to give them a tour. The driver was more than happy to accommodate.

He first drove down Market Street, where Mary Ann could see the homeless problem up close.

"Where do they all come from and why do they come to San Francisco?" she asked.

"That's a good question, lady," the cab driver replied. "But I think there are two reasons. Number one, the weather here is pretty nice and, except for the fog off the ocean, it does not get too cold. Second reason, San Francisco is just the city that can't say no to anybody. They try very hard to make everyone happy, but you know what happens when you try to make everyone happy?"

"You make no one happy?" Mary Ann speculated.

"Could not have said it better myself," the cab driver said.

"Nor could I," Tim added.

"How 'bout we take a ride up through Haight Asbury?" the cab driver suggested.

"Sure, why not?" Tim responded.

The driver took a right-hand turn onto Castro Street and headed north. The street appeared dimly lit as they passed the homes in the area known as the Castro District.

"This part of town has always reminded me of the Dupont Circle area of DC," Tim said.

"Yes, there is a woman at work named Jill who lives over there with her wife, Molly," Mary Ann said in a low voice. Tim had noticed before that his wife was not exactly comfortable with the whole LGBT segment of the population.

"So, are you two in from DC?" the cab driver asked. "What brings you out to our fair city?"

"We are spies for the United States government and someone has put a contract on us," Mary Ann blurted out. Tim was somewhat amazed that his wife had revealed exactly what they were doing in San Francisco, but also figured that the cab driver would not take her seriously. He was right.

"Really?" replied the driver. "Well, I happen to be a Russian agent myself."

Everyone laughed as the cab stopped at a traffic light on Divisadero and Haight Street.

"Hold on, something is going down," the cab driver said as Tim observed a marked San Francisco police cruiser block the intersection with its flashing blue and red lights. Two other cruisers passed the cab on the right-hand side while another was coming down Divisadero Street from the north. The four marked police units were then joined by a fifth unmarked unit and then a sixth unmarked car. The woman who jumped out of the sixth car bore a striking resemblance to FBI Special Agent Cindy Andrews.

"God, is that who I think that is?" Tim asked.

"Yep, it is our own Special Agent Cindy Andrews on the job," Mary Ann replied.

"You know, I still want one of those jackets," Tim said to Mary Ann, referring to the blue windbreaker with *FBI* embossed on the back.

"Maybe for Christmas honey," Mary Ann replied, although Tim could tell that his wife was still concentrating on the police activity.

"Mary Ann, I know you really want to go over there and see what is going on, and usually I would not have a problem with it; however, in this case, it may be difficult for them to believe that we were just driving by."

"You do have a point, Tim,"

"Are you two really cops?" the cab driver said, overhearing Tim and Mary Ann's conversation.

"Yeah, we are kind of cops," Tim replied.

The cop blocking the intersection now got out of his car and began to wave the traffic through the intersection.

"Do you guys want me to pull over and let you out?" the cab driver asked.

"No," Tim replied. "You better take us back to the Fairmount."

The driver proceeded north on Divisadero Street until he came to Broadway and turned right. Once the cab driver had figured out that Tim and Mary Ann were not just tourists taking a tour of the city, he stopped talking. Mary Ann meanwhile continued to stare out the window at the passing houses. Tim guessed that his wife was missing the days of being a field agent, or perhaps just missing the adrenaline rush cops get while rushing to a scene or making an arrest. Tim also knew that feeling, but had decided a number of years back that he no longer enjoyed it. Sure, being in law enforcement was kind of cool in the sense that you could walk into a situation and receive immediate respect (at least, most of the time), but the real question of police work was why you wanted to do it in the first place.

Police work was a very lonely job. You found yourself having very few non-cop friends, plus you developed a healthy mistrust of just about everybody else in the world. Tim figured that women cops had it a bit rougher since many also wanted to start families. Tim had read someplace that 60 percent of women did, and that must have also included the ones who were cops. Tim was aware that Mary Ann suffered for the choice she'd made. She had confessed to Tim one night that giving up Molly and Amy so she could go undercover had actually not been worth it. Her ex-husband Dennis had ended up raising the two girls and had only allowed them to visit Mary Ann and Tim in Virginia once.

The cab had now pulled up in front of the Fairmount and the driver turned to Tim.

"Look, dude, we usually don't charge cops since we can get paid back by the city, but you got to understand that I did not know you two were on the job and—"

Tim interrupted the cab driving by handing him two one-hundred-dollar bills for a seventy-five-dollar fare.

"Oh man, this is way too much and—"

"That is not a problem," Tim said. "Do you have a business card?"

"Yeah, man, I do," the cab driver said as he reached behind the sun visor and produced one.

Tim glanced at the card and saw that the driver's name was Brent Wilkins.

"We may need some help in the next few days and the wife and I were wondering if we could depend on you?"

"You can depend on me, sir."

"The name is Hall, but you can call me Tim."

"Got it Mr. Hall—I mean, Tim."

"Great, then we will see you around, Brent."

Tim walked into the Fairmount and found Mary Ann at the bar ordering a drink. Tim ordered one himself and then looked at his iPhone.

"Room looks clear, babe. Are you ready to come to bed?" Tim asked.

"I will be after this," Mary Ann said, referring to her vodka tonic. "Did you make a new friend?" she asked, referring to Brent, the cab driver.

"Yes, it may come in handy having a driver who knows the city."

"Well, you're the boss," Mary Ann replied.

"I'm not sure about that, Special Agent Wilson-Hall,"

"Well good, because I have plans for us in bed tonight," Mary Ann whispered in his ear.

"Can't wait," Tim said as Mary Ann took him by the hand and led him back to their room.

Chapter 12

Tim woke to the ringing of an iPhone. The standard or the default ring; the ring you get when you first buy the phone. Anyway, it was not Tim's phone, so he placed his head back under the pillow, hoping that the ringing would go away.

"Special Agent Hall," said the voice of Mary Ann. Tim waited for that period of time between when someone says hello and then begins speaking once again. Tim considered himself an expert of the one-sided phone conversation, and he certainly felt that enough time had passed since Mary Ann's initials greeting.

"Yes, Agent Andrews, and what can we do for you this morning?"

God, Tim thought to himself. His wife was giving no quarter to the young agent. He listened a while longer and decided that he needed to surface from the bowels of the bed. He felt a pain on his backside and began to recall the sexual intercourse he'd had with Mary Ann the night before. She was certainly exploring her sexual side.

"OK, Agent Andrews, we will expect you at ten AM. Call when you are out front. OK, great. See you then."

"Good morning, cowgirl," Tim said. "And who was on the phone this morning?" Tim asked, though he already knew it was Special Agent Cindy Andrews.

"Guess who was assigned to escort us over to Oakland?"

"Our new friend, Special Agent Cindy?"

"The same. Senior Special Agent Russo thought that it would be a good idea, just in case."

"Just in case of what?" Tim asked.

"I am really not sure. I have been in law enforcement for over twenty years and now some kid starts laying out the rules of investigation to me? Like, fuck her."

Mary Ann, who had apparently just climbed out of the shower, was wearing a white bathrobe and had wrapped a towel around her head. Tim felt that she looked adorable.

"Mary Ann, everyone in every profession goes through this kind of thing. What I mean is that there will always be younger people looking to prove themselves. That is just how it works."

"But I am only forty years old, Tim."

"And you have been some kind of cop for over twenty-two years now. There is a book you should read called *Passages*, by Gail Sheehy. Pam read it and it helped her a lot."

"Tim, although I don't mind you bringing up your late wife Pam, do you think we could go a couple of weeks without you mentioning her name?"

Tim had not read Mary Ann's mood very well that morning; she obviously was not in the mood to listen to any of Tim's self-help advice. He thought he would try again.

"Why don't you finish getting ready and I will order up something to eat?"

THE DECOYS

"I just need some coffee, hon," Mary Ann replied as she shut the bathroom door.

Tim picked up the room service menu and ordered something called the "All-American Breakfast" along with a pot of coffee. Although Mary Ann claimed that she did not want anything to eat, Tim knew that she would eat at least half of his eggs and bacon.

Tim really did not mean to bring up his late wife's name as often as he did, but she'd been a big part of his life and he could not just erase her. In Tim's view, it was women who seemed to have no problem just cutting an ex-boyfriend or ex-husband out their lives—or, at least, that was his experience.

Room service arrived at about the time Mary Ann emerged from the bathroom. She had already dressed in her working clothes, as Tim referred to them: a black pair of slacks with a cream-colored silk blouse. The only accessories missing were her jacket, shoes, and her Glock 22 9mm pistol. It was now 9:30 AM and both Tim and Mary Ann were sure that Special Agent Cindy Andrews would be there at exactly 10:00 AM.

"I'm sorry, honey, I did not mean to snap at you when you mentioned Pam. It's just that these kids are so presumptuous that it drives me nuts. This kid is calling me up and telling me how we will approach this Bernard Haskell guy and what we should ask and what we should not ask and I am on the other end of the phone thinking, *what in the hell do you know?*"

Tim sensed that Mary Ann's real issue was that Special Agent Cindy Andrews was not showing her the respect that she felt that she had earned over the years. Tim also knew that feeling and did not like it either; however, he also figured that Special Agent Andrews was simply repeating what her boss, Carol Russo, had told her to say. That just told Tim that Carol Russo knew a lot more about Bernard Haskell than she was admitting to. It was almost like she was protecting him.

Tim noticed right away that Mary Ann was now eating the All-American Breakfast that he had ordered so he decided to take a shower.

At 10 AM, Mary Ann's iPhone rang, indicating that Cindy Andrews had arrived. Tim did a quick check of the room to make sure that his room camera and door devices were both operating.

"Come on, honey, we don't want to keep the FBI waiting," Mary Ann said as she carefully stepped into the hallway.

The housekeeping cart was parked in front of another room, which was certainly not suspicious, but they could not take anything for granted. Mary Ann walked ahead of Tim but quickly turned around as they passed the room. That way, they could both watch both ends of the hallway. The last thing they needed was someone coming up from behind.

Having safely made it to the lobby, Tim and Mary Ann were met by Special Agent Cindy Andrews. Both FBI agents were wearing almost exactly the same outfit except for the sky-blue blouse that Cindy Andrews had on.

"Good morning, Agent Hall and Mr. Hall." Special Agent Cindy Andrews beamed with all of the false sincerity that she could muster. "I am parked out front," she said, turning and heading to the front door.

"Actually, I would like to get some coffee to go it that is all possible," Mary Ann said.

"Sure, but I am double parked and—"

"Tell you what, why don't you two gals go around the corner to that little coffee shop on Mason while I watch the car," Tim said. "That way you two can discuss how you would like me to behave during this interview."

"Sounds like a plan," Mary Ann replied and began to walk around the corner. Special Agent Andrews for a moment appeared confused about what to do, but decided to follow Mary Ann.

"Hey, boss, any work for us today?"

Tim looked up and saw his new friend, taxi cab driver Brent Wilkins, waving to him from across the street. Tim walked over to meet him.

"No, not this morning, Brent, but probably at some point tomorrow," Tim said as he pulled out his wallet in order to give Brent some money as a retainer.

"No, boss, only pay me when I do some work."

"Well, I do have some work for you to do, Brent. We have a rental car parked in the hotel garage that you will be driving; however, I just need to put you on the rental contract. Is there a Hertz location around here?"

"Yeah, boss, actually there is one in the hotel," Brent replied.

"Great, that makes it easy. If you would go in and just show them your driver's license, I will take care of the rest when we get back from Oakland."

"Why in the hell are you going to Oakland, boss?" Brent asked.

"On FBI business," Tim replied casually.

"Does it have anything to do with the cute redhead driving the black Taurus?" Brent asked.

"Boy, you don't miss anything do you, Brent?"

"Not if I can help it, dude," Brent said as the two agents appeared from the coffee shop around the corner.

"So, we're good," Tim said as he handed Brent a one-hundred-dollar bill"

"Yep, we are. I'll take care of everything. And boss?"

"Yes, Brent?"

"That is one sharp suit, dude," Brent said, referring to Tim's Armani.

Tim laughed and returned to Mary Ann and Cindy Andrews. Mary Ann was holding a cup of coffee for Tim and some kind of pastry.

"Thank you, my love," Tim said.

"That's the least I can do after I finished off your breakfast," Mary Ann replied.

Not wanting to start any discussion about where anyone should sit in the FBI vehicle, Tim opened the rear door but first made sure that the child safety lock, which was also used to secure prisoners, was not engaged. This did not go unnoticed by Mary Ann.

"Nothing gets past you, does it, honey?"

"Well, when that starts to happen, it will be time to retire."

Tim noticed that Cindy Andrews was not reacting one way or another to Tim and Mary Ann's banter. *She's probably wondering why we both have not retired*, Tim thought to himself. Although Mary Ann technically outranked the

THE DECOYS

young agent, she was not a manager and no longer a field agent. Plus, most of Mary Ann's achievements as an FBI special agent were classified. So, to Cindy Andrews, Mary Ann was just some paper-pusher from DC and did not have any of the "street creditability" that she had obtained over her five-year career. At least, that was how Tim read the situation.

"So, I see you were speaking to your new friend, Brent the cab driver," Mary Ann said as Cindy began to drive away from the hotel.

"Yes, just passing the time," Tim responded.

"You have to be careful with some of these guys, Agent Hall." Cindy was now talking, which Tim saw as progress. "They are always looking to take advantage of some poor tourist. If you have the guy's name, I would be happy to run a background check on him."

"Sure, that would be great, Agent Andrews, just as long as it is no bother. The guy's name is Brent Wilkins and he drives for Diamond Cab,"

At a stoplight, Tim watched as Special Agent Andrews wrote the information in her notebook. He also noticed Mary Ann's eyes in the rearview mirror, which seemed to say, "why are you having her do something that we can just as easily do ourselves?" Tim and Mary Ann had become very good at picking up each other's body language.

Special Agent Andrews next reached into her bag and produced a folder, which she handed to Mary Ann.

"Here is some information on our target," she said to Mary Ann.

Mary Ann opened the folder and then handed it to Tim. He certainly disagreed with the term "target," since, in Tim's mind, Bernard Haskell had not been accused of any crime as of yet. They just wanted to have a simple interview, but it did not look like that would happen. Tim opened the folder to find a photo and a profile of Bernard. Which read:

Name: Bernard Allen Haskell
Address: Vicinity of the 1200 block of 8th Street
City: Berkeley
State: California
Zip: 94709
DOB: 03/01/1944
Occupation: Analyst, Central Intelligent Agency; Retired
Description: 70-year-old white male, 185lbs, blue eyes, shoulder-length gray hair.

> *Profile: Bernard Haskell is a known advocate for the homeless primarily in the East Bay area of the San Francisco-Oakland Metropolitan Area. He is also thought to be connected with the California Environmental Impact Group, also known as CEIG. The CEIG is a known environmental terrorist group that is thought to have been involved in a number of domestic terrorist acts (See Appendix A). Mr. Haskell has often acted as an apologist for environmental terrorism thought to be connected with CEIG and has often acted as a spokesperson for the group. In an interview conducted on May 23, 2018, Mr. Haskell denied any direct knowledge of activities related to the CEIG. The subject was*

placed under surveillance from [date and time redacted] until [date and time redacted] by [redacted] and [redacted], however, no significant activity was observed.

Bernard's profile continued for another page and listed a number of acts thought to be related to environmental terrorism, but there was nothing that could prove his association, at least not directly. The interesting thing, however, was the signature at the bottom of page number two. Under the unreadable signature was written *Special Agent Caroline Russo, Federal Bureau of Investigation*; and, under that, was a courtesy copy sent to Robert Oscar Fredericks, CIA.

"Oh my God, his middle name is Oscar?" Tim said out loud from the back.

"What was that, Tim?" Mary Ann asked from up front.

"Oh, nothing," Tim replied, sounding almost absentminded. He really did not need for Cindy Andrews to know that he had discovered something interesting. When Tim had mentioned Bernard Haskell to Carol Russo over tea the day before, she'd never indicated that she had indeed started an investigation on the man. Why was that?

Tim looked up and saw that they were now on Interstate 80, taking the Bay Bridge into Oakland. Traffic was moving very well so Tim figured they would arrive in Berkeley in maybe twenty minutes. He was not sure where 8th Street was exactly but knew it was somewhere west of the UC campus. Tim had rarely left the Berkeley Campus when he was a student, which had been fine by him. The city of Berkeley had certainly been no garden spot in the early 1970s.

As a matter of fact, it had been downright dangerous, but these days everything had changed. Part of this was due to the amazing housing shortage in the entire Bay Area, where cracker box-type houses were selling for over one million dollars.

Mary Ann and Cindy Andrews were doing their best to make small talk, but even that seemed to be strained. Mary Ann had earlier asked if Cindy was married or had a boyfriend, which had resulted in a ten-minute rant by Cindy about how you could not find suitable men in the Bay Area because at least half of them were gay and the other half self-involved, whatever that meant. She then went down the "why men won't date female cops" road, which Tim had walked too many times. He wanted to suggest that perhaps Cindy should not try to control every situation, including dating, but he knew he was outnumbered.

Tim began to think about how the interview with Bernard would probably go. Special Agent Cindy Andrews obliviously would want to control the interview. Tim did not have to wait long to have his suspicions confirmed.

"Agent Hall?" Cindy Andrews asked.

"You can call me Tim," Tim responded.

"Well, Tim, please don't take this the wrong way, but this is an FBI interview, not a CIA or federal marshal one. Therefore, please do not ask Mr. Haskell any questions without asking me beforehand."

Tim was not sure how he was going to ask Special Agent Cindy Andrews anything beforehand without knowing what he was planning to ask beforehand, but he let the matter go.

THE DECOYS

"Perhaps your wife, Special Agent Wilson-Hall, should ask any questions that you might have, since she is a special agent."

"Yes Cindy, she is an FBI special agent, but I call her Mary Ann," Tim replied, trying not to lose his cool.

"Yes, of course," Cindy Andrews responded. "Just please cooperate."

Tim pulled out his iPhone and began to type a text message. When he next looked up, he saw that they were on 8th Street, where there was a line of decrepit Winnebagos, campers vans, and campers on the backs of pickup trucks parked on both sides of the street.

"I think that is Mr. Haskell's camper right there," Cindy Andrews said as she slowed down.

There, on the back of a 1981 Ford 150 pickup, was a beat-up camper, which was probably around the same age as the truck. Agent Cindy Andrews proceeded to the corner and parked at an angle. She turned on the car's flashers.

"You know, maybe I should just stay here. What I mean is, if I can't ask any questions, then what the point of me going?" Tim said.

"Tim, please don't be like this. I think it is important that Bernard sees you. After all, that was the whole point of us coming out here."

"Look, guys, I have other things to do today and I would like to get this over it. If your husband does not want to come with us, that's fine with me," Special Agent Cindy Andrews said.

Mary Ann gave Tim one last look and shut the passenger-side door. A little too hard, Tim thought.

Tim began to look at the second hand of his watch. Exactly one minute and forty-seven seconds later, both Agents Andrews and Hall came running back to the car.

"Mr. Hall, you have to get out of the car right now," Special Agent Andrews exclaimed.

"Why? What is going on?" Tim wanted to know, acting as if he was in no hurry to leave.

"Tim, honey, it is an FBI matter and you can't come."

"Oh, you are breaking my heart, but if you two really have to go," Tim said as he got out of the back seat.

Tim watched as he saw the blue dashboard and grill lights come on. Special Agent Andrews turned on the siren and made a U-turn onto 8th Street.

"I never met an FBI Special Agent who could not respond to a bank robbery in progress," Tim said to himself as he watched Cindy and Mary Ann head west on 8th.

Tim walked to the camper that Cindy had identified as the one belonging to Bernard. He knew it was most likely the correct one since he imagined that it was Cindy who was running the surveillance mentioned in the report on Bernard's camper. Tim walked to the back and banged on the door.

"Barnyard, open up!" Tim yelled.

Tim heard a groan coming from within the camper and then footsteps to the door.

"There are only two people in the world that know me by that name and I hear one of them is dead," the voice said as the door swung open. "Tim Hall, you SOB. What in the hell are you doing out here?" Bernard Haskell asked.

"I'm in trouble, Bernard, and I think you are the only person left that can help me."

Chapter 13

"Tim, my boy, it is good to see you," Bernard Haskell said as he gave Tim a bear hug. "Come in, come in. Find yourself a seat."

Tim entered the cramped camper and saw absolutely nowhere to sit down. "Actually, Bernard, it may be a better idea if you and I take a walk. I am visiting you by way of the San Francisco office of the FBI, and I don't think that they will be happy when they find out that I am visiting you without their supervision."

"So now the fucking FBI has to give permission for an old friend to visit me?"

"Well, I am kind of on official business, Bernard. Carol Russo insisted that I be escorted by one of her junior agents."

"Oh yes, my pal Carol. How is Special Agent Russo? I have not seen her for a couple of months now."

"As right as rain from what I can tell, but I did not find out until this morning that you two have a history."

"Yes, Carol and I go back a few years and I have to admit, Tim, that Russo is some kind of woman. I would be with her right now but she won't agree to share this camper with me," Bernard said, following his words with a deep belly laugh.

THE DECOYS

Tim had no clue if Bernard really was romantically involved with Carol Russo, but decided not to follow up on his statement.

"By the way, Tim, I understand that you hooked up with an FBI gal yourself. So, where in the hell is she?" Bernard asked.

"My wife Mary Ann and Special Agent Cindy Andrews needed to respond to a possible bank robbery in progress at the local Bank of America branch."

"Which was most likely called in by one of your guys at Langley, right, Tim?"

"Perhaps. I did want Mary Ann to meet you, Bernard, but I also needed to get rid of Special Agent Cindy Andrews for a while."

"Yep, I know her. She and some dweeb had me under surveillance on and off for over a month. The dweeb was a clown but Andrews is an A1 bitch, Tim. I would not underestimate her if I was you."

"That is what my problem is, Bernard. Someone has it in their mind to kill me and take out Mary Ann for good measure, but I have no clue who it is. If it was only me then I would just disappear for a few years, but—"

"But now you are married to the girl of your dreams and all you are trying to do is live a normal life in the suburbs of Northern Virginia, right? Yes, Tim, you and I had better take a walk."

It was a beautiful seventy-degree East Bay day when Bernard Haskell and Tim Hall set out on their walk. The neighborhood where all of the campers were parked, one after another, mostly consisted of old one- and two-story warehouses. Oakland-Berkeley was the Baltimore of the West Coast (or at least that was what someone had once called it back in the 1970s), yet Tim could see that was all changing before his eyes. A new coffee shop over there, a new restaurant here.

"So, is this your retirement job, Bernard?" Tim asked.

"Yes, it is, Tim. Who would have ever thought that people would be lining up to live in Oakland and Berkeley?" Bernard asked. "Even if you have a job that pays fifty thousand per year, you still won't be able to afford a shitty apartment. That's why I'm here with the rest of them, Tim. If somebody does not bring attention to this situation, the government will just sweep it under the rug."

Tim had no way of knowing if Bernard was telling him the truth or lying. He had never known Bernard Haskell to be particularly altruistic during his days as an analyst for the agency but, then again, after Bernard's wife had died of cancer in 2005, he had moved back to California and he and Tim had lost touch. Anyway, Bernard would not be the first guy to have some kind of epiphany later in life. That happened all of the time.

"Have you heard from your kids, Bernard?" Tim asked.

"Benny and Judith are both doing fine. Both are married and both have two kids apiece. Yep, I'm a grandad, Tim; however, I never see them. I'm afraid both my children feel that I am a little nuts."

Tim could understand why but still wondered if his old friend was now really an advocate for the homeless or whether he was just pretending to be.

THE DECOYS

"Bernard, do you have any clue how can I stop this organization from killing me and my wife?"

"I do and I don't, Tim, but let me explain over a cup of coffee," Bernard said as he walked ahead of Tim. The pair finally stopped at the corner.

"Let's stop here, Tim. The coffee is decent and will not cost you five bucks."

The coffee bar looked like one hundred others that Tim had been in. He went ahead and ordered two medium-sized black coffees. The tattooed young woman behind the counter showed no interest in either Tim or Bernard and went back to reading her book. Bernard and Tim were the only two in the place.

"I never figure out how these places make money," Tim commented as he sat down.

"It is a different world now, Tim," Bernard said, but he was not looking at Tim. Instead, he was watching the door—almost as if he expected someone to walk in.

"So, as you were saying Bernard, you do know but you don't?"

"Do you know how government contracts work, Tim?"

"Yes, I do," Tim replied. "In case you don't know, I run a safe house now."

"Sure, the place on the Potomac that your late wife Pam used to operate. By the way, I was sorry to hear about that."

"Thanks, Bernard, but yes, I know how contracts with the government work."

"And you know what a statement of work is?"

"Sure, it describes what a contractor needs to accomplish in order to get paid," Tim said.

"Well, someone has placed your name and probably your wife's name in the statement of work. Once you find that contract and remove your name from the SOW, you will be home free. However, Tim, as long as your name remains in the SOW, the contractor will keep trying to kill you and your wife. You see, the contractor does not get paid unless they kill or are attempting to kill you. They have to submit a report each month along with their invoice."

"Well, Bernard, we think it was the Department of State or someone like that who placed the contract, but I am not entirely sure or, for that matter, convinced."

"They are a powerful organization, Tim, and have their hands in many pots, as the saying goes."

As crazy as it sounded, Tim knew that Bernard Haskell was probably correct. If there was anyone in the world who understood the inner workings of the United States government, it was Bernard Haskell.

"OK, so assuming that is true, how in the hell am I supposed to find out who has this contract?" Tim wanted to know.

"Not as hard as you may think, Tim. First, you may want to try and catch one of these assassins instead of killing them, but what you really need to do is find the right contractor. I mean, there are only around five or six outfits that even do this kind of work. The man or woman pulling the trigger may not know who they are working for, but there will always be someone close by supervising and, more importantly, documenting their work. After all, that is how anyone gets paid these days. There are no more briefcases under the bed filled with cash. Those days are long gone."

"So, do you have any suggestions as to how I might catch one of these assassins?" Tim asked.

"Yes, that will be the hard part. These types of people try to use the element of surprise to their advantage, so time is on their side. They could try today, but most likely will not try again for a couple of weeks. One thing that will be on your side, Tim, is that they will most likely need to kill you by September thirtieth, 2020, which is when the government fiscal year ends. The government may not opt to renew the contract."

As Tim was digesting what Bernard Haskell had just told him, a now all-too-familiar voice interrupted his thought process.

"Mr. Hall, I thought that I conveyed to you that I did not want you to interview Mr. Haskell without me," Special Agent Cindy Andrews said as she walked into the coffee shop with Mary Ann.

"Agent Andrews," Bernard said as he stood up. "You are in no position to tell me who I can or cannot speak with. Deputy Marshal Hall is an old work colleague of mine and we were simply catching up. Now, if you are unsatisfied, I am ready to contact my attorney, who is more than willing to file a harassment complaint at the United States district court and—"

"That will not be necessary, Mr. Haskell," Special Agent Cindy Andrews said as she tried to calm the situation. "We will be leaving now."

"Special Agent Andrews, you are the one that will be leaving. I will be remaining here with my husband. You, on the other hand, are free to return to San Francisco."

"Special Agent Hall, I really don't care what your husband does at this point but my instructions are—"

"Take you fucking instructions and shove them up your ass, Cindy," Mary Ann said in a quiet but stern voice. "The last I looked, I outrank you and I am giving you a direct order. Now get the fuck out of here."

Special Agent Cindy Andrews turned and left the coffee shop without saying another word. Tim, Mary Ann, and Bernard watched her get into her Ford Taurus and drive away.

"You know, Tim," Mary Ann said, "a bunch of police cars responding to a crime scene is a very dangerous thing. More officers are injured responding to crimes then they are from any other activity. That is just something you should remember."

"I think that you are totally full of shit about that, Mary Ann," Bernard Haskell said, "but I can now see what Timmy here sees in you."

"Timmy?" Mary Ann responded. "I thought I was the only person on the planet allowed to call him that."

"Hell, that was his name back in the day. You know, the kid on *Lassie* was named Timmy. That was who Tim reminded us of. He was not born an adult like some people think."

"By the way, Mary Ann, the man who resembles Santa Claus here is my friend Bernard Haskell, and I'm sure he would love to flirt with you while I try to get us a ride out of here," Tim said as he started to look up Brent's phone number.

"Go ahead and take your time, honey, I am in no hurry. At least, not now."

Chapter 14

It took cab driver Brent Wilkins about one hour and thirty-two minutes to make it over to the 1200 block of 8th Street in Berkeley. In the meantime, Bernard Haskell explained government contracting to Mary Ann, or at least how it applied to her and Tim. Mary Ann still had a hard time believing that the government would place a contract on their lives and thought that it was more likely that Bernard Haskell was just a crazy old man, but Tim asked her to keep an open mind. The three then walked back from the coffee shop for a quick drink in Bernard's camper when they heard a car horn blaring on the street outside.

"Boy, I thought I just drove into a used RV lot," Brent said as Tim and Mary Ann got in the back of the rental car. "Did that FBI girl dump you two out here to fend for yourselves?"

"No, the FBI woman did not, Brent," Mary Ann said, correcting him.

"The FBI woman finished with what she had to do over here, Brent, so my wife sent her home," Tim said, trying to keep the peace. "Mary Ann? Would you like to drive through UC Berkeley to see where I went to school?"

"Sure, but can we do it another time, honey? I'm beat and I'm hungry and God knows how long it will take us to get back to San Francisco."

"I know a great Mexican place downtown if you would like to eat there," Brent suggested.

"Sure, that would be great, Brent," Tim replied.

"Please wake me when it's over," Mary Ann said as she placed her head on Tim's shoulder.

Tim knew that Mary Ann wanted to talk about Bernard and Cindy Andrews and the FBI, but she did not want to do so in front of Brent. At least, not until she knew him better. Tim, on the other hand, had already checked out Brent and was satisfied that he was OK, although Mary Ann was probably right about not talking out of school. Tim knew that cab drivers loved to gossip with one another and there was no need for them to know about the internal squabbles at the local FBI office.

Since Mary Ann was now taking a nap, Tim decided to converse with Brent.

"So how was your day up until now, Brent?"

"Not bad, boss, I had a couple of fares today but it really sucks driving a cab nowadays. Uber and that other ride service are really killing the business."

"You don't seem like the type who would be driving a cab," Tim said but was sorry as soon as the words left his mouth.

"Why is that, boss? Because I'm a white guy?" Brent replied but was laughing as he did.

"Well, no," Tim responded uncomfortably. "You seem like a bright person. Are you from San Fran?"

THE DECOYS

"Nope, I'm from Milwaukee, Wisconsin," Brent replied, using a Wisconsin accent. "I was in the Navy, stationed over at the support center in Alameda."

"How long were you in the Navy?"

"Altogether, twelve years. I was planning on being a lifer but I got hurt and then developed a little bit of a substance abuse problem, so it was suggested that I become a civilian. They did, however, allow me to retire on disability, and my little problem did not follow me into civilian life."

"Meaning you were able to get your hack license?"

"You know, boss, it is harder to get a hack license than it is to get one to fly an airplane, but then this Uber comes along and now every stoned-out freak is operating a ride service"

"Well, that does suck," Tim replied.

"It sure does, boss, it sure does."

When Brent pulled up in front of the Taqueria Cancun, both Tim and Mary Ann had fallen asleep. *We are certainly making it easy for assassins to take us out*, Tim thought to himself as he looked over the restaurant façade.

"Honey, wake up. Time for dinner."

"Huh, oh, OK," Mary Ann responded.

"I will be around, boss, so just give me a call when you need me," Brent said as he held the door open for Mary Ann.

The restaurant was about half full, so Tim and Mary Ann had no trouble finding a booth toward the back of the room. They ordered two margaritas and looked at the menus.

"I'm sorry that I tricked you into responding to that robbery-in-progress call," Tim said.

"You did not trick me," Mary Ann said before taking a long sip of her margarita. "I knew that a 211 in progress only four blocks away was really just too convenient."

"What about Nancy Drew?" Tim said, referring to Special Agent Cindy Andrews. "Did she suspect that the call was a fake?"

"No, she bought it hook, line, and sinker. Cindy really does not appreciate how the CIA can magically just make things happen. Someone has given her the impression that the agency is nothing but a bunch of white guys drinking martinis in DC. She also feels that the FBI will soon be doing much of the international intelligence work anyway, and that you, my friend, are a dying breed," Mary Ann said as she finished her drink and looked for the waitress so she could order another one.

"So, what happened at the bank?" Tim wanted to know.

"Oh, it was about what you would expect. About ten Berkeley and Oakland black-and-white police cars converged on the scene, guns drawn and all, but it did not take them very long to determine that the branch was indeed not being robbed. Next, they started thinking that maybe another bank in another part of the city was being robbed, but that did not pan out either. Cindy was pissed but she did not suspect you. At least, not yet."

Tim ordered two more margaritas and four tacos with no sour cream. Four tacos were what Tim Hall ordered in any Mexican restaurant anywhere, while Mary Ann had enchiladas covered with a lot of cheese and some sort of savory sauce. To Tim, it just looked like too much food to digest.

"Let's hope that she will be out of our lives from now on," Tim said.

"I have a funny feeling that she is not going anywhere. For some reason, Carol Russo does not want you anywhere close to Bernard. At least, that was the impression that I got from Cindy on our way back over to 8th Street. As a matter of fact, she said 'Russo will have my ass if she finds out I left your husband alone with Haskell.'"

The food arrived and both Tim and Mary Ann started eating as soon as their plates landed on the table. Tim was on his third taco before he asked another question.

"So, why don't you think that Cindy Andrews is out of our lives, Mary Ann?"

"Well, number one, Carol will not allow it and, number two, Cindy Andrews hates you and has so much as told me so."

"You mean Cindy has convinced my loyal wife that I am nothing but a useless a-hole?"

"Cindy thinks you represent everything that is wrong with federal law enforcement, but you belong to me and I think I demonstrated that this afternoon by not returning to the city with her."

Mary Ann reached across the table, squeezed Tim's hand, and blew him a kiss.

"Anyway, I'm not sure why Carol Russo is so intent on keeping you away from Bernard. Tim? You don't believe that cockamamie explanation about government contracting, do you?"

"Let me put it to you this way, Mary Ann: I do not disbelieve it."

"Oh, please," Mary Ann replied. "You mean to tell me that in some filing cabinet in one of those gray buildings in downtown DC, there is a contract with our names on it?"

"Not as such, honey, but there is a mechanism in place that is paying a company somewhere to kill us. As Bernard said, no one walks around with briefcases of cash anymore."

"Yes, I get your point, Tim, but what agency would even do such a thing? I mean, the CIA does not kill off its old employees, does it?"

"Well, if it did then I would have been gone years ago," Tim said with a half-laugh. "No, it would have to be someone else. Maybe the Department of Agriculture."

"Agriculture," Mary Ann said, loud enough for the entire room to hear, which resulted in Tim placing his finger over his lips.

"Yes, agriculture," Tim said as he lowered his voice. "Think about all the things that the Department of Agriculture is involved with. Think about all of the food the USDA distributes around the world. Food is probably more important than rocket launchers to most of these third-world countries, and I know for a fact that the department contracts with several outfits to provide security. So, what would stop them from placing something in one of their contracts about us? Yes, I know it sounds farfetched, but a lot of things do until you find out otherwise."

Mary Ann stared at Tim for what seemed like an eternity until she finally said, "Yes, I can see your point, but be honest with me for a minute, Tim." Mary Ann took a deep breath. "Have you done anything lately to piss off the USDA?" She laughed.

THE DECOYS

"Well, I'm glad you are finding my theory so amusing," Tim said and was actually a little hurt by Mary Ann's teasing, but what had he expected? Nobody perceived the USDA as anything other than a benign organization, even though they were probably the most powerful federal agency next to the Department of Defense.

"Mary Ann? Three days ago, you shot and killed two men in a drug store and, to the best of my knowledge, these are the first people you have ever killed. I am curious how you feel about that."

"I think I do what everybody else does, Tim. I bury it all deep inside of me and hope that it does not come back to haunt me at a later date. Why do you ask? Have you found a better method?"

Mary Ann had asked a question that Tim could not answer. Tim had felt obligated to speak with Mary Ann about the shooting but now he really had no clue what to say.

"So, Tim? Are you going to wow me with your vast insights on taking a human life? Tell me, how do you handle the guilt of taking a life?"

"Can I get you folks anything else to eat?" the waitress had interrupted the tension.

"Yes, can you bring us two shots of Sauza Gold tequila and the check?" Tim said.

Tim and Mary Ann sat in silence while the waitress obtained the tequila shots from the bartender. Tim felt dumber than a box of rocks for going down this particular road with his wife at this time. Tim did feel an overwhelming need to protect his wife, but often he forgot that Mary Ann had been a cop for a very long time and knew all the ins and outs of the job. The waitress returned with the tequila.

"Well, this is what I do, Mary Ann, when I have a bad experience. I tie it all up in a ball and I bury it all deep inside of me and hope that it does not come back to haunt me at a later date." Tim laughed and both he and Mary Ann drank their shots.

"So, if you are ready, my dear, let's go back to the hotel."

"Best idea I've heard all day," Mary Ann said as she grabbed hold of Tim's arm.

Chapter 15

Brent Wilkins drove Tim and Mary Ann to the front of the Fairmount Hotel, where he parked and opened the door. *Just like a real chauffeur*, Tim thought. He gave Brent two one-hundred-dollar bills and told him that they would not need him anymore tonight.

"Do we really need a driver, honey?" Mary Ann asked.

"We do if I keep drinking four margaritas at dinner, yes. Besides, I am expensing this back to the agency."

"OK, as long as it does not put us in the poorhouse," Mary Ann said and she and Tim walked arm and arm past a statue of the singer Tony Bennett. Mary Ann had not noticed the monument before and stopped to look.

"So, this is where he sang the song 'I Lost My Heart in San Francisco'?" Mary Ann asked.

"Yes, it sure is," Tim said

"Tim? I know what you were trying to do back at the restaurant and I want you to know that I appreciate it because it shows me how much you do really love me. About the shooting last week: I am still processing it and I do, in a way, feel bad for the two guys who tried to kill us, but that's just the thing, they were trying to kill us—I was just defending us."

"Yeah, I know that, Mary Ann. Sometimes I feel a need to protect you but you probably do not really need it."

"No, that is where you are wrong, Tim. Yes, I do know a lot of women agents that might say that to their husbands—that they don't need to be protected—but I do. We all need to be protected."

"Well, I'm sorry if I am coming off like your dad," Tim said.

"Oh God, I only wish my dad had protected me. You know, Tim, it occurred to me the other day that my father has been ripping me off for the last five years, most likely to support his gambling habit. I was a fool to send him my entire paycheck but, when I was undercover with Toby, I had no other choice."

"Don't worry about it, Mary Ann. We will fix that when we get home."

"Speaking of home, I am just about ready. San Francisco has been fun but I think that we have accomplished what we needed to do here. I mean we have spoken to Bernard and have found out almost nothing. In other words, I do not feel this investigation is going anywhere."

Tim and Mary Ann lingered a bit longer in front of the statue of Tony Bennet and also watched a cable car go by. They next walked into the lobby of the Fairmount.

"Honey, let's go to bed," Mary Ann said.

As Tim and Mary Ann rode up the elevator, Tim looked at his wife. He really was lucky to have her, he thought to himself. At least he had found someone that actually cared about him.

THE DECOYS

Morning came and Tim rolled over and grabbed the clock radio. It was 9:55 AM. Almost 10 o'clock. Tim and Mary Ann had slept late, and why not? They had nothing planned, beyond beginning to pack for the trip back home. Tim figured he would be in a better position to solve the mystery of who was going to kill them back home in Virginia than in San Francisco. Plus, no one had been very welcoming in the three days since they'd arrived. Tim's iPhone began to ring but he decided not to answer it. The call could only be from Bob Fredericks, who would once again give him conflicting information about their purpose in San Francisco or about the parties trying to kill them. Tim wondered if he could convince Mary Ann to quit the FBI and go underground with him. The iPhone rang once again. This time Tim picked up. As he expected, the caller was Bob.

"Good morning, Bob. Yes, we are alive."

"Tim?" Bob said. "Is Mary Ann there and are you both all right?"

"Yes, we are both fine and are about to order breakfast. Why, what's up, Bob?"

"It's about Carol Russo. She was found dead this morning in her apartment and the police suspect foul play."

Tim sat up in bed but remained silent. He really did not know what to say about the woman who he had only met the day before. He did understand that Carol was a friend of Bob's, but he still felt no real reaction to the news of her death.

"I'm sorry to hear that, Bob. Carol seemed like a nice person," Tim finally said, although he really did not feel that way. As a matter of fact, Tim had been suspicious of Carol from the moment he had met her.

"It does appear that she was murdered at some point around midnight this morning. She did not report to the office for an eight AM meeting and they sent a police officer to check on at nine AM your time. The cop found the door partially open and, when he entered the apartment, he found her dead. She'd been shot in the face."

"Do they always send a cop to check on your welfare if you are an hour late for work?" Tim asked. "The agency has never done that for me."

"Tim, you have to understand that Carol is—or was—a key player."

"A key player in what, Bob?"

"A key player in the operation that I can't talk about, Tim. We have all been concerned for her safety."

"Well, thanks for letting me know about it, Bob. Now, after Mary Ann and I have breakfast, we plan to start packing for our return home."

"Tim, please hold tight. FBI management would like to speak with Mary Ann. I believe they may have an assignment for her."

Oh great, Tim thought. He knew that Mary Ann would be a sucker for anything the bureau wanted her to do, especially if some FBI brass asked her personally.

"OK, Bob. We will hold tight for now—and Bob? I'm sorry about Carol. I know that she was a friend of yours."

"Oh yes, she was," Bob said, but Tim suspected that Bob had really not been very close to Carol Russo.

THE DECOYS

"So, what's up, Tim?" Mary Ann had woken up and had been listening to Tim's half of the conversation.

"Carol Russo was found dead this morning in her apartment."

"How?"

"Gunshot wound."

"Oh my God," Mary Ann said. "Did Bob say anything else?"

"She was shot in the face."

"Hmm, that's interesting," Mary Ann responded.

"How so?"

"When someone is shot in the face, it often means that the killer had lost trust in the victim over a period of time. It is also an indication that the perpetrator wanted to be sure that the victim saw who was shooting them. It is a really intense and emotional act," Mary Ann said.

"I didn't know that you knew so much about homicide, honey."

"Well I worked homicide in Cleveland before I joined the FBI, and we did have a lot of gang members taking it in the face. It is also a real insult to the victim and the victim's family since it usually means that they cannot have an open-casket funeral."

"Well, that certainly is interesting, but Bob also said that Carol was a key player."

"A key player? What kind of key player?"

"A key player in the operation—the operation that no one can tell us about. Bob also said that the FBI may want you to do something special."

"Really? What kind of something special?"

"That I can't say because—"

Tim was interrupted by the sound of Mary Ann's iPhone. The default ring, as Tim referred to it. Mary Ann was quick to answer it.

"Special Agent Hall," Mary Ann said into the phone. Tim observed that his wife was listening intently to someone.

"Yes, sir. No, that will not be a problem. Thank you, sir, I will do my best."

Mary Ann put down her iPhone and looked at Tim.

"They would like me—I mean, us—to lead the investigation into the death of Carol Russo, and they would like to meet with us at five PM in the lobby."

"That certainly gives us some time to kill. Why don't I order breakfast?"

"I don't think I could eat a thing," Mary Ann remarked.

"Well, just try," Tim said as he picked up the phone and ordered two All-American Breakfasts.

Mary Ann, of course, finished her All-American Breakfast and then retired to the bathroom for a beauty bath. Tim, on the other hand, had almost five hours to kill and was not happy about it at all. Of course, Mary Ann and Tim could have gone out and toured the city some more, but neither of them wanted to risk missing the meeting. No; the best thing to do was hang out in the hotel room.

After her bath, Mary Ann found a movie to watch while Tim went on the Internet. He checked the safe house email and saw that everything seemed to be running OK. Anyway, Bob had asked Tim not to get involved with any safe house business while he was away. *Good old Bob, always taking care of business*, Tim thought to himself. Tim had to wonder whether Bob Fredericks had arranged for Mary Ann to head the investigation into Carol Russo's murder. After all, Bob Fredericks knew as well as Tim did that Mary Ann would never have been able to resist such an assignment. It was not lost on Tim that the FBI had not been happy with Mary Ann's decision to marry a CIA agent. Tim figured that this was the main reason his wife was no longer considered for plumb FBI assignments. Bob Fredericks had stepped up and found Mary Ann a job with the CIA as a liaison between the two agencies, which was the type of position that no one took seriously, and Tim could tell that Mary Ann was becoming frustrated with the job. However, if Mary Ann decided to return to the FBI as a regular agent, she would be destined to serve as a field agent in some backwater Virginia or Maryland resident agent office. These offices were basically sub-stations of the larger main offices. They were offices where you spent the majority of your time investigating bank robberies and other small-time federal crimes, certainly nothing high-profile, and that was one thing about Mary Ann Hall: she was all about high-profile crimes. Leading an investigation into the murder of a senior FBI special agent would be considered a *career case* and was something Mary Ann would probably have done for free.

At 4:55 PM, Tim and Mary Ann started for the lobby of the Fairmount, performing their regular routine of checking both ends of the hallway. At 5 PM, Tim and Mary Ann entered the dining room of the Fairmount Hotel to meet Agent in Charge Perez.

Albert Perez stood six feet and two inches tall, with dark salt-and-pepper hair. He was flanked by two white male FBI special agents, but Albert stood out. He immediately stepped forward to introduce himself.

"Special Agent Wilson-Hall and Agent Tim Hall? My name is Albert Perez and I would like to speak with you on a matter of the utmost importance."

"Honey?" Tim said as he leaned into Mary Ann, "I can meet you up in the room if you two need to speak privately."

"No, Agent Hall," Albert Perez said. "What I have to say concerns the both of you. If you would, let's step into the bar."

Tim and Mary Ann followed Albert Perez into the bar and to a table where a third agent was sitting. The third agent got to her feet and offered Mary Ann a seat. She then walked to the front, where she joined the other two, who appeared to be standing guard.

"Would the two of you care for a drink?" Albert Perez asked.

"No, just coffee," Mary Ann replied.

"Same for me," Tim said.

"I will have a Johnnie Walker Black Label on the rocks," Albert Perez told the waitress.

"Oh, can I have a Grand Marnier with the coffee?" Tim added.

"I apologize for interrupting your evening," Albert Perez started off by saying, "but you are aware that one of our special agents was murdered this morning?"

THE DECOYS

"Yes," responded Mary Ann, "my husband's manager called him this morning and gave him the news. Tim and I both met Carol yesterday and feel awful about it."

"Yes, it is very hard when we lose someone in our FBI family, especially in this way. Mary Ann—may I call you Mary Ann?" Albert Perez added.

"Yes, of course," Mary Ann quickly responded, "and please call my husband Tim."

"Wonderful, I'm glad we got that out of the way," Albert Perez said with a smile as the drinks arrived from the bar.

"Anyway, Mary Ann, you may already know this, but I have only been at the San Francisco office for a little over six months now and I have to confess that I am not totally familiar with the staff as of yet. There are over five hundred agents in the Bay Area, not counting support people, and, in all honesty, it is a difficult assignment. On top of that, this is San Francisco—the employees here all seem to have a different mindset, or at least it seems that way to me. I started off in Los Angeles, but LA is nothing like it is up here," Albert Perez said as he took a sip of his Johnnie Walker Black Label.

"Special Agent Caroline Russo was a popular manager and many of the agents who were under her, as well as the agents who knew her, are quite frankly in a state of shock. That being the case, I was hoping, Mary Ann, that you would consider taking the lead in her murder investigation. All of the agents working for Carol will need to be interviewed, as well as her associates. The Berkeley Police Department and the Alameda County Sheriff Department are leading the homicide investigation and I need someone to coordinate with them. Since we are the FBI, a lot of our agents feel that we should handle the investigation ourselves, but past experience has shown us that this is not always a good idea. Of course, our resources—our lab and forensic team, for example—will be used as required, but no agents working in the Bay Area will be taking an active part in the investigation."

"You mentioned my husband, Agent Perez; how is he involved?"

"Yes, well, I feel that your husband is more than qualified to assist you in your investigation, although I do not feel we should advertise the fact that he is a CIA agent. Therefore, Agent Hall will be officially on loan from the United States Marshal Service—I have already cleared that with them both locally and nationally. Now, Tim"—Albert Perez was looking straight at Tim now—"a United States deputy marshal may not impress our agents, so perhaps you would be better served working in the field with the Berkeley police or the sheriff department, but that is all up to Mary Ann. She will be in charge."

"Mr. Perez, I would be happy to accept this assignment, but do you feel that I am qualified?" Mary Ann asked.

"Although your file is classified to many, Mary Ann, it is not classified to me, and I am fully aware of all of your achievements. I assure you, you are more than qualified."

Albert Perez looked up and nodded to one of the agents standing at the door to the restaurant. The woman agent walked to the table.

"Mary Ann? This is Special Agent Angela Rice. She is will be your personal assistant and liaison to me or anyone else that you need to speak within the San Francisco or Oak-

THE DECOYS

land offices. You can coordinate with her concerning any needs you and your husband may have. Oh, and yes, you report to me and only to me. I am a big believer in the seventy-two-hour rule, so let's catch the person who did this to Carol. Any questions?"

No one seemed to have any.

"OK then." Albert Perez got up to leave and so did Tim and Mary Ann, until Albert put his hand out.

"Please sit and get to know one another. And Tim?"

Tim looked up, not sure how he should refer to Special Agent in Charge Albert Perez.

"Tim, say hi to Bob Fredericks for me. The two of us go back a long way."

"Don't they all," Tim said under his breath, but Albert Perez had already walked away.

Mary Ann and Tim had a quick meeting with Special Agent Angela Rice. It was decided that Angela Rice would pick Mary Ann up at 9 AM and take her to the San Francisco FBI office. There, she would be introduced to the entire staff and would explain what she hoped to accomplish. Tim, on the other hand, would go out to the crime scene and report back to Mary Ann. Angela Rice was pleased to learn that Tim had already rented a car, since there was a shortage of vehicles at the office—government cutbacks and all. Once that was completed, they each said their goodnights and went their separate ways.

"Well, this is certainly an unexpected turn of events," Tim said.

"Yes, you could certainly say that again," Mary Ann replied.

"So, what is your take on this?" Tim wanted to know.

"It sounds to me that Carol knew her attacker and freely let them into her condominium. First things first, we have to find out if she was romantically involved with anyone here at work," Mary Ann said.

Tim immediately recalled Bernard Haskell's comment about Carol Russo being "one hell of a woman," which Tim had taken as just an odd type of compliment an older man might make. He did not really think that Bernard had a romantic relationship with Carol Russo, but Bernard did know her and that would need to be checked out. They also apparently lived only two miles apart. Tim would follow that up tomorrow but did not feel he should mention it to Mary Ann, at least not yet.

Tim and Mary Ann slowly exited the elevator and, as usual, checked the hallway before they proceeded to their room. They had not forgotten that they were still targets.

"Tim? Now that we are working, do you think we should ask for some protection?"

"I was thinking the same thing, Mary Ann."

"Tim, I am going to have a very hard time running this investigation if I'm constantly having to look over my shoulder," Mary Ann said. For the first time, Tim thought that his wife sounded stressed.

"OK, I get it, Mary Ann, and I think I know someone who I trust enough to take on the job of protecting us. I will call him first thing in the morning."

"Wonderful, honey, I knew that you would not let me down," Mary Ann said as she turned and kissed Tim.

THE DECOYS

They both decided to have dinner in the hotel room that night while watching a movie.

Later on, they both got into bed and made love. Mary Ann, who'd been on top of Tim, moved off to his left side and almost immediately fell asleep with her head on Tim's chest. It had occurred to Tim that he and his wife made love almost every night. Tim was not sure of the exact numbers, but he knew that had to be well above average. He was happy about the sex and was happy that he was still able to perform, but he also wondered if Mary Ann's sexual appetite—not to mention her increased desire for more off-beat or kinky sex—was indicative of something else. Not to make a pun, but Tim did not want to screw up a good thing, especially considering that he knew several couples who just no longer had sex or several others who didn't have it often. He did not want that to happen, but still, he was concerned.

The other elephant in Tim's head was Mary Ann's father, his gambling habit, and the fact that he had been stealing money from his daughter for the last four years. That had to stop, but Tim knew it would most likely result in a fight. Gambling was the one vice that Tim Hall hated and he had no sympathy for victims of the addiction. Tim could understand drug and alcohol addiction because many felt a need to escape life, but losing money because you needed that short-lasting high from the anticipation of winning or losing made no sense to him. In his heart, Tim knew that the reasons for gambling addiction were much more complicated than the so-called "gamblers' high," but Tim found the fact that gamblers could somehow justify stealing money from their own children inexcusable.

At least Tim had finally thought of the one man who he could trust to protect him and Mary Ann; that was at least some kind of accomplishment. Tim needed a bodyguard who would not get distracted by boredom. A bodyguard who, for example, would not be fooled by a woman in distress, even if the situation involved a baby or a child. A bodyguard who knew all of the tricks in the book. That person was Darrell Murphy, a bodyguard who'd been trained by Tim's late wife, Pam. The only problem was that, since he had been gut-shot by Toby Wheeler, Darrell was a little nuts. To make matters worse, he also blamed Tim for the death of Pam. Regardless, Tim felt that it could all be worked out. At least, he hoped so.

Chapter 16

Tim woke up at 8:30 AM to find Mary Ann already dressed. She was wearing the black pencil skirt that she had brought from DC along with her cream-colored blouse and dark stockings. Her hair was tied back in a bun, which made her look especially sexy to Tim.

"Good morning, honey, I ordered you some bacon and eggs," Mary Ann said as she brought Tim a cup of coffee and sat down on the edge of the bed. She also had a folder, which she handed to Tim.

"These are pictures of the crime scene and, unfortunately, pictures of Carol Russo. I would like you to catch up with a detective named Walter Ashton of the Berkeley PD. He is in charge of the case. I think it is best that we let them handle the investigation, unless you feel that they are total screw-ups. If that is the case then we will take it over."

Tim looked at the file and handed it back to Mary Ann.

"No, you keep it. That is your department," Mary Ann said. "Honey, I am really depending on you to be my eyes and ears on the street."

Tim half-expected Mary Ann to next say, "so please don't screw it up," but she did not. This was the first time that he had worked with Mary Ann and Tim was not sure how he felt about her being in charge; however, he knew enough to keep his mouth shut about it.

"Not a problem, babe, I will do my best," he said.

"Oh, I know you will, which is why I love you so very much," Mary Ann said as she picked up her coat.

"Mary Ann? Before you leave, I have decided who to hire as a bodyguard for us. At least around the hotel."

"Really? Do I know them?"

"Yes, in a way you do. It is Darrell Murphy, the guy who ran safe house security for Pam."

"Really?" Mary Ann said as she stepped into the bathroom to check her makeup. "The guy that Toby shot? I thought you told me that he was crazy?"

"I think he is OK now. The thing about Darrell is that he will not be fooled by a fainting woman or a fire in the next room. He will be totally focused on the task and—"

"Tim?" Mary Ann interrupted. "If you think Darrell Murphy is the right person then he is the right person. I just don't want to keep looking around corners," Mary Ann said as she returned to the bedroom and kissed Tim on the forehead. Tim suddenly felt turned on and tried to pull her back into bed but Mary Ann stopped him.

"Careful, don't mess up my makeup, you silly boy. Wait until after dinner tonight. Then I am all yours."

"I'm afraid you won't be home until midnight," Tim replied.

"Look, I'm not planning on moving into the San Francisco FBI office, meaning that I expect to have dinner with you at around six this evening. You will be surprised by how fast I blow through these interviews," Mary Ann said as her phone rang.

"Good morning," Mary Ann said to the caller. "Great, I will be right down." She hung up. "That was my new PA, Angela Rice. Now, text me when you know something new." Mary Ann kissed Tim goodbye.

Tim got out of bed, grabbed his Glock, and followed Mary Ann to the door.

"OK, let me at least check the hallway for you."

He did and watched his wife walk to the elevator. Tim knew that was sloppy, since a would-be assassin could have been anywhere, and there he was standing naked in the doorway. He really did need Darrell Murphy or someone like him, so he sat back down on the bed and began making phone calls.

Tim first called the contractor Darrell Murphy worked for to check his availability. They told Tim that they would get back to him. Tim next called the hotel desk to reserve a room for Darrell and his team—preferably one on the same floor. The front desk also said that they would get back to him. Tim next called Brent Wilkins and told him to turn in the Ford Taurus and get an SUV instead. He also told Brent that he would be needing him for at least one more week and would pay him five hundred dollars a day to be on call for twenty-four hours. This news appeared to make Brent very happy. The next call was to Detective Sergeant Walter Ashton of the Berkeley Police Department's homicide division. For a change, the cop was actually nice and respectful to Tim and seemed to be happy to meet with him at the crime scene at around 1 PM. The last call of the morning was to Bob Fredericks.

"Good morning, Bob, is there any new information on your end?"

"Well, with regards to Carol Russo, apparently she was romantically involved with Bernard Haskell and he was semi-cohabitating with her."

"What is the exact meaning of semi-cohabitation?" Tim asked.

"Well, I guess it means that Bernard was sleeping at her condominium on a regular basis and was only using the camper van as a front for his social activism."

"Are the Berkeley police aware of this, Bob?"

"They are and, as a matter of fact, he is a person of interest, but you know the cops, Tim—they always first look at the husband or boyfriend any time a woman turns up dead."

"OK, well, that is good to know as I am meeting with them this afternoon. Is there anything else they have that we do not?"

"Well, they are pursuing other leads because, after all, Carol was an FBI special agent and has put several people away over the years."

"What about this Albert Perez guy? He said that you two go back a long way," Tim asked.

"Albert and I worked one of those joint FBI-CIA details in the nineties, Tim. That is pretty much all I can say about that, but he is an up-and-coming career bureaucrat who is in line for the director's job one day. He is also a lawyer and becoming the attorney general one day is not out of the question for him. I would stay on the right side of him if I were you, Tim," Bob said and Tim knew enough to take that as a warning.

Tim noticed that Bob was not his usual upbeat self and decided to ask why.

"Are you doing OK, Bob?"

"Well, you know that all roads lead through me, and I guess I am the common denominator in all of these mysteries, so there has been some talk about having me step back for a while."

"Do you want to step back for a while, Bob?"

"Not on your life, Tim. Right now, the mood in DC is that if you are not on the side of the progressives in Congress and the media then you are a bad person; however, the conservative Republicans are also taking names and they are waiting to pounce as soon as the opportunity presents itself. The best thing to do right now is to keep your mouth shut until we have a winner."

"OK, Bob, well keep up the good fight," Tim said.

"Oh, don't worry about me, Tim, I always land on my feet. And Tim, please be careful. Mary Ann's new position at the San Francisco FBI office does not make you two any safer."

"Thank you, Bob," Tim said, but Bob had already hung up the phone. To Tim, Bob's comment about staying safe was just a way of saying, "Good luck because you are on your own now."

Tim's iPhone rang, which made him look at the clock next to the bed. It was now 11 AM and he needed to start getting ready for his visit to Berkeley.

"Tim Hall," he said into the iPhone.

"Mr. Hall? This is Darrell Murphy. The office called me this morning and said that you needed my help?" Darrell asked in his unmistakable monotonal voice.

"Yes, Darrell, my wife Mary Ann and I have been targeted for assassination by some group who have already tried to kill us twice over the last seven days."

"Are you the target, Mr. Hall, or is it your wife?"

"It is me, Darrell, but they also appear to be willing to take Mary Ann out as well."

"Has it occurred to you that the contract may be on your wife, Mr. Hall?"

Darrell had just made a very good point. Tim had just assumed that the hit was meant for him, especially after Bob Fredericks had said that it was all about Tim pretending to be a drug dealer in Colombia, but could it be about Mary Ann? *Well*, thought Tim, *I guess it's possible.*

"To be honest, Darrell, I don't know. The hit may be on Mary Ann."

"Well, it does not matter, Mr. Hall. Yes, I am available."

"We are in San Francisco, Darrell. When can you be out here?"

"As long as price is not an issue, Mr. Hall, my team and I can be out there by this evening."

"How many in your team, Darrell?"

"I will be bringing two with me. If any additional members are required, we can pick them up out there."

"OK, Darrell. We are registered at the Fairmont Hotel. Call or text me when you get in."

"Sure, Mr. Hall."

"And Darrell? Thank you."

THE DECOYS

"Not a problem, Mr. Hall." With that, Darrell hung up the phone.

It really had not occurred to Tim that the hit might have been on Mary Ann and not him. Sure, it was possible, but most likely it was about something that Tim had done in the past.

With that in mind, Tim needed to take a shower and get across the bay to Berkeley. After all, he had a crime scene to see.

Chapter 17

Brent Wilkins stood out the front of the Fairmont by the brand-new Lincoln Navigator SUV that he had rented from Hertz. Today, Brent had also decided to dress in a suit. Tim, on the other hand, was dressed more casually in light Dockers, a button-down blue shirt, and a sports jacket. He affixed his Glock to the holster on his belt, deciding against the old-fashioned shoulder holster, and even carried a pair of handcuffs, although he doubted that he would have an occasion to use them.

"Good morning, boss, where to today?" Brent asked.

"Today, Brent, we are once again heading for Berkeley. This time, to Tenth Street and Dwight Way. Looking for a condo complex. We are going to be meeting two homicide detectives."

"We will be meeting two homicide detectives?" Brent asked nervously.

"I should have said that I will be meeting two homicide detectives, Brent. You see, my wife and I were asked last night if we could help out on a murder investigation," Tim said while wondering if he had given Brent a little too much information.

"If it is all the same to you, boss, I would just prefer to stay in the car. I am not a big fan of the police. No offense or anything."

"No offense taken, Brent. I am not a big fan of them myself, and I am one," Tim replied. "Actually, now that you mention it, I do need to speak with you about a couple of things. First of all, here is a present for you."

Tim handed Brent a pair of Bluetooth earbuds.

"Thanks, boss, I have been wanting a pair of these but they are a little expensive. So, why do I need them?"

"There may be occasions when I have a conversation in the back of the SUV that I would prefer that you did not hear. This would be more for your protection than mine, because there may be some discussions that the bad guys would want to know about; however, if you don't hear anything then you do not know anything. Of course, this would all be on the honor system, since I can't really stop you from listening. Does that make sense?" Tim asked, realizing that he had provided a somewhat convoluted explanation.

"Yeah, sure, boss," Brent replied somewhat uncomfortably. "What you are telling me is that there will be some stuff that you just don't want me to hear. The only problem is that I think wearing these earbuds while driving may be illegal."

"Well, don't worry about that, Brent. If we get stopped, there will not be a ticket," Tim said.

"Sure, if you say so, boss."

"So, what is it about cops that make you nervous, Brent?" Tim asked.

"Cops just don't like me very much, boss. When I was a kid and anything happened at school or in our neighborhood—you know, stuff like vandalism—well, the cops always came to our house first and I was the one they always suspected of perpetrating the crime."

"Well, did you?" Tim asked.

"Yes, most of the time, but that is beside the point, boss," Brent said, and both he and Tim started laughing.

"What it's really about, boss, is my body language; or, at least, that is what my girlfriend says. Sometimes I have trouble looking people in the eye because I am kind of shy and I think that cops pick up on that and start believing that I am hiding something."

"Yes, they will do that, Brent, and that is because cops are taught that in cop school. The cops get something like a forty-five-minute course in 'how to tell if someone is lying to them,' and not making eye contact is one of the signs. Of course, that is complete bullshit, but all cops like to think that they can tell when someone is lying to them. That's why, in an interrogation, they always ask you the same questions over and over again. They are looking to see if you change your story. Now, that technique *does* work, but not making eye contact does not tell you anything," Tim said.

"Yeah, I guess so, boss," Brent said, but still sounded dejected.

"Brent, looking at someone directly in their eyes is very difficult, especially if you are shy. That's because someone's eye movements tell you a lot about how they are reacting to you, and shy people are uncomfortable with that. So, what you do to get around that is look directly at the tip of someone's nose. That way, it appears that you are looking at someone directly even when you're not. Give it a try sometime. It really does work."

"Wasn't that on the TV show *The Americans*?" Brent asked.

"I think that was the best spy show ever, Brent, and that is coming from a real spy, but the looking-at-the-tip-of-the-nose trick has been around for years," Tim said.

"How did you become a spy?" Brent asked.

"I was recruited while I was in graduate school over here at UC Berkeley. The United States was still fighting the Cold War and the agency was really looking for people with degrees in chemistry; but, of course, they never used me for any of that." Tim laughed.

"But why did you do it? They did not make you, did they?"

"I guess it was because my favorite TV show was something called *The Man From Uncle*. I thought those guys were very cool, but the job turned out to be nothing like it is on TV or in the movies. It really is not all that exciting." *Or, at least, most of the time it's not*, Tim thought to himself.

Luckily, Brent and Tim were now in downtown Berkeley and Tim would no longer need to answer any dumb question about the agency, at least for the time being.

Brent slowed down as they approached 10th Street and Tim looked for the telltale signs of an unmarked police car. Most police departments had switched from the standard Ford Crown Victoria model to either the Ford Taurus or Dodge Charger, since Ford no longer manufactured the Crown Victoria. Some departments, however, held onto their Crown Victoria fleet, especially for their detectives.

Detectives did not put their vehicles through the same wear and tear as patrol cops, or at least that was Mary Ann's explanation. Tim saw that the Berkeley detectives did indeed still use the Crown Victoria when he spotted a white one on the corner of 10th Street and Dwight. The car displayed the newer stubby-type antennas used for the digital radio systems, but otherwise made no secret about its purpose. Tim saw that there were red and blue lights in the back window, plus a divider between the front and back seats that kept the prisoners separated from the officers.

"You can let me out at the corner, Brent, but don't go too far. I don't know how long I am going to need to hang around."

"Not a problem, boss, I will be close by," Brent assured him as he drove off.

Tim stood on Dwight Street and realized that the street was now somewhat different than it had been in the 1970s. Berkeley and Oakland were both enjoying the same renaissances as Brooklyn, Queens, and even the Bronx were in New York City.

Tim reached for his cell phone and dialed the number that he had called that morning.

"Walter Ashton," the voice on the other end of the phone answered.

"Walter, Tim Hall here. I am standing right outside."

"Yes, Tim, we see you now."

A man and a woman emerged from the unmarked police car. The man was six foot seven and very thin for his build. The other detective was a blonde woman and was what one would call a "big gal," although she was in no way fat; she was

THE DECOYS

big-boned. Tim guessed that she was between 160 and 180 pounds.

"Hi, Tim, my name is Walter Ashton but everyone calls me Walt. This is Detective Diane Clifford."

Everyone showed everyone else their identifications until they were satisfied that they were who they said they were. Diane spoke first.

"So, you're a United States deputy marshal? Why are you performing FBI work?"

"The short story, Detective Clifford, is that Mary Ann, my wife, is the special agent in charge of the internal investigation of Special Agent Russo's murder. We happened to be out here interviewing Bernard Haskell in regards to a fugitive warrant and were about ten hours away from flying back to DC. That was, until Agent in Charge Perez requested that my wife open an investigation. I'm really out here to interview you and Walt so that Mary Ann will not need to call you in; that said, if you would rather speak with her—"

"Diane, shut up," Walt said to Detective Clifford. "I'm sorry, Deputy Hall, but Diane here likes to ask questions. Sometimes too many."

"Questions are good, Walt, and please, call me Tim. You too, Diane."

Tim figured that all he would need to do was threaten the two detectives with the prospect of hauling them over to San Francisco to be interrogated by some special agent from DC. That would be the last thing they would want, so there would be no more questions about why Tim was performing FBI work.

Tim followed the two detectives as they made their way to the second tier of the condominium and to Special Agent Russo's unit, 2B. The door was still sealed with crime scene tape and it was Diane's job to remove it. After all, that is what you did when you were the junior investigator. As they entered the room, Tim smelled the various chemicals that the crime scene technicians used for fingerprints, bloodstains, and DNA collection. Everything was outlined in the report that Tim was pretending to look at.

Tim walked to where Carol had been found face down. He could see where blood had stained the wood floor.

"So, Diane? What does getting shot in the face tell you?" Tim asked the younger detective.

"It says to me that Special Agent Russo knew her attacker and did not believe that he or she would fire the weapon. She was obviously mistaken."

"I agree with that. Do you have anything to add, Walt?" Tim said.

"Not really, Tim. I believe that Carol's attacker was standing about here," Walt said as he walked over to where he thought that Carol's attacker had been standing, "and was pointing the gun at her. Now, Carol is talking with him or her and she says something that pisses them off and he or she fires and hits Carol in the face. They then turn and run, but no one hears or sees anything."

"And I guess a working security camera would be asking too much?" Tim inquired.

"As a matter of fact, there was a camera and we are waiting for that to be examined; or, I should say, for the FBI to examine the recording. Special Agent Russo's camera interfaced with her iPhone and—"

"And no one has her passcode," Tim said, finishing Walt Ashton's sentence. "So, as of right now, do you two have a prime suspect?"

"Agent Hall, we are certainly not ready to divulge that information, even to the US attorney," Diane Clifford said.

"Walt, why does Diane keep talking?" Tim said, fully realizing that he was being an asshole but knowing he had a reason for it.

"We like Bernard Haskell but we are also trying to gather more evidence; plus, we have not found a murder weapon yet."

"Have you searched his camper?" Tim asked.

"No, but we are working on a warrant right now," Walt replied.

"And you are watching Bernard to make sure he does not dispose of any evidence?"

"We have two people watching him now, Tim."

"Then I'm happy to see that you two have matters under control and see no need to bring in any other resources," Tim said. "All I ask is that you let me know if you decide to arrest and charge Mr. Haskell. From there, the state and US attorneys will determine who tries the case. Mr. Perez and the US attorney will be extremely pleased if this case can be closed in the next day or two so please, keep up the good work you two," Tim said, although he did not mean any of it. "So, I am finished here and will be heading back across the bay. Do you two have any questions for me?"

Detectives Walt Ashton and Diane Clifford both looked at one another and then back to Tim.

"No Tim, I think we understand one another," Walt replied.

Tim was not sure what he and Walt Ashton understood, but he had done what he'd set out to accomplish: get Bernard Haskell arrested for the murder of Carol Russo.

"OK then, I am out of here. All that I ask is that you stay in touch," Tim said as he turned to leave.

"Sure thing, Tim, not a problem. Diane and I just need to seal up the door," Walt said as Tim started down the steps but, on the first landing, he stopped to see if he could eavesdrop on the two detectives. He did not have to wait long.

"See, I told you, Diane. The guy just wanted to make sure we are on top of everything," Tim heard Walt say.

"Yeah, maybe, but I don't appreciate you telling me to shut up, Walt," Diane said.

"Look, I just wanted to get rid of him. They obviously want us to arrest Haskell and—"

Tim heard the voices of the two detectives move closer, indicating that they were now coming down the steps. Tim turned, jumped down to the bottom landing, and speed-dialed Brent.

"Come get me," Tim said

"I'm right here," Brent replied and Tim saw the black SUV pull up.

"Is everything OK, Tim?" Walt asked as he and Diane came up from behind.

"Yep, just waiting for my driver, Walt. Once again, thank you."

Tim saw that Walt and Diane were still standing on the sidewalk, watching him, as Brent drove away, but he really did not care if they suspected he was eavesdropping on them. After all, what did they expect him to do?

"That is what I hate about cops," Brent said as he watched Tim. "They are all just so goddamn suspicious."

Chapter 18

It was almost 5 PM by the time Tim and Brent made it back into the city. Tim had spent most of his time on the drive back checking text messages. He'd received two from Bernard Haskell asking for Tim to call him, but Tim decided it would be better not to—at least, not until he spoke with Mary Ann about it. Tim's gut feeling was that Bernard Haskell did not murder his girlfriend but it was a good idea to let the true murderer think that they were free and clear. Tim also wanted to place Bernard in a position where he would need Tim's help. That way, Bernard might be more willing to help Tim find out who was trying to kill him.

There were also two text messages from Mary Ann telling Tim what a fantastic day she was having. One message read:

I'm having a wonderful day making Cindy Andrew's life miserable.

Tim could only imagine what that was all about. The second message read:

I am starving, where are you?

After reading that one, Tim figured that he'd better give his wife a call.

"Where are you?" Mary Ann said, picking up after only one ring.

"I'm much closer than you think, darling. Why? What's up?"

"Oh, I'm just hanging in my new office overlooking the city. I think I could get used to this."

"Great, perhaps you could be the next agent in charge at the Tulsa, Oklahoma office," Tim joked.

"Well, let's not get crazy," Mary Ann replied. "Anyway, I have a lot to tell you, plus I understand you made quite the impression on two homicide detectives in Berkeley this afternoon."

"Let's just say that I feel that I got our point across," Tim replied.

"We will have to discuss that over dinner. My new PA has suggested a place close by the federal building. Let me text you the name and I will meet you there."

"Ten-four, Chief," Tim replied.

"OK, wise-ass, see you in a minute."

Tim showed Brent the name and address of the restaurant. "Know this place?"

"It is about three minutes away," Brent replied.

"OK, and Brent, thank you for today. I know driving around all day can really suck," Tim said, momentarily forgetting that Brent drove a cab for a living.

"Yes, Mr. Hall, it certainly can," Brent replied as he pulled up in front of Joe's Italian Restaurant. "Call me when you finish dinner," Brent said as Tim climbed out of the SUV.

Slightly embarrassed at his gaffe, Tim just smiled and walked toward the restaurant.

Tim was met by the maître d' but heard and recognized his wife's laugh from the other side of the room. Mary Ann appeared to be having a drink with her new friend Angela Rice, although Special Agent Rice did not seem to be drinking.

"I'm with her," Tim said and walked to Mary Ann's table. Special Agent Angela Rice got up as Tim arrived and, although he tried to have her remain seated, Angela insisted that she did have to go. As Tim shook her hand, he noticed an unusual tattoo on her wrist.

"Does your tattoo have any religious significance, Angela?"

"On no, it was just something I liked," she replied as she headed for the door.

Both Tim and Mary Ann watched as she left the restaurant.

"Angela is just wonderful, Tim, and has been such a help to me. She really made my day."

"Wonderful," Tim said as he leaned over to kiss his wife.

"What I mean, Tim, is that she arranged my entire schedule today, including all of the interviews. The day just flew by."

Tim could tell that Mary Ann had become energized by her new position as the lead investigator and he was in no way going to ruin that. He did, however, suspect that Agent in Charge Perez had ordered Special Agent Rice to smooth her way and make Mary Ann as comfortable as possible. That said, he was happy to see his wife happy again.

"So, tell me about your afternoon with Berkeley homicide," Mary Ann said in a low voice.

THE DECOYS

"How many martinis have you had, Mary Ann?" Tim laughed.

"Oh, two I think. I ordered two before Angela said she was still on duty, so I drank hers."

A waiter arrived and Tim ordered a vodka martini for himself and another one for Mary Ann.

"You have me at three to one right now hon so you'd better order something to eat," Tim advised.

"Anyway, about Berkeley?" Mary Ann asked.

"Well, Detectives Ashton and Clifford look to be close to arresting Bernard Haskell for the murder of Carol Russo. They planned to search his camper today and I would think that, if the murder weapon was not there before, it will be found now."

"That's good, Tim. Thank you," Mary Ann said. "And you did not throw in your two cents about not thinking that Bernard was capable of murder?"

"No, not a hint. I told them both that I thought that they were doing a wonderful job and that I would tell you as much. They believe I am just your stooge; plus, they really want to close this case, gun or no gun."

"Tim, you do know that it is possible that Bernard killed Carol," Mary Ann said.

"Sure, I guess, but I don't think so. You know, another reason to shoot someone in the face is to make it difficult to identify the victim. We do know that this was Carol Russo, don't we?" Tim asked.

"Yes, I did think of that, Tim, and we have requested a DNA test. And before you ask, Carol Russo did not have a twin sister."

"Twins don't share exact DNA," Tim said. "That has been proven."

"Yes, I know, darling, so tell me something that I don't,"

"The individuals responsible for the death of Carol Russo will have rock-solid alibis, so that's one aspect to consider."

"Now that is an interesting concept, Tim. Ninety-nine-point-nine percent of the population are now suspects." Mary Ann laughed.

"Mary Ann, what if Bernard and Carol were both working on a project together that they both cared deeply about?"

"And what do you think that might be, Tim?"

"Affordable housing."

Mary Ann stopped to consider what Tim had just told her.

"OK, sure. Carol and Bernard both care about affordable housing and Carol secretly supported Bernard's advocacy, but so what?"

"I just keep wondering why Carol Russo seemed to go out of her way to stop us from interviewing Bernard. I get the feeling that she was under the impression that we were sent out here to somehow stop his efforts."

"I'm still wondering why Bob sent us out here in the first place—other than to get us out of DC, I mean," Mary Ann said. "Anyway, I'm too hungry to think. What are you going to have for dinner, hon?"

"I'm going to have the steak in mushroom sauce," Tim replied.

"Wow, just like our first date," Mary Ann replied. "By the way, how are your teeth holding out?"

THE DECOYS

"I am going to need a major overhaul, I'm afraid, Mary Ann. Just hope I live long enough to get some new ones."

"Let's hope we both live that long."

Tim's iPhone made the iPhone text message sound. Tim picked up the phone and looked at the screen.

The text read: *At the hotel lobby, waiting for instructions. DM.*

"Who is that, Tim?" Mary Ann asked.

"It is the one and only Darrell Murphy who is currently at the Fairmount awaiting instructions."

"We can meet him after dinner," Mary Ann said.

"Mary Ann? Do you have a problem if I visit Bernard? He has been calling me."

"Sure, go ahead, but remember, you are an investigator, not his lawyer. You are working for the FBI, not for Bernard. And Tim, remember it is possible that Bernard really did murder Carol Russo."

"Yes, I am fully aware of that, Mary Ann," Tim said. "Fully aware."

Chapter 19

Darrell Murphy was waiting for Tim and Mary Ann in the lobby of the Fairmount Hotel. With him were two rather nondescript men and one woman, which made Tim happy. He did not need any goons with shaved heads and tattoos up and down their necks standing or sitting outside of their room, scaring the other hotel guests.

While Darrell's crew, as they would now be known, remained in the lobby, Darrell accompanied Tim and Mary Ann to the hotel bar. Darrell ordered a club soda while Tim and Mary Ann ordered coffee and Grand Marnier.

"First of all, thank you for flying out on such short notice, Darrell," Tim began. "Mary Ann and I do appreciate it."

"Not a problem, Mr. Hall. Glad to have the work. Since I was shot, my phone has not been ringing off the hook."

"You mean, you have been out of work since that shooting?" Tim asked.

"Not out of work—or, at least, not out of a paycheck—but running security for an office building was not why I got into this business," Darrell said.

Tim suddenly felt guilty—he could have employed Darrell at the safe house but, during their last meeting, Tim had detected some hostility from Darrell in relation to Tim's late wife Pam. Tim was ready to launch into an explanation when Mary Ann decided to provide one instead.

"Darrell, Tim did not feel you were ready to return to your regular duties at the safe house, which is why you were not called back. Now, I am not sure whether you have been briefed on the entire story because much of it is still classified, however, we are here to answer any questions you may have."

"I am just a little confused, ma'am. The last thing I remember before waking up in the hospital was walking down the steps to the basement and seeing you tied up on the floor and Mr. and Mrs. Hall—I mean, the first Mrs. Hall—standing over to my right. Next thing I know, that Toby guy shoots me and I go falling down the stairs. Then I find out that you and Mr. Hall are now married and the first Mrs. Hall is dead so yes, I am a little confused."

"Darrell, I was working undercover for the FBI, investigating Sebastian Oak, Toby Wheeler, and Mr. and Mrs. Hall. My cover had been blown and I was captured and held by Toby Wheeler. Mr. Hall helped me escape while the first Mrs. Hall, Pam Hall that is, shot and killed Toby Wheeler. Unfortunately, Pam Hall, along with Sebastian Oak, was struck and killed by a vehicle traveling south over the Route 15 bridge at Point of Rocks, Maryland. Afterward, Mr. Hall and I began seeing each other socially and have since married. Needless to say, my employer, the FBI, was not happy that I'd married the man I was investigating, but such is life. So, now that you know all of this, do you have any questions?"

Darrell Murphy seemed to consider everything that Mary Ann had just told him.

"One question. Did Mrs. Pam and Mr. Oak do anything wrong?"

"The FBI, along with the CIA, has just about classified everything pertaining to my investigation, but I can tell you, Darrell, that no further action was taken against Mr. Hall or anyone else related to the investigation, living or dead. What Tim and I need to know from you, Darrell, is whether you can with a clear conscience provide protection for Mr. Hall and myself?"

"Yes, Agent Hall, I'm sure that I can," Darrell replied.

"Then that is all I need to know, Darrell. Now, Tim will fill you in with what you need to know. I just need to be escorted back to our room so I can get some sleep," Mary Ann said as she finished her drink.

Darrell called his female crewmember, whose name was Susan, to escort Mary Ann back to the hotel room.

"Susan used to work the gang unit in PG County," Darrell said, referring to the Prince George's County, Maryland Police Department. "I don't know of anything she can't handle," he continued.

"Yes, I think she will be perfect," Tim said as he watched the two women head toward the elevators.

"You know, Darrell, these people, the ones trying to take us out, are very good. Unless we stop them, eventually they will succeed."

"The only way to stop them, Mr. Hall, is to find the person who is responsible for the contract in the first place. They are the ones who need to call this off but, in the meantime, I am confident that we will be able to prevent anything from happening to you or your wife. At least for the time being."

"Darrell? Is there anything that you need from either Mary Ann or me?"

"I am concerned about your wife, Mr. Hall. Is she going to work every day?"

"Yes, but her office is only about four blocks from here."

"OK, well, first of all, someone will be sitting in front of your room at all times and someone needs to be with your wife when she is not with the FBI. That is why I brought Susan with us. She was a great cop but she got into a little trouble and they had to let her go."

"What kind of trouble, Darrell?"

"She head-butted some gangbanger and the video made it onto YouTube. You know, a cop beating up a black dude just don't look good," Darrell said with a laugh as he handed Tim his iPhone.

The video on the iPhone showed a group of African American kids surrounding a white female police officer. The kid doing the most talking started pointing his finger at the woman, who grabbed the young man by his shoulders and head-butted him. This resulted in the young man falling to the ground. Although the sound was turned down, the group appeared to be laughing at the kid on the ground while the woman officer turned and walked back to her police car.

"So, this is thought to be a racial thing, Darrell?" Tim asked.

"I guess so" Darrel replied and for a moment, no one in the room could think of anything to say which led to an uncomfortable silence. Fortunately, Darrel spoke once again.

"So, Tim, what is your current security setup?"

"I have a driver named Brent Wilkins. He was a cab driver who drove us around on the first night that we were here. I did run a check on him and he appears clean. Brent is a disabled US Navy veteran."

"I'm sure he is probably OK, Tim, but I think that I should ride with you from now on. It won't hurt to have another gun."

"Yes, and it may also help calm Brent's nerves. He is kind of a nervous guy, and is not a big fan of the police."

"That makes two of us," Darrell said and began to laugh. "So, are you ready to go upstairs now?"

"Yes, Darrell, I am—and Darrell, I am happy that you decided to take this assignment."

"Yes, Tim. As a matter of fact, so am I."

Chapter 20

When Tim entered the hotel room, he was pleased to find Mary Ann still awake. Tim saw that she was reading the contents of a manila envelope. Before Tim could ask about the folder's contents, Mary Ann spoke.

"Tim, Bernard has been arrested by the Berkeley police for the murder of Carol Russo."

"That certainly did not take long, Mary Ann. Was this your decision?"

"No, the Berkeley PD found the murder weapon under the rear bumper of Bernard's truck. It is a Glock 22 that has recently been fired. The weapon was taken to the lab for analysis, but we are ninety percent sure we have the murder weapon."

"No matter that every FBI special agent carries a Glock 22, and God knows how many cops as well."

"Tim, we promised each other that we would not take this personally."

"I'm not, Mary Ann, but it smells like a setup to me."

"Look, Tim, this isn't some Perry Mason murder mystery where the suspect was set up. I will even admit that much of the evidence we have so far is circumstantial, but you might be shocked to find out how many real murder cases go to trial with just that: circumstantial evidence."

"You know what bothers me, Mary Ann? Each time I hear that some group or organization is against affordable housing, the real estate industry is usually behind it."

"Whoa!" Mary Ann exclaimed. "Where is that coming from? We have a domestic violence case, not a vast conspiracy involving the real estate industry."

"I don't think Bernard murdered Carol Russo. They were a couple committed to affordable housing and someone wanted them eliminated."

"When I first became a detective, Tim, an old sergeant told me that if it walks, swims, and quacks like a duck, then it's probably a duck."

"Oh, I'm sure that your sergeant did say that, Mary Ann, just as I'm sure he probably had over a hundred homicide cases that needed to be cleared. However, you and I are supposed to be better than that."

Mary Ann leaned over and gave her husband a kiss.

"Honey, it is OK with me if you want to interview Bernard. Just be clear that we are moving ahead with charging him so, if you do think that there is anything to back up your theory, we need to know about it as soon as possible."

"It is not lost on me, Mary Ann, that this case is moving rather quickly."

"The DOJ is not fond of anyone killing our own."

"I agree," Tim said as he got up and walked to the door. "Just as long as they get the right person or right people."

Tim slowly opened the door to find Susan, the ex-police officer fired for head-butting a suspect, sitting in a chair across the hall. She looked up from her book.

"Is there anything wrong, Mr. Hall?" she asked.

"No, everything is fine, Susan. I was actually checking on you," Tim replied.

"Oh, that's sweet of you, Mr. Hall, but remember, we are protecting you and your wife."

"Just be safe, Susan. These people are capable of anything."

"Are you flirting with my new bodyguard?" Mary Ann teased as Tim walked back into the room.

"You know I just have a thing for women cops," Tim replied. "I believe it's a Freudian thing relating to a weak father, a dominating mother, and—"

"Tim?" Mary Ann said as she climbed on top of him and pinned both of his arms to his side. "Shut up, I want to show you something."

And Mary Ann did just that.

The next morning, Tim woke up and could hardly move either of his arms. The sexual position that Mary Ann had Tim try the night before had done something to Tim's back, and not in a good way.

Tim did not mind trying new things and was happy that Mary Ann was into their sex, but the position they'd tried last night reminded Tim of the torture known as waterboarding, only without the water. He was going to have to have a talk with Mary Ann about this, but not right now. Right now, Tim had to get over and visit Bernard Haskell at the San Francisco County Jail 4.

Although Bernard Haskell had been arrested by the City of Berkeley Police Department, he'd been turned over to the San Francisco office of the FBI and was being held in one of the San Francisco county jails. Tim was not quite sure why

San Francisco had five jails for a population of 884000 residents, but the United States, in general, had a lot of jails and a large prison population. At least Bernard was being held at Jail 4, which was located on the seventh floor of the Hall of Justice. The newest San Francisco jail, County Jail 5, was located in a different county. At least they'd not placed Bernard there.

It was 7:30 AM when Tim kissed the still-sleeping Mary Ann goodbye and headed to the lobby. Susan had been replaced by a guy named Bobby who, to Tim, looked about sixteen years old.

"Good morning, Mr. Hall," Bobby said as he stood up.

"At ease, Bobby," Tim replied jokingly, though he doubted that Bobby knew he was joking.

Tim never thought the term "generation gap" would enter his lexicon, but he'd been noticing more and more that there certainly was one. Tim felt that the United States had become somewhat prudish, with its current sensibilities seeming almost as if they belonged in the 1950s or early 1960s, prior to the Vietnam War. Tim's parents—and everyone else's parents, for that matter—were of the generation that made it through World War Two. These WW2 parents perhaps did not understand what the Vietnam War protests were all about, but they seemed to care very little about what their own kids were doing. For example, how could the parents of the 1960s have allowed their kids to run off to Woodstock for three days of debauchery? The kids who'd attended Woodstock in 1969 would, ironically enough, never allow their own children to attend such an event today.

"Do you need an escort to the lobby, Mr. Hall?" Bobby asked.

"No, thank you, Bobby. Just as long as the hallways are clear," Tim replied.

To Tim Hall, Bobby the bodyguard was the perfect example of the modern-day twenty-four-year-old. Most likely, Bobby was a product of the modern all-volunteer military that had, to everyone's surprise, become the best-trained fighting force in the world. The military had also become the vehicle to transport these kids out of small-town and rural America and turn some of them into killing machines. These types of kids had no intention of returning to the farm. Tim figured that Bobby was one these types; but then, the two guys in the drugstore probably had been too.

"We have certainly come a long way," Tim said out loud, which seemed to confuse Bobby.

"What was that, Mr. Hall?" Bobby asked.

"Oh, just thinking out loud, Bobby. Anyway, be careful today, these guys trying to kill my wife and I are very capable."

"So are we, Mr. Hall," Bobby replied and Tim had no doubt that he meant every word.

In the lobby, Tim was pleased to see both Brent Wilkins and Darrell Murphy. Brent held two cups of coffee and handed one to Tim.

"Thank you, sir," Tim said to Brent as he took a sip of the freshly brewed beverage. "Today, the three of us have to take a drive over to a San Francisco county jail—the one located at the Hall of Justice."

Tim noticed that the news of the drive to the courthouse and jail had made Brent Wilkins turn white as a sheet.

"Are you OK with that, Brent?" Tim asked.

"Sure, boss," Brent replied, "that place just makes me nervous, that's all. Let me go and get the SUV and I will meet you two around the front, by the Tony Bennett statue."

Tim turned to Darrell as Brent left the lobby.

"So, what do you think of our driver, Darrell?" Tim asked.

"He seems OK to me, Tim, although he is just a little too squirrelly for my tastes."

"Yeah, I know what you mean, but it is a little too late to find a new driver now—at least one we can trust," Tim said as the two walked out the lobby door.

Brent was parked at the corner of Mason and Sacramento Streets. He got out of the SUV as Tim and Darrell approached to open the rear door for them. Officially, it was a ten-minute drive from the Fairmount to the Hall of Justice but, at eight AM, Tim figured it would take around twenty or thirty minutes. Due to a disabled truck, the trip took closer to forty minutes.

Mary Ann had arranged for Tim to meet FBI Special Agent Angela Rice out in front of the building and Tim found her impatiently waiting for him.

"Good morning, Agent Rice. I apologize for being late but—"

"Never mind that now, Mr. Hall," Special Agent Rice barked. "Just please follow me."

Tim did hold up his finger, indicating to Special Agent Rice that he needed a second. He walked back to the SUV.

THE DECOYS

"Who's your girlfriend?" Darrell said, referring to Special Agent Rice.

"She is my wife's personal FBI special agent, and is not showing me the same kind of love she shows Mary Ann. Anyhow, I will be here for at least an hour, so you guys stay out of trouble. I will give you a call when I'm done," Tim said as he turned to catch up with Agent Rice. Tim found her standing in front of the x-ray machines at the security checkpoint.

"Mr. Hall, if you have a firearm please place it in this tray so it can be checked in. Only local federal agents and police officers with special permission are allowed to carry in this building."

"That's not a problem, Agent Rice," Tim said as he complied with her requests. Tim was then given a temporary ID, which indicated he was a visiting federal law enforcement officer. Tim and Special Agent Rice next headed to a bank of elevators. Special Agent Rice pressed the button for the seventh floor and watched as the old elevator car door slowly shut.

"This elevator takes forever to get upstairs," Special Agent Rice remarked, but Tim decided to no longer try to be nice with her. She obviously had some issue with Tim visiting Bernard Haskell, but Tim had no time to find out why.

"Good morning, Special Agent Rice," said a man that appeared to be a sheriff's deputy. "Are you here to see Mr. Haskell?"

"No, but this man is," Special Agent Rice said, referring to Tim. "I will be leaving him in your care, John," the agent said, apparently knowing the sheriff's deputy. "Is there anything more I can do for you, Mr. Hall?" Special Agent Angela Rice asked Tim.

Tim thought of a hundred different things to ask for just so he could screw with the FBI agent but decided to be mature. He did have a lot of things he needed to discuss with Bernard, so he decided he'd better get to it.

"No, Angela, but you have been great," Tim said.

Special Agent Rice stared at Tim for a second as if she was planning on saying something but instead decided to just turn and leave.

"Angela?" the sheriff's deputy said as they watched Special Agent Rice get into the elevator. "I have never heard anyone call her Angela before. As a matter of fact, we were not sure if she even had a first name," the deputy continued as he led Tim down a hallway.

"She is working for my wife this week," Tim said. "So she has to pretend to like me."

"Yeah, women do always seem to be pretending. At least around us guys," the deputy replied.

"They certainly do," Tim said. "They certainly do."

Chapter 21

The San Francisco deputy sheriff named John took Tim to what looked like a room used for interrogations. *This is good*, Tim thought; he'd expected to have been taken to the regular visiting room, which would not have allowed for very much privacy.

There were two doors in the room: the one that Tim had come through and another that Tim figured must lead to the cell block. The deputy and Tim had walked by a window where Tim could see an older-looking jail with two tiers of cells on top of one another. The doors to the cells faced out to a row of windows, which at least provided some natural light. The interrogation room also included a large mirror that Tim had to assume was a two-way type, where one would be able to both observe and hear their conversation from another room. Since Tim was not Bernard's lawyer, he could not expect privacy.

Tim heard a buzzer and what sounded like a very heavy door lock disengage. The door swung open and there was Bernard. He was dressed in an orange jumpsuit and wore full leg irons. He was also handcuffed around the waist. *True FBI overkill*, Tim thought. Bernard was being escorted by two deputies: the one Tim knew as John and another.

"Is all of the hardware necessary?" Tim asked.

"Sorry, Mr. Hall, but those are our orders," Deputy John replied.

"It's not a problem, Tim," Bernard said. "Actually, it pleases me that someone feels that I am dangerous."

The two deputies helped Bernard into his seat and turned to leave. At the cellblock door, Deputy John turned to Tim.

"Mr. Hall? There is a button to your right. Please press that when you are ready to leave. We will be right outside." With that, the two sheriff's deputies left the room.

"Gosh, Tim, you took your sweet time coming over to see me. What have you been doing besides stitching me up for murdering my girlfriend?"

"So, I take that to mean that you did not murder Supervising FBI Agent Carol Russo?"

"No, I did not, and I am very mad that someone did. I did think for a second that you had something to do with it—why else would you just all of a sudden show up out here with your FBI girlfriend?"

"You mean my wife," Tim corrected.

"Yes, your FBI agent wife, Mary Ann Wilson: the one planted to take down Sabastian Oak and your first wife, Pam. Have you ever asked your current wife why she was even around in the first place?"

"She told me that she was investigating a guy named Toby Wheeler when Sabastian showed up. Her bosses just told her to see where it all led. Makes sense to me."

"Well sure, that does make sense," Bernard said sarcastically. "After all, that is how the FBI likes its young agents: young and dumb."

THE DECOYS

"As usual, you are confusing me, Bernard. Is this about your current situation or is it about my wife?" Tim asked.

"It is about your wife having no problem railroading me for a murder that I did not commit."

"If you have any information, Bernard, then you'd better tell me now; otherwise, I will not be able to help you."

"That is just it, Tim; I am not sure if I can trust you. If I tell you what I think is going on and you take that back to your wife, Mary Ann, then I really am a dead man."

"Have you mentioned this to your lawyer, Bernard?"

"Yes, I have, but he seems more concerned about a plea bargain. But they still have not decided who will take my case: the state or the feds. The state will probably offer me second-degree murder and ten years, but god knows what the federal attorney will ask for."

"Look, Bernard, if you know something then tell me, but keep in mind that someone is probably listening to our conversation."

"There is no love lost between the FBI and the City of San Francisco. My friend, Deputy John Law, will not pass any of our conversation on."

"John Law? You can't be serious," Tim said.

"Ask to look at his driver's license if you don't believe me," Bernard replied, laughing.

"OK, so tell me what this is all about."

"Affordable housing, Tim. There is a large parcel of land close to the old naval installation on the bay that would be perfect to build affordable housing units. HUD in DC and the State of California are both on board, but there is one group that is not."

"And that is?" Tim wanted to know.

"The real estate lobby," Bernard stated. "They have their tentacles in everything. For example, the real estate industry funds or contributes to every environmental group in the United States, Tim. They want to control what gets built and where it is built, and they do not want affordable housing—simply because there is no money in affordable housing."

Tim recalled how, in the 1990s, the real estate industry had single-handedly stopped the Walt Disney Company from building a theme park in the small town of Haymarket, Virginia. They'd planted stories about how the theme park would encroach on a Civil War battlefield and told everyone how the theme park would negatively affect the environment. They funded grassroots groups across the country that opposed the theme park.

Disney, not wanting to dive into any controversy, decided to cut and run, but any rejoicing by the anti-Disney theme park crowd was short-lived: the land for the proposed park was rezoned shortly afterward for townhouses and new single-family homes. The bedroom community that replaced the theme park resulted in an increase in taxes and traffic.

Yes, Tim Hall did believe that there was a real estate lobby that perhaps looked out for its own self-interests, even selfishly, but was it responsible for the murder of Carol Russo?

"Bernard," Tim said in a low voice, "do you have any proof that you did not murder Carol? Anything at all?"

"Well, I do have a video."

"Where do you have a video, Bernard?"

"On my iPhone."

"Where is your iPhone, Bernard?"

"The FBI has it."

"And they have not looked at the video?" Tim asked.

"I won't give them the password. They have the iPhone now and they are trying to figure the password out."

"But why don't you give it to them and clear yourself?" Tim exclaimed.

"Tim? Do you really think that the video clearing me will be there five minutes after they, the FBI, see it? Have you listened to anything I have told you?"

Bernard used to have a homemade sign that read *The Real Enemy is the Government*, but Tim had never really understood or cared what it meant.

"Tim, the FBI has been trying to take the CIA down since we were the OSS," Bernard said, "and if it was not for men like Allan Dulles, that crossdressing SOB Hoover would have probably pulled it off. So no, I don't trust the FBI, or your fucking wife, Tim, but I have decided to trust you. The password for the iPhone spells out 'camper': 226737. All in lower case. If you can get a hold of the phone and send the video to someone other than the FBI, then maybe I have a chance of clearing myself."

"All I can do is speak with Mary Ann about it," Tim offered.

"You may as well smash the iPhone with a hammer, Tim. Look, I'm not saying that your wife Mary Ann would purposely destroy evidence, but somebody at the San Francisco office would."

"Once again, how do you know any of this, Bernard?"

"I wasn't sleeping with an FBI special agent for nothing, Tim. Carol told me all kinds of things that go on in the federal building. Look, we at the CIA hire people that can think for themselves, whereas the FBI hires robots."

"Was Carol a robot?" Tim challenged.

"Carol Russo was different," Bernard replied, lowering his voice. "She never bought into any of that FBI fascist BS. Carol cared about the welfare of the people."

"Sounds like a fellow traveler," Tim said, referring to ones that sympathized with communists.

"Tim, there has always been a very thin line between capitalism and fascism and if you think that the United States does not exercise control over economics then just look at the real estate industry."

Tim noticed that Bernard's face was turning beet red, not to mention that beads of sweat were forming on his forehead. He decided that he'd better stop the interview before his old friend had a stroke.

"OK, Bernard. I hear what you are saying and I will check it out. Just try to have a little faith in me," Tim said.

"Tim," Bernard said, seeming to calm down. "The reason Carol tried to keep you away from me was because she felt that Bozo Bob Fredericks sent you and your wife out here to take us down. Now I feel just the opposite. You came here to help me and I wish Carol had seen that. She might still be alive if she had. Now go ahead and ring the buzzer. I want to lie down and take a nap."

Tim pressed the buzzer and in came two deputies to escort Bernard back to his cell. Deputy John Law also came in

THE DECOYS 173

to escort Tim outside. Tim watched as Bernard shuffled out of the room and the door slammed shut.

"Bernard is correct when he says there is no love lost between us and the feds. I really hope that you can find the real murderer," Deputy John said.

"So, you don't think that he murdered Carol Russo?" Tim asked.

"Bernard has been a guest here a few times and Special Agent Russo would visit him. No, the old guy loved her. I don't think he would hurt a fly."

Tim knew better. He had watched Bernard in action during the war in Central America but he also believed that the deputy was telling him the truth.

"Thank you, Deputy Law, I will certainly take that into consideration," Tim said as the elevator door closed.

Back on the street, Tim took a deep breath of San Francisco air. He next called Brent and walked down to Bryant Street. Tim saw Brent pull up on the other side of the street. Tim looked both ways to make sure that the street was safe to cross. It was, and Tim started for the SUV but, in the middle of the street, Tim was suddenly approached by a woman.

"Sir? Is this where the jail is located?" the woman asked.

Just as Tim was about to answer, he noticed that the woman's hands were held in a position to grab him. Tim took the woman by her forearms and, for a second, they appeared to be dancing in the middle of the street.

"Look out, Tim," he heard Darrell scream from behind. That was the last thing Tim Hall remembered.

Chapter 22

"Goddammit, I thought that you were there to protect him."

It was the voice of Mary Ann that Tim heard, but where in the hell was she? Tim slowly tried to open his eyes but his vision was somewhat blurry, and there was something covering his right eye. Tim reached up and felt a bandage on the right side of his face.

"Special Agent Hall, you requested that I escort your husband to the city jail, which is what I did. I did not think you meant that I needed to babysit him all day."

"Just get out of my sight, Agent Rice," Mary Ann demanded.

"Mary Ann? Where are you?" Tim said as his vision began to refocus. He was once again in a hospital room. Tim did a quick check to make sure that all of his limbs were present and could move. They were and could.

"Tim?" It was Mary Ann. "Are you OK?" she asked as she sat down on the bed next to him.

"Yeah, I think so. Where in the hell am I? What happened?"

"There was a woman—a woman who is known to the police as someone who has been accused of personal injury fraud. Darrell says that she approached you in the middle of the street and tried to push you into oncoming traffic."

"What does the woman have to say about that?"

"We won't know, honey—she was the one who ended up getting killed."

"So, what am I doing here?"

"The woman's body was somehow thrown into you and you ended up about ten feet away, knocked unconscious. The woman had a hold of you, according to Darrell."

"I just remember a woman approaching me with her hands out to grab me," Tim said as he winced in pain.

"The doctor says that you have a rib injury. That makes two since I've been with you,"

"You just about gave me a rib injury in bed last night," Tim said, referring to their sexual position. "Anyway, this was no accident—it was another attempt on our lives; or, at least, my life. Bernard told me that there is something on his iPhone that people do not want us to see. I did not take him completely seriously, but now someone has tried to push me into traffic. This all has to be somehow related."

"We have the iPhone, Tim, but Bernard has refused to provide us with the passcode. They have it in the lab, where they are trying to break it."

"Bernard told me that his iPhone has a video that shows the real murderer of Carol Russo, but he is afraid of giving it to the FBI. He says that it will disappear, and I am beginning to believe him."

"I'm not sure if I'd be able to get my hands on the iPhone even if I wanted to," Mary Ann said. "There is a discussion about sending it to Quantico or even up to Apple headquarters, however, as you know, Apple is not real keen on unlocking their phones."

"Well, they claim that they are unable to unlock them, Mary Ann, but it is hard for me to believe that Steve Jobs would not have built a back door into the iPhone operating system."

"Tim, I should not be giving advice to Bernard, but Bernard's lawyer needs to get a court order to have the phone unlocked before a neutral party. That way, there can be no question of anyone tampering with the phone. Why Bernard's lawyer did not already tell him this is a mystery to me."

"I don't think Bernard has told his lawyer about his iPhone and how it might have evidence affecting his case. Bernard is very paranoid, Mary Ann."

"I'm becoming a little paranoid myself, Tim. The whole situation is becoming crazy, and the fact that I almost lost you today, I—" Mary Ann could not finish her sentence and turned toward the window so Tim would not see her begin to sob. Mary Ann felt that women became emotional too often and she did not want to show her husband that side of herself. Tim could count on one hand the number of times he had seen his wife cry. He tried to change the subject.

"Let's just for a moment consider the notion that Bernard did not murder Carol Russo. So, if that is the case, then who did? It has to be someone that Carol knew and trusted, since there was no sign of any struggle or forced entry. So, whom in Carol Russo's circle of friends would have that privilege? In other words, who could just walk into her condo without question?"

THE DECOYS

"A neighbor, a good friend, a family member, or a work colleague. We have already covered this in the investigation, Tim."

"Yeah, I know, but it needs to be covered again."

"Everyone that Carol worked with has a rock-solid alibi, Tim."

"Which tells us that maybe this was a hit job set up to eliminate Carol and Bernard. Carol must have thought that it was Bernard returning—but it was not Bernard, it was the murderer, who had a key to Carol's condo that someone had given to him or her. It also tells me that Bernard Haskell knows more than he is telling us. Mary Ann, Bernard is the key to all of this. If something happens to him, we are all screwed."

Mary Ann got on the phone right away and ordered Bernard Haskell to be moved to the San Francisco jail ward at San Francisco General Hospital, figuring that he would be safer there. Being held in a regular jail was certainly not very safe.

Mary Ann received pushback from several supervising agents at the San Francisco FBI office, who cited many reasons why Bernard should not be moved. This gave Mary Ann even more reason to move Bernard. She ended up contacting Agent in Charge Perez and, true to his word, Agent Perez sent out an email informing everyone to cooperate with Mary Ann. Within an hour, Tim was watching Bernard, dressed in an orange jumpsuit, being escorted down the hospital hall, surrounded by several deputies.

"Where is the jail ward, Mary Ann?" Tim asked.

"Right down the hall. You almost made it there yourself until I stopped them. The city cops were not sure about your involvement."

"You mean, they thought that I may have had something to do with the lady getting run over?"

"Well, you have to admit, Tim, it must have looked kind of suspicious."

"Cops think everyone looks suspicious."

"Yes, honey, I am afraid that we do. It is just part of the job, but it is nothing personal."

"You know what? I am getting a little sick of that phrase, 'It is nothing personal.' It sure is personal to me."

"Try to get some rest, Tim, and I will try to get you released and back to the hotel," Mary Ann said as she gave her husband a kiss.

Tim closed his eyes and tried to think who could have killed Carol Russo. He had a few names in mind as he fell asleep.

Chapter 23

It was not until the next morning that Tim was released from the hospital. According to the doctor, Tim had just avoided an orbital fracture of the right eye socket. This left him with one hell of a black eye, which Mary Ann, for some reason, found sexy. Besides the eye, Tim also suffered bruised, but not broken, ribs. However, this rib injury was nothing compared to the injury he'd endured from escaping the submarine over the summer. The doctor wrote Tim a prescription for ninety Percocet 5/500 and some anti-inflammatory pills. The doctor also advised Tim to consult with an eye doctor once he returned to the DC area.

"I can sell those in about five minutes," Darrell said, referring to the Percocet.

"I have a feeling that I may need these now that I am off the pain machine," Tim replied as he pulled a sweater over his head.

"Who is selling what?" Mary Ann said as she walked into the room.

"Nothing, honey, Darrell and I are just fooling around."

"Be careful, no one has a sense of humor about pain pills anymore," Mary Ann said, sounding like someone's mom. She had spent the night with Tim in the hospital room and had left that morning to change outfits.

"I have set up a meeting with Bernard for this morning. His lawyer will be there. Tim, this meeting will be like any other police interrogation, with you and I and the US attorney on one side of the room and Bernard and his lawyer on the other side. The reason I am telling you this is so you will not treat it as some kind of joke. Bernard's lawyer can use anything you do or say to their benefit so please, be careful what you say. Now that I think about it, you should say nothing. You are there as a courtesy to Bernard, who has requested your presence. However, do not say anything unless you are addressed directly. Do you understand, Tim?"

Tim had never been spoken to in such a manner by Mary Ann and he certainly did not like it, although he did understand. That said, Tim made a mental note to never work with Mary Ann again.

"Sure, Agent Wilson-Hall. I promise not to say anything to screw up your persecution—oh, I mean prosecution—of Bernard Haskell."

Mary Ann gave Tim one of her looks.

"I will come and get you when we are ready," she said as she turned and walked away.

"Wow, you certainly are pissing off your old lady," Darrell remarked.

"Darrell? What happened to all the 'Yes, Mr. Hall' and 'No, Mr. Hall'?"

"Oh, that was when I was working for BXG Consulting. Now I am freelance. However, if you would like me to head back to DC, I will."

"I'm just asking, Darrell. As a matter of fact, I like you better this way as opposed to the ex-Navy Seal act."

"Well, I did a lot of that for your late wife, Tim. I think she got a kick out of the enlisted man serving her."

Tim did not like where Darrell was going with his comments about Pam so he decided to cut it short.

"Like I said, Darrell, I like you better this way. Oh, and by the way, thank you for yesterday. If you had not come up from behind, that crazy lady may have succeeded."

"I should have been there sooner, Tim, but that dipshit driver Brent parked on the wrong side of the street. I was yelling at him to make a U-turn but you'd already started crossing. Then the crazy lady came at you, deliberately. It was like she was waiting for you."

"Brent is not a professional bodyguard, Darrell, so he would not know that kind of basic stuff but yes, it all smells like a setup. Would you do me a favor, Darrell? Will you recheck Brent? Just to make sure that he is who he says he is?

"Sure, but it will take a couple of days; plus, I will need to ask around."

"No hurry, just want to put my mind at ease."

Tim heard the voice of Mary Ann plus the clicking of her high-heel shoes. It was unusual for his wife to wear high heels, which told Tim that this must be a special occasion.

"Tim? This is Robert Declan. Robert is an assistant US attorney for Northern California. Robert, this is my husband, Tim Hall. Tim is a case officer for the Central Intelligence Agency."

"Good to meet you, Tim—and by the way, everyone calls me Bob," he said as he gave Tim one of the firmest handshakes he had ever experienced. It suddenly occurred to Tim that perhaps Mary Ann should be married to a guy like Bob Declan and not a broken-down spy like himself.

"Good to meet you too, Bob. Everyone calls me Mary Ann's husband," Tim said, and was surprised when Bob Declan picked up on his joke.

"I know exactly what you mean, Tim. My wife is the chairman of the Walnut Creek City Council and I am known around town as Beverly Declan's husband."

Everyone seemed to have a good pretend laugh over Tim and Bob's roles as modern-day husbands that no one took seriously.

"So Tim, Mary Ann tells me that Bernard has a video of Carol Russo's murderer on his iPhone but is afraid to share it for fear that the local FBI office will tamper with it."

"Yes, that is about the size of it, Bob. I have known Bernard Haskell for several years. He was my first field supervisor back in the eighties and is an extremely intelligent individual. As a matter of fact, he holds a PhD in mathematics from MIT. He does, however, have a somewhat crazy side, and is also somewhat of a conspiracy nut. For example, he feels that the real estate industry is out to stop a proposed affordable housing project at the former Alameda naval base and will do anything to stop it—including committing murder."

"I'm sure the real estate industry is against the affordable housing project but I doubt that they are ready to commit murder. At least, not yet," Bob Declan said with a laugh. "But I'm sure we can have the iPhone opened in front of a federal judge and any other person Mr. Haskell requests. Why don't we all go in and ask him?"

THE DECOYS

Bob Declan turned and headed toward what Tim expected to be the jail ward. Bob led the way and Tim followed. He felt someone grab his hand and saw that it was Mary Ann.

"Look," Mary Ann began in a low voice, "I'm sorry, but it is not—"

"Don't say it," Tim said, cutting her off mid-sentence.

"Don't say what?" she asked.

"Don't say it is nothing personal, because it is personal. I embarrass you in front of all your straight FBI friends, but—"

Tim had to stop his rant because they had caught up to Bob Declan, who was trying to gain entrance into the jail ward. A buzzer finally sounded and a female deputy escorted Bob, Mary Ann, and Tim into an interrogation room much like any other interrogation room.

Bernard and his lawyer sat across the table and Tim could see that, while he was still handcuffed, they had at least removed the leg irons. Meanwhile, Mary Ann set up the recording device and introduced everyone in the room. Bernard Haskell's lawyer was named Max Shuler and was the first to speak.

"So, am I to understand that Mr. Hall here is an agent for the CIA and that his wife is the lead investigator in my client's case? I do find that highly unusual."

"Mr. and Ms. Hall were here on the West Coast for a different matter when the murder of Carol Russo was committed. FBI Agent in Charge Albert Perez requested Ms. Hall to lead the investigation because she is a senior FBI special agent as well as a former detective with the Cleveland, Ohio police department. She is more than qualified to handle such a matter."

"I have no problem with Special Agent Hall. It is Mr. Hall, who worked under my client at one time, who I take issue with. My client told Mr. Hall, in confidences, that a video existed. My client did not expect Mr. Hall to run and tell his wife about that. Since my client was tricked into revealing the existence of the video, we would like the video to be excluded from any trial."

"Max," Bob Declan began, "your client had no expectation of privacy during his meeting with Tim Hall yesterday and he knew that going into the room. On top of that, the United States is not concerned about the existence or nonexistence of a video belonging to Mr. Haskell. The United States plans to seek a grand jury verdict to indict Bernard Haskell on the charge of first-degree murder. If Mr. Haskell has any information that may help his case then I suggest that he reveals it sooner rather than later."

"Bob?" Max Shuler said. "Can I have a couple of minutes to speak with my client?"

"Sure, Max, take as much time as you need."

Tim, Mary Ann, and Bob got up from their chairs and walked out of the room.

"I feel sorry for Max Shuler," Bob Declan said. "He used to be one of the best lawyers in the city and I did some pro bono work with him a number of years back, but he has lost a step. You were wrong to see Haskell yesterday, Tim, especially without Max being there, since you are someone who is officially involved in the investigation, but I'm not going to point that out to him. That is basic stuff, but what is funny is

THE DECOYS

that Max thinks he is playing with the house's money, but he has nothing to offer. We don't need what is on the video and even if it shows the pope committing the murder, we still can contend that it was somehow doctored. In other words, the video is no smoking gun."

The female deputy who had opened the door to the jail ward appeared and requested that Bob return to the interrogation room to confer with Max.

Mary Ann waited until Bob Declan was out of earshot before she spoke.

"Tim, honey, please forgive me. I'm sorry and I did not mean to hurt your feelings. You don't know how much pressure they have me under to close this case and—"

Tim took Mary Ann by her shoulders and kissed the top of her forehead.

"It hurts me when you feel that you have to beg for my forgiveness, babe. Everything is OK."

"Glad to see you two have made up," Bob Declan said as he snuck up from behind.

"Look, Max has agreed to let us open the iPhone in front of a judge as soon as I can make that happen, so we are good."

Bob then looked at Tim's black eye as if he had just seen it for the first time.

"That is one hell of a black eye you got there, Tim."

"I think it makes him look sexy," Mary Ann teased.

"Bernard also asked about it. I said that I understood that you were almost run over yesterday and Bernard said that he told you so. Do you have any ideas what he meant by that?" Bob Declan asked.

"Yes, I do, Bob. The problem is that I don't know what to do about it."

Chapter 24

Tim made it back to the Fairmount Hotel at 4 PM that afternoon while Mary Ann and Bob Declan drove back to the federal building.

Four Percocet and two martinis later, Tim was feeling no pain. He sat next to Darrell in the hotel lobby, just watching the world go by. It was easy to see how quickly a person could become addicted to these pills. As a matter of fact, Tim had in the late '80s been a true heroin addict. He'd been on a mission and had been forced to inject heroin in order to maintain his cover. In the process, Tim had become addicted to the drug.

He had mentioned this to Mary Ann but had not told her the full story of his recovery. In reality, it had taken Tim almost two years to totally kick the habit. Although he had been warned by numerous drug counselors about gateway drugs, which included alcohol, Tim had never become addicted to drugs again; or, at least, Tim did not believe he was addicted.

Tim did consult one of his doctor friends, offline of course, about addiction. Tim's doctor friend basically told Tim that, in his opinion, the potential for addiction varied between people. While one person might become a fully-fledged addict, others would just stop after treatment. Also, not everyone became addicted after exposure to narcotics. All of this was, of course, a moot point in Tim's current life. Mary Ann would confiscate the remaining Percocet as soon as she determined that Tim no longer needed them.

Tim was beginning to wonder why he was even married to Mary Ann in the first place. The two of them were some twenty-two years apart in age, so what exactly did Mary Ann like about him? He always seemed to be embarrassing her in one way or the other, and she seemed to have no respect for his abilities. *Abilities*, Tim thought to himself. Yes, he could be sneaky and underhanded if those were considered "abilities." Throughout his career with the agency, Tim had simply collected data and passed that on to the analysts. The analysts were supposed to be the brains in the organization. Tim just went to countries and pretended to be someone he was not. Tim was realizing for perhaps the first time that he was pulling Mary Ann down, not up. FBI management just did not like Tim or the CIA, no matter what they might publicly say to the contrary.

Darrell had got up to use the restroom. When Tim caught someone in the corner of his left eye sit back down in his chair, he just assumed that Darrell had returned. Instead, he was surprised to see Mary Ann seated there instead.

"How many of those Percocet have you taken today, Tim?" Mary Ann asked.

"Oh, I don't know, Mary Ann. Maybe two," Tim lied.

"Then give me a couple so I can catch up."

Tim reached inside his pocket and opened the bottle. He shook out three pills and handed them to Mary Ann.

THE DECOYS

Mary Ann popped one in her mouth and placed the other two in the breast pocket of her blouse.

"You do realize that we both just broke a couple of laws, Mary Ann. One is not supposed to give away or sell controlled substances."

"Oh, don't I know it, Tim, but politicians just do not understand that they can't legislate the moral behavior of the citizens they serve. Not to mention that some US attorneys are just complete assholes. I know this one guy, a US attorney in Pennsylvania, who ended up charging the friend of some junkie for finding the junkie some dope. You see, the junkie died because the heroin his friend scored was cut with fentanyl, so this US attorney charged the guy with murder and you know what? They had an office party because they nailed some junkie for murder. These are the kinds of assholes I work with."

"Sure, Mary Ann, but I have been thinking about us and—"

"Oh, I know that you have been thinking, Tim. I can see the wheels turning inside that head of yours, but you know, Tim, how you love to tell me about your business? Well, let me tell you a bit about mine."

Mary Ann had slurred a couple of her last words, which indicated to Tim that she'd had a couple of drinks somewhere else. Meanwhile, the waitress brought Mary Ann and Tim two more martinis. Mary Ann took a sip of hers and continued speaking.

"I am in the revenge business, Tim. The citizens of the United States have crimes committed against them every day and they take it very personally and want me or people like me to go out and do something about it. This is especially true with the opioid crisis. Very few of the junkies I have encountered over my career have been upstanding citizens, Tim. Most are just deadbeats who would have found trouble in some other way if there was no opioid crisis. Their lives suck and getting high is a way out. Real stand-up men and women don't blame the pharmaceutical companies; they blame themselves."

Tim could tell that his wife was upset. He needed to get her upstairs and into bed.

"Come on, cowgirl, time to hang it up for the night."

"Tim? If I wanted to marry someone like Bob Declan then I would have found someone like him. You seem to think that I was sitting in the old maid's home waiting for you to show up, when the fact is that I was dating a ton of guys. One guy I was dating was putting so much pressure on me to get married that I ended up volunteering to go undercover. Do you know what he did for a living?"

"Was he a US attorney?" Tim asked.

"Damn right he was, and a good one, but I was really looking for a guy like you and I knew that the day you walked into the Blue Goose. Now, let's go back to the room," Mary Ann whispered. "I got another thing I want to show you."

By now, Darrell had appeared along with Susan to help Tim get the drunk Mary Ann up to their room. When they arrived, Mary Ann went directly to the bathroom and started to throw up. Tim found that a bit of a relief. He helped get Mary Ann into her sweatshirt and pants and into bed.

She curled up in a fetal position and Tim thought that she looked adorable.

"Tim?" Mary Ann asked. "You're not leaving me, are you?"

"The thought never entered my mind, babe. Now go and get some sleep. I'll be right here, all night long and forever."

Chapter 25

Tim awoke to an empty bed. The clock on the bedside read 7:30 AM and the sound of water running in the bathroom told Tim that his wife was probably in the shower. *See, there is nothing to this detective work*, Tim said to himself. Tim decided that he'd better go in and check on Mary Ann. After all, she had been acting a little strangely the night before. Tim, on the other hand, felt fine, especially considering the martinis and the Percocet he'd ingested.

As Tim moved from the bed to stand up, he felt a sharp pain in his right side. He had forgotten the injury to his ribs, but the ribs had not forgotten to be painful—painful to the point that Tim collapsed on the floor. He planned to just lie on the floor until the pain subsided but, just then, Mary Ann emerged from the bathroom.

"Tim? Tim, where are you?"

"I'm on the floor, honey."

"Oh my God, what happened?"

Mary Ann was now standing next to him but all Tim could see was her ankles. She did have nice ankles, Tim thought to himself.

"Why are you on the floor?"

"I'm on the floor because I forgot about my ribs and I did not wrap them up last night. I blame you," Tim said, but

THE DECOYS

he was only kidding about blaming Mary Ann. Still, he did want to speak to her about why she'd been so drunk. Something must have happened at work that she had not told him about.

Mary Ann dropped down to her knees and started to examine Tim. This resulted in her bathrobe coming open and Tim enjoyed the great view. His wife did have an excellent body.

"I'm going to have to call Darrell and Bobby and maybe the other guy that we have not met yet. I can't get you back in the bed by myself."

"That's OK, Mary Ann. I'm OK right here as long as I don't move. Just get me a couple of Percocet—they are in the drawer of the bedside tab—" Tim laughed but that hurt as well.

"The Percocet party ends in a couple of days darling so enjoy them while you can."

"I am in pain, Mary Ann," Tim protested as Mary Ann gave Tim two of the pills.

"Yes, I am aware of that, honey. Do you need any water?"

"No, I will just suck on them. So, tell me, what happened last night, Mary Ann?"

"We lost Bernard Haskell's iPhone, Tim. It disappeared from the evidence room and there is no record of it being sent anywhere."

Somehow, the news that the local FBI office had lost the iPhone that could perhaps clear Bernard Haskell of murder was of no surprise to Tim. As a matter of fact, Tim had almost expected the iPhone to be lost.

"So, was that why you came home a little bit loaded?"

"Well, kind of, but there was more. So, when it was reported to me that the iPhone is missing, I called Albert Perez. He tells me to meet him at this bar in thirty minutes—the bar where everyone from the office hangs out. I go and Angela Rice meets me and escorts me to a private room. In the room are Albert Perez and Bob Declan. Angela also stays. Turns out that Angela Rice is Albert Perez's number one, but I should have figured that one out. So anyway, I sit down and someone brings me a martini without me even asking. Next, Perez tells me that they have already cracked or backdoored the iPhone and have watched all of the videos and there is nothing. Not only is there nothing, but there is also nothing on Carol Russo's phone except of course a record of Bernard entering her condo at around the time of the murder."

"So, is the prosecution planning on using the iPhone as evidence?" Tim asked.

"No, and that is the interesting part. Bob Declan says that they plan on offering Bernard second-degree murder and ten years in a nice low-security federal penitentiary somewhere in Pennsylvania."

"That does not sound like a very long sentence for killing an FBI special agent."

"It is not, Tim, but they want this case to go away. Perez and Declan have decided to bury it. In a year, no one will even remember Carol Russo."

"What happened next?" Tim asked.

Well, by martini number three, they are asking me if I—or we, rather—would consider relocating out here. Perhaps replacing Carol Russo. I just laugh and tell them that I will need to think about all of that, but I do tell them that it is an intriguing offer. In reality, though, I am sick to my stomach, but I do not let on."

"Anything else happen worth noting?"

"Yes, as a matter of fact, something did. While Special Agent Angela Rice was giving me a ride back to the hotel, she starts telling me how many nice guys there are out here in the Bay Area and how, if I were to move out here, she would certainly introduce me to her friends."

"Did you happen to remind her that you are married?" Tim asked.

"Oh, she told me about her first husband who was apparently some loser detective in the San Jose PD. She dumped him and is now sharing a bed with our agent in charge, Albert Perez."

"And what about the murder of Carol Russo?" Tim asked.

"Well, if Bernard takes Declan's deal then whether he murdered Carol or not becomes a moot point. But to answer your question, the case is essentially closed, Tim, and we are free to return to DC. Of course, this contract to murder us is still hanging over our heads."

"What do Declan and Perez say about the fact that people are trying to kill us?" Tim asked.

Mary Ann took her bathrobe off and laid it flat on the floor. She then pulled a blanket from the bed to cover both her and Tim. Tim meanwhile was able to slowly turn onto his side so they were facing each other.

"The reason I said everything I did to you last night, Tim, is that I want you to know how much I love you and how sorry I am that my FBI colleagues have no respect for you. I am finding that, in general, they have little respect for anyone. When I mentioned that there have been at least two attempts on our lives, they just laughed. They laughed and said that that's what happens when you play fast and loose with the rules. They also said that if I dumped you, the hit men and women would no longer be coming after me. That it was you that they wanted."

"The thing is, Mary Ann, is that they may be right. If you leave me, the attempts on your life may indeed stop. The problem is that these assassins are not foreign agents but other Americans—other Americans who believe I am some kind of drug dealer."

Mary Ann moved closer to Tim and began to kiss him, beginning at the top of his head and slowly moving down.

"Mary Ann, you have to understand that this will not stop until we figure who is behind this contract on my life."

Mary Ann was now at Tim's belly button, where she stopped for a second.

"What I was trying to tell you last night, Tim, was that I love you and I am on your side. On your side forever. Now stop talking and let me finish what I have started."

And Mary Ann did finish, sending Tim into ecstasy.

Chapter 26

Tim and Mary Ann continued to lie on the floor for at least another two hours until there was a knock on the door.

"Are you two OK in there?" said the voice of Susan the bodyguard.

"Hold on a minute, Susan," Mary Ann said.

"I'm going to have to answer the door or else our security team will kick it in," Mary Ann said as she picked up her bathrobe and tied it around her waist.

"That's OK, I think I can get up off the floor now," Tim replied and slowly pulled himself back onto the bed.

When Mary Ann opened the door, Susan walked in with her Glock drawn and took a look around.

"I'm sorry, Mr. and Mrs. Hall, but I heard some sounds that I could not identify and—"

"That's all you need to say, Susan. My husband and I understand. You can now re-holster your weapon," Mary Ann said, now laughing.

"Oh yeah, sure, Agent Hall." Susan now sounded embarrassed.

"It's OK, Susan. I would rather you be safe than sorry," Mary Ann said as she pushed Susan out of the room.

"Gosh, these kids today," Tim said as he chewed two more Percocet.

"We are old enough to be that girl's parents, Tim," Mary Ann said. "And she probably never heard her parents have sex." Mary Ann was still staring at the door.

"Well, you were pretty loud, Mary Ann."

"I was because I was having a good time, Timothy," Mary Ann said as she lay back down on the bed.

"You do know that it is almost noon, Mary Ann. Are you not going into the office today?"

"Well, since I am the boss, I can go in when I like, but I am having a hard time right now thinking of a reason to even go. If Bernard takes the deal then the case is closed from our end. Jack and Jill over in Berkeley will have to testify, but we don't need to be here."

"You mean Detectives Ashton and Clifford of the Berkeley Police Department?" Tim asked.

"Yes, those two. I think they spent exactly two hours investigating Bernard's case; they will say anything in court that Declan tells them to say."

"All of a sudden you don't sound like a big Bob Declan fan, Mary Ann. What happened?"

"Declan just reminds me of the US attorney I know who got that junkie convicted of murder because he got his friend some dope. These assholes really think they are protecting society, whereas what they're really doing is racking up numbers. I have not met one prosecuting attorney who does not keep his or her eye on their conviction rate."

"Wow, you have certainly done a one-eighty since yesterday, why the change of heart?"

THE DECOYS

"Because yesterday I was finally invited to join the club, which is really all I ever wanted, but now I know that I really don't want any part of it. Not if it means dumping my own Jack Ryan," Mary Ann said, referring to Tim.

"I don't know any guys like Jack Ryan in the CIA. I know a few contractors a little like him, but—"

"OK, you win, I mean my own Tim Hall," Mary Ann said as she began to kiss Tim. "I thought that I could have it all. I thought that I could have the job I wanted, the kids I wanted, and the husband I wanted, but now I realize how close I came to losing everything."

"So, do you have any ideas about what to do next? Because I am running out of them," Tim said.

"I think that we need to re-interview Bernard Haskell, because I believe you were right. Bernard is not telling us everything he knows."

"Won't Bob Declan get mad at us if we interview Bernard without him and Bernard's lawyer?"

"I think that is exactly why Bernard is not telling us everything. He is afraid of revealing something. You and I may have more luck working on him."

"You mean you will not be bothered by my unprofessional demeanor?" Tim asked.

"Shut up and get dressed, Tim, we have work to do."

Chapter 27

Brent and Darrell were standing by the elevator as Tim, Mary Ann, and Susan made their way down to the lobby.

"Afternoon, guys. We need to head back over to San Francisco General Hospital," Tim said cheerfully.

"Are you feeling OK, Tim?" Darrell asked.

"Never better, Darrell. The reason we're going to the hospital is to re-interview Bernard Haskell once again," Tim replied.

Mary Ann had wrapped an Ace bandage tightly around Tim's ribcage, which helped him move with much less pain. Also, the sex Tim and Mary Ann had enjoyed that morning had also seemed to re-energize him.

The early afternoon San Francisco traffic helped Brent make it over to the General Hospital in a little less than thirty minutes. Tim had found out recently that the kid who'd come up with Facebook had donated some seventy-five million dollars to the hospital. That had resulted in his name being added and so the official name was now the Zuckerberg San Francisco General Hospital and Trauma Center.

"The name of the hospital just rolls off the tongue now, doesn't it?" Tim remarked.

"Not a lot of people are happy with the new name," Brent said, "plus, one of the supervisors introduced a bill to take the name off, but I don't know what will happen with any of that."

The SUV pulled up to the ER entrance and Brent parked in one of the spaces reserved for the police.

"Don't really know how long we will be up in the jail ward, fellows, but I will stay in touch," Tim said as he followed Mary Ann out of the SUV and into the hospital.

Mary Ann's FBI ID allowed both Tim and her direct access to the jail ward via the emergency room.

"Mr. Haskell is preparing to be transferred back to the Hall of Justice detention facility, but he is still here," said the same woman deputy that had opened the door to the jail ward the day before.

"On whose authority?" Mary Ann asked.

"Lady, I just take the paperwork and do what I'm told."

"And I'm telling you that Bernard Haskell stays here," Mary Ann replied. "Now go and bring him here."

The deputy gave Mary Ann a kind of sideways glance but got to her feet and complied.

"Boy, you're sexy when you get mad," Tim said.

"They're playing games, Tim. Something is going on here but I have no clue what."

The female deputy soon escorted Bernard into the interrogation room and sat him in a chair.

"I'm calling my supervisor, Agent Hall, so we can determine what is going on," the female deputy replied as she turned and walked out of the room.

"So why are you pissing off Doris?" Bernard said, giving a name to the deputy sheriff.

"OK, Bernard. First of all, cut the shit and tell Tim and me what this really is all about."

"It is about ten years, according to Mr. Declan, since I did agree to his deal," Bernard replied.

"And how long do you think you will survive in California detention?" Tim asked.

"In case you did not know, Tim, I will be residing in Pennsylvania for the next four years, assuming I get good behavior."

"Which will be great, Bernard, provided you make it there, but do you really believe they will let you live?"

Bernard lowered his head and sat still, as if he was frozen. He then looked up at Tim. "How long have you known?"

"How long have I known that you were responsible for Carol Russo's murder? I guess when I first interviewed you at the Hall of Justice jail," Tim said.

"Nice that you mentioned it to me, Tim," Mary Ann remarked.

"I wasn't sure until this morning when you told me about your meeting with Declan and Perez," Tim replied.

"They told me that they just wanted to speak with Carol," Bernard blurted out. "That they were not going to hurt her. All I had to do was leave someone the key. On the windowsill. They just wanted to reason with Carol."

"Suppose you tell me what they wanted to 'reason' with Carol about?" Mary Ann asked.

"Carol found out something, something big, and she was going to take it to the *New York Times* and *Washington Post*."

"You mean Carol found out something about moving the homeless over to the old naval base?" Mary Ann asked.

"No, it was something bigger than that and it involved Perez and his girlfriend, Angela Rice. I asked her to tell me but Carol said that her life was already in danger and there was no point in putting my life in danger as well."

"Bernard? There is some rumor going around DC that there is some operation that only ten people know about," Tim said. "Do you think that is what Carol found out about?"

Bernard Haskell sat stone-faced for almost one minute before he spoke.

"I don't know, Tim. I would not think that Carol Russo would have access to that kind of information, but she did work closely with Perez and she might have accidentally overheard something. Look, Perez is no lightweight, so don't underestimate him."

"Yes, so I have been told, Bernard. Do you think that Perez was capable of killing Carol?"

"Albert Perez is really not the kind of guy who would personally kill someone. He would, however, have no problem having someone else do it for him."

"OK Bernard, Mary Ann and I need to step outside, so don't go anywhere."

Bernard held up his hands to show that he was still handcuffed to the desk and called to Tim as he was leaving the room. "Tim, you have to get me out of here and look, I can help you with your problem. You know, your problem of people trying to kill you."

Tim and Mary Ann stepped outside.

"So what do you think, Mary Ann?" Tim asked.

"I think that we may have to get Bernard here out of San Francisco and back to DC. You are going to have to call Bob Fredericks and get a federal court order to release Bernard from the San Francisco county jail and get him on a plane to DC. We can place him at a safe house until we get back. Technically speaking, he did not murder Carol Russo and, if he is telling the truth about not believing she was going to be harmed, then he really has not committed any crime."

"What about Declan, Perez, and the rest of our new friends?"

"Unless we can prove that they conspired to murder Carol Russo, we have nothing on them; however, I would really like to find out who really killed her."

"I have some ideas," Tim replied, "but I'd better get on the phone with Fredericks. Would you like to keep Bernard company?"

"I would like nothing better, but first I think I need to have a talk with Doris, the sheriff deputy, and find who has been visiting Bernard."

Tim put in a call to Bob Fredericks only to find that he was in a meeting. Meanwhile, Bernard had been taken back to his room while Mary Ann was having a rather animated discussion with Deputy Sheriff Doris. Tim was getting ready to join the conversation when his iPhone began to ring. The phone number appeared as *Unknown*.

"Tim Hall."

"Tim, Bob here. What in the hell is going on out there?"

"Bob, we have to bring in Bernard Haskell. I don't know if he is really retired or still active, but we have to get him out of San Francisco before he is killed."

"OK, Tim, calm down. I was under the impression that Bob had been arrested for the murder of his girlfriend, Carol Russo?"

"Mary Ann and I no longer believe Bob was directly involved in her murder. It looks as though Carol Russo had stumbled into some conspiracy and paid for it with her life. Mary Ann and I are still working on who killed Carol; we have to get Bernard out of here."

"OK, Tim, I can send an extraction team that will remove Bernard and seek a federal court order under the Patriot Act; however, you and Mary Ann are going to have to take the heat from the locals."

"Who do you plan to use for the extraction?"

"Probably Seal Team Seven out of San Diego."

"OK, just please ask them not to blow any doors unless they absolutely have to."

"You know they will do what they like. I will text you a time to expect them. You should probably be there to run interference."

"Ten-four, boss," Tim replied.

Tim hung up his iPhone and returned to the interrogation room, where Mary Ann was still speaking with Deputy Doris.

"Hi, Tim, it turns out that Doris here is from Cleveland. We went to the same high school!"

"Except I was six years behind Agent Hall," Doris added.

"Please, call me Mary Ann."

"Well OK, if you think that is OK," Doris replied.

"So, Doris, what brought you out to San Francisco?" Tim asked as he sat down next to Mary Ann.

"I was following a guy who wanted to live and work here but I did not know that he was gay, which is probably the reason he wanted to move here to begin with. I guess I should have seen that coming."

"Some people never find out that their partners are gay. Some men are gay but just do not want to come out of the closet, Doris. There is nothing you can do about it," Mary Ann said.

"Look, I have to get back to work now, Agent—I mean, Mary Ann. So, if you no longer need me for anything—"

"No, that will be it for now, Doris, but thank you again."

"Not a problem. Always good to meet someone from back home," Doris said as she walked out of the room.

"Well, I'm glad you have made a new friend because in about five hours some US Navy Seals will be extracting Mr. Bernard Haskell from San Francisco General Hospital's county jail ward."

"In other words, breaking him out," Mary Ann said.

"Yes, breaking him out, and they will use any means necessary, including blowing off the doors and using stun grenades. Now, I don't know what kind of weapons the deputies have locked up here, but if anyone tries to shoot at them, they will shoot back."

Mary Ann placed her head in her hands and then on the table.

"How did some dumb plan to relocate homeless men escalate to the point that we've got Navy Seals perpetrating a jailbreak?" Mary Ann said.

"I'm sure there are homeless women involved as well, honey."

"No, Tim, it is always men that start everything. They are the ones that started coming out here to San Francisco.

THE DECOYS

The women, as usual, just followed. We women are the idiots, Tim."

"Hey, we men invented the toilet, Mary Ann. I think that is the greatest invention ever!" Tim joked, trying to cheer up his wife. "Anyway, Mary Ann, Bob Fredericks wants me to run interference for the Seals so that nothing bad happens."

"No, Tim, I am the senior domestic law enforcement official and I will run the interference. What time do we expect the boys?"

Tim looked down at his iPhone at a new text message: *Fun starts at 7 PM PST.*

"In about four hours," Tim said.

"OK, when they get here, I will do the talking. Will there be an officer?"

"Yes, usually a junior-grade lieutenant."

Yeah OK, makes sense, I guess. Tim, you need to be in the back with Bernard. Make sure the other three guards do not interfere. We then just hand over Bernard, make sure he gets away, and then wait."

"Wait for what?" Tim asked.

"Wait to explain. You and I may be the ones spending the night in jail."

"There is no one I would rather be locked up with," Tim replied.

Chapter 28

At 6:45 PM, Tim, Mary Ann, and Bernard were sat in the interrogation room waiting for Navy Seal Team 7. Tim had told Bernard that he would be extracted that evening and flown back to DC; however, Bernard still refused to tell Tim the entire story of Carol Russo's murder.

"Sorry, Tim," Bernard told him once again. "As soon as I tell you everything, you and the other boys from Langley will no longer need me."

At 6:55 PM, there was a rumble that shook the entire building. At the same time, an automated announcement was broadcast over the hospital intercom system.

"Attention, ER staff. Incoming helicopter alert. Attention ER staff. Incoming helicopter alert."

Both Tim and Mary Ann had heard the same automated announcement during the day as medevac helicopters came and went, but not in response to the US Navy Black Hawks which were now approaching.

The automated announcement suddenly stopped and was replaced by what sounded like a fire alarm; however, that also soon stopped. There was now just an eerie silence.

Doris walked into the integration room. She looked concerned.

THE DECOYS 209

"Agent Hall? Something is happening. I have lost all power to my board, plus my computer is down and the door to the jail ward will not unlock. The phones are down and even my radio does not work."

"Federal agents! Everybody down," yelled a man.

The hallway outside the interrogation room was suddenly filled with soldiers holding automatic weapons and dressed in body armor. Their faces were covered by masks and they appeared to all be wearing safety glasses. One of the men approached Doris.

"I have a federal warrant to take Bernard Haskell into custody," he said as he showed the warrant to her.

Mary Ann, who had already taken out her FBI ID, stepped in front of Doris.

"I'm Special Agent Mary Ann Hall. To whom am I speaking?"

"Lieutenant JG Sam Banerjee, ma'am, United States Navy."

"Please show me your warrant, Lieutenant."

The lieutenant showed Mary Ann the warrant, which she pretended to read.

"It looks good to me, Doris. You'd better give them Mr. Haskell."

"I'm Bernard Haskell," Bernard said as he stood up.

"Mr. Haskell, I have a warrant from the Eastern District Court of Virginia for your arrest. Would you please accompany me?"

"Now wait a minute, you guys can't come in here and take one of my prisoners without authorization," said Doris.

She was a lot braver than had Tim expected; most people would have just put their hands up.

"Well, we are, lady, and unless you want to be arrested yourself, I suggest you shut up."

"It's OK, Doris. I will explain it to your boss," Mary Ann said, trying to console her.

Two Navy Seals had meanwhile taken hold of Bernard Haskell and were carrying him down the hallway. When they reached the stairway, they turned right and disappeared.

"This is your copy, ma'am," the lieutenant said as he handed Mary Ann the warrant. This done, he began to walk back out the door. The men covering him each peeled off the wall and followed as he passed. They all reached the door to the stairwell and disappeared. It was beautifully choreographed, like a dance you would see on Broadway, Tim thought to himself. Next was the roar of the Black Hawk helicopters, this time taking off. Tim walked to the window and caught a glimpse of the two choppers, red lights flashing, as they flew off to the south.

"My board is back up and so is my computer. I activated the escape alarm," Doris announced. "I don't know what happened; everything just went dead."

"What exactly is this board you keep referring to, Doris?" Tim asked.

"My board controls all of the door locks in the rooms and in the ward. Nothing worked; I could not lock or unlock anything. Then the front door just unlocked by itself. How did it all happen?"

"I don't know, Doris," Mary Ann replied while looking directly at Tim, "but I'm sure a lot of other people will have the same question."

Over the next fifteen minutes, the hospital jail ward filled with cops. The first to arrive was the San Francisco SWAT team, who seemed surprised that there was really nothing for them to do. All the bad guys were gone and, five minutes later, so were they.

Next came the actual sheriff of San Francisco with all his top deputies. He wanted to know how someone could break into one of his jails and take away one of his prisoners but, once satisfied that it was a legitimate transfer, he and his entourage also left.

That left the FBI to deal with—only, no one from the FBI showed up. That surprised both Tim and Mary Ann, who had expected the FBI to arrest the two of them on some kind of charge and then drag them through hours of interrogation about why they had engineered Bernard Haskell's transfer to the DC area. None of that happened.

Even Deputy Doris no longer seemed to be interested and asked Tim and Mary Ann how long they planned to hang about the hospital jail ward.

"So, I guess we should be heading back to the hotel?" Tim said.

"That was really anticlimactic, Tim. I mean, I thought that there would be stun grenades and that they would zip tie our hands and—"

"But instead they simply bypassed the main lock and walked in. Stun grenades make a lot of noise, Mary Ann, plus they create smoke. That would not be appropriate for a hospital ward and—"

"Tim, I get it, honey. I know all about stun grenades. I guess I did not expect everything to go so smoothly."

"Let me call Brent and get back to the hotel."

"OK, I'll say our goodbyes to Doris."

Brent's phone rang three times. Then, Darrell picked up.

"Tim, Brent split," Darrell said, "but he left his phone."

"Split? Where did he go?"

"Don't know, Tim. I went to get coffee and, when I get back, no Brent."

"No note or anything, Darrell?"

"No, Tim, but Tim? I found out today that Brent Wilkins is dead. He's been dead for over a week."

Chapter 29

It was 10:30 PM when Tim and Mary Ann made it back downstairs to the SUV and to Darrell.

"So, what happened to Brent? Tim told me that Brent just disappeared," Mary Ann said.

"Brent Wilkins is dead; or, at least, the real Brent Wilkins has been dead for at least a week," Darrell replied.

"Dead for a week? We just saw him this morning," Tim said.

"That is the issue, Tim—the guy who has been driving you and Mary Ann around the last few days was not Brent Wilkins. The real Brent was an unidentified body residing at the office of the San Francisco medical examiner. Unidentified, that is, until today. I thought that you and I would spring this on the fake Brent together, just to see how he would react, but someone must have tipped him off because he beat feet out of here when I went for coffee."

"Which tells us that somebody must have tipped him off somehow," Tim said.

"Yes, I think Darrell just made that point, Tim," Mary Ann said.

"But I never saw him on the phone or texting anyone, and I checked him out twice."

"He was probably reading and writing text messages without you knowing about it, Tim," Mary Ann said. "However, I'm a little annoyed—how you could let some guy get that close to us?"

Mary Ann did have a point, which made Tim wonder if maybe he was getting a little bit too old for this kind of game. Taking someone out and then assuming their identity was one of the oldest tricks in the book; you just needed to find somebody who would not be missed. At least, not missed for a few days. The big question was why did the imposter go to such lengths to get close to Mary Ann and Tim? He'd had plenty of chances to kill both of them, which ruled him out as a contract killer. So, if not that, then what? Just to watch and report their movements? Seems like a lot of trouble to go through."

"I spoke with an SFPD inspector named Mindy Smallwood this afternoon. She would like to speak with us about the phony Brent in the morning," Darrell said.

"Sounds good, Darrell, but, for the time being, Mary Ann and I would like to go to bed. Just try to get us home alive."

In the hotel room, Mary Ann quickly changed into her sweats and climbed into bed without saying a word. Tim was at a loss as to whether his wife was mad at him or not, and decided that he'd better ask.

"Are you mad at me, Mary Ann?"

"I'm mad because you hired some maniac to drive us around, but I will get over it.

"Well not to get technical, but it appears that I hired an imposter and not the real Brent Wilkins and" but Tim caught Mary Ann giving here one of her looks and decided to quite while he was ahead. It was beginning to seem to Tim that each time he was able to find some common ground with his wife, he managed to do something else to upset her.

"I am also finding it strange Tim that no one from the San Francisco FBI office has called me about Bernard Haskell. They have to know he flew out of here."

"Maybe they no longer care?" Tim suggested.

"Yeah, maybe, but I doubt it. I guess we will find out in the morning," Mary Ann said as she placed her head on Tim's shoulder.

"Let go ahead and get some sleep," Tim said, and soon they were both asleep. Morning came and Tim woke to find Mary Ann on top of him. He did not recall having sex with his wife the night before, but it appeared that he had.

"Would you like me to order an All-American Breakfast for you, my darling?" Mary Ann asked.

Tim wondered why his wife was being so nice to him, especially after he'd screwed up by hiring the Brent Wilkins imposter, but he was not going to question a good thing.

"Yes, I would love an All-American Breakfast. Should we order two?"

"No, I'm watching my weight so I will just eat some of yours."

Tim knew that meant that Mary Ann would be eating at least half, if not more, of his All-American Breakfast, but he did not mind. Keeping your wife happy was priceless.

At 10 AM, Susan escorted Tim and Mary Ann to the lobby, where they met Darrell. Brent's absence was noticeable to Tim mostly because Darrell did not bring any coffee with him.

"Need to get some coffee, Darrell," Tim remarked and headed for the main entrance.

"Tim, let's start leaving directly from the hotel garage. We can get to the coffee shop by going this way," Darrell said as he led Tim and Mary Ann down a long corridor.

Tim knew exactly what Darrell was doing. *"A person's routine is the assassin's best friend,"* someone had once told him. Therefore, one should never take the same route to work or go to the same place for lunch. Of course, changing ingrained behavior was a lot easier said than done.

After obtaining coffee, Darrell drove the SUV out of the hotel garage with Tim and Mary Ann in the back seat and headed to the office of the San Francisco medical examiner. The office was located off of Third Street, close to Hunters Point, the neighborhood that Tim had driven through on the day he and Mary Ann had arrived in San Francisco.

"This is the same area where you were trying to lose Cindy Andrews and Matthew Boykins," Mary Ann said.

"What do you mean *trying* to lose them?" Tim said. "I recall that we did."

"I think that they just decided that we were crazy and not worth pursuing. Anyway, that seems like it happened a year ago, but it was really only last week."

"More like six days," Tim replied. "What happened to Cindy? I have not heard you mention her name."

"Cindy Andrews has been keeping a low profile since I was placed in charge of the Carol Russo murder. I did inter-

THE DECOYS

view her and she told me that she was out serving a warrant that night; the one that you and I witnessed."

"The one you and I witnessed while the phony Brent was driving us around. Funny how we just happened to come upon that," Tim said.

"Yes, that's one hell of a coincidence; strange how we witnessed Cindy Andrews making an arrest the first night we were in town," Mary Ann replied.

"Here we are," Darrell announced as he pulled in front of the medical examiner's office.

"Come in with us, Darrell; they may want to speak with you as well," Tim said, but then saw a man and woman who appeared to be waiting for them.

"Hi, I'm Joanne Dombrowski and this is Tom Harvey. We are with the San Francisco police and are investigating the homicide of Brent Wilkins."

The two inspectors showed their identifications to Tim while ignoring Mary Ann and Darrell. *Why do they always assume that the white guy is in charge*, Tim thought to himself and almost laughed out loud at the absurdity.

"I'm FBI Special Agent Mary Ann Hall," Mary Ann said, stepping in front of Tim. "I am investigating the murder of Carol Russo over in Berkeley but I am working out of the San Francisco FBI office."

"So, you're the bitch from DC," Inspector Dombrowski said to Mary Ann. "That is what they are calling you over there. We work with those people a lot which is how I know."

Inspector Dombrowski then turned her attention back to Tim. "And is this your old man? The guy who is supposed to be a spy?"

Inspector Dombrowski spoke with a strong New York City accent. Perhaps even a Long Island accent.

"So, Inspector Dombrowski, how long have you been out here from Long Island?" Tim asked.

"So, you still can tell, huh? Oh, five years now. My old man got transferred out here with the ATF and I was the trailing spouse. Actually, I've done OK here. If I had stayed in New York, I would still be driving a patrol car out of the one-thirteen precinct in Queens."

"The one-thirteen? That is out of Jamaica, right?"

"Yep, down and around JFK. Not a great beat, but there are worse."

"By the way, this is Darrell Murphy. Darrell runs personal security for my wife and me."

Darrell just nodded his head at the two inspectors.

"Tell you what, why don't we all go in and take a look at Mr. Wilkins. Then we can sit and talk about all of this."

Everyone entered the medical examiner's office and met the lead technician. He escorted everyone to the basement and to the autopsy room. The smell of death was everywhere. Tim had never understood how anyone could get used to that stench.

Next they were greeted by Doctor Kinder. After all the introductions had been made, Doctor Kinder spoke. "Goodness, I did not expect so many people this morning," he remarked as he walked over to the table where the true Brent Wilkins lay. Tim looked down at the real Brent and found that he did have a striking resemblance to the fake Brent.

"The patient has deep bruising and ligature marks around the neck and CT imaging detected intramuscular

THE DECOYS

hemorrhages, indicative of manual strangulation. I would guess it was done by a scarf due to the size of the marks. Now, if you take a look here, you can also see signs of ligature marks."

"So, you're telling me, Doc, that someone had this guy tied up and then strangled?"

"In a word, yes, Inspector. That is what it looks like to me."

Inspector Dombrowski turned to Tim, Mary Ann, and Darrell.

"I really think that you guys need to discuss all of this with me and my partner—we should compare notes and all. There is a room upstairs we can use if that is OK with you."

"Yes, that will do," Mary Ann replied. Tim was not so sure—to him, it sounded more like an interrogation—but he was willing to let Mary Ann take the lead. He just hoped it would work out.

"I need to use the boy's room," Tim said.

"Down the hall and to the left," replied Dombrowski.

Tim had his iPhone out and was texting Bob Fredericks as he entered the stall.

"Being interviewed by SFPD homicide, woman named Dombrowski. Need to get out."

With that, Tim returned.

Chapter 30

"So how did you meet Brent Wilkins?" Inspector Dombrowski began.

"My husband Tim hired him," Mary Ann replied.

Dombrowski looked at Darrell.

"He was hired before I came out here," Darrell said.

"And you, Tim?"

"Can't tell you because it is a matter of national security."

"Let's get one thing straight, pal," said Inspector Tom Harvey, who was speaking for the first time. "Dombrowski and I have already spoken with Agent in Charge Perez and he tells us you two are no longer working for the San Francisco FBI office, so don't try to hide behind them."

"Look, honey, it talks," Tim said to Mary Ann, referring to Inspector Harvey.

Inspector Harvey was out of his seat and heading for Tim when Inspector Dombrowski stood up to stop him.

"Tom, the guy is just trying to screw with you. Don't let him."

Tom Harvey sat down but Tim could almost see steam coming out of his ears. In Tim's mind, it was obvious that both San Francisco inspectors suspected Tim of some kind of crime, which scared the hell of him. Once a cop thinks that you are guilty of something, it is almost impossible to

THE DECOYS

convince them otherwise. Mary Ann decided to try and make peace.

"Look, Inspector Dombrowski, my husband hired someone pretending to be Brent Wilkins and we do not know why he pretended to be someone he was not. Our private investigator, Mr. Murphy here, only discovered this fact last night. We do not know who the imposter was but we are working hard to find out. We really do not have much more to tell you at this time."

"We have a lot more questions to ask you and—" Inspector Dombrowski's cell phone began to ring. She took a look to see who was calling.

"Excuse me, I need to take this," she said and walked outside the room.

Tim could only catch bits and pieces of the conversation which seemed to be made up of "Yes sirs," "No sirs," and "Right away sirs."

Inspector Dombrowski came back in the room wearing a look of defeat.

"Mr. Hall and Agent Hall and—"

"That is Darrell," Tim added.

"And Darrell, I would like to apologize for any disrespect that I may have shown you this morning."

"What the fuck?" Inspector Harvey said as he got to his feet.

"Shut up, Tom, you are about one minute from going back on patrol." She turned back to Tim and Mary Ann. "As I was saying, I am very sorry if—"

"Inspector Dombrowski, you don't need to apologize to me or anyone else. You were not made aware of the situation and you were actually used to impede our investigation. Now, if you would please take us to where Brent Wilkins' body was found, I think that will be all we need from you."

"Sure, Tom and I can take you there right now. It is actually only a few blocks from here."

Inspectors Dombrowski and Harvey got up and walked out of the front door followed by Tim, Mary Ann, and Darrell.

Darrell, who was driving, followed the SFPD unmarked police car out of the parking lot of the medical examiner's office back to Third Street, where it turned left.

"Who in the hell called that cop?" Darrell asked.

"I sent a quick text to Bob Fredericks and told him that we were getting the 'third degree' by the two homicide inspectors," Tim replied.

"Their captain or even the police chief may have called them," Mary Ann added.

Tim's iPhone made the text message sound and Tim pulled it out of his pocket to take a look. It was a text message from Bernard Haskell. Tim read it out loud.

Back in DC safe and sound and staying at your safe house. Sent you a present. Check your email. Love, B.

"If he is staying in our bedroom then we are buying a new mattress," Mary Ann declared.

"I'm sure he is in the marshal's house and not the main house. Besides, the decoys are still there," Tim reminded Mary Ann.

THE DECOYS

The unmarked police car slowed down and made a left-hand turn on Key Ave. Darrell followed and passed a number of modest homes; certainly not homes that Tim would consider unsafe. The road turned from pavement to dirt and they entered what looked like a large vacant lot.

"According to the GPS map, this is Bayview Park," Darrell said.

"It looks like the set for *West Side Story*," Tim said, but it was apparent that neither Mary Ann nor Darrell knew what he was referring to.

The police car pulled off the road and Darrell pulled in behind them.

"I would lock your doors if I were you," Inspector Harvey yelled as he got out of the Ford.

"I will stay here if you two don't mind," Darrell said as Tim and Mary Ann followed the two inspectors.

The four walked about fifty yards behind a small clump of trees. Tim could just make out what was left of the yellow police tape used to seal off the crime scene.

"Some kids were playing back here when they smelled the body. That is not that uncommon around here. Tom and I caught the call last Wednesday afternoon, but we could not find any ID. Finally, his fingerprints came back on Friday. Is it OK if I ask you two how long you have been out here?" Inspector Dombrowski said, this time in a much friendlier tone of voice.

"Sure, my husband and I arrived last Monday evening," Mary Ann answered.

"And when did you meet Mr. Wilkins?"

"We met him on Tuesday," Tim replied. "He picked us up on the Embarcadero and took us on an impromptu tour of the city. He was out the front of our hotel, the Fairmount, the next morning, which is when I hired him to be our driver. At the same time, I ran a background check on him."

"What kind of background check?" Inspector Harvey asked, not in a friendly manner.

"The same background check that you guys use except mine is a lot better," Tim shot back. "Our security guy is the one that figured out that the Brent driving us was a phony."

"Yeah, and how did he do that?"

"By taking a picture and showing it around to other cab drivers," Darrell said as he walked up from behind. "The phony Brent must have seen me showing his picture to the other cab drivers. I'm sorry for that fuck up, Tim."

"Look, if you two have not figured it out already, Tim and I, along with Darrell, are on a special assignment for the Department of Justice. We are investigating the FBI along with the United States attorney for Northern California. I fully understand if you don't want to get involved but we do need some information," Mary Ann said.

"Look, lady, Tom and I aren't no members of the Rat Squad," Inspector Dombrowski said, referring to the police internal affairs division, "but we ain't no fans of the snot-nosed kids at the FBI. No offense or anything. So, what would you like to know?"

"On Tuesday night, between eleven-thirty and twelve AM, Tim and I observed four or five city police units at the corner of Divisadero and Haight Street. We witnessed an FBI agent named Cindy Andrews involved in some kind of arrest. We need any information that you may have about that arrest, if there was indeed an arrest. The thing is, we have to keep it on the QT."

"Yeah, I know the girl. She is a real princess. Anyway, that sounds like the Northern Station on Fillmore Street," Inspector Dombrowski said. "We can take a ride by and ask around, nothing official, and get back to you, Agent Hall."

"You can call me Mary Ann."

"Great, I'm Joanne. We will be in touch."

With that, everyone returned to their vehicles and drove back to Third Street.

"Where to now?" Darrell asked.

"Let's go back to the hotel and see what kind of present Bernard emailed us," Tim said.

Chapter 31

Darrell drove the SUV into the garage where Tim and Mary Ann were met by Susan. Susan then escorted Tim and Mary Ann back to their room.

"Do you feel like some lunch, honey?" Tim asked.

"Sure, but let's eat in the room. I can't wait to see what Bernard has sent us."

"Well, don't get your hopes up. Bernard is famous for getting your hopes up," Tim warned.

In the room, Tim walked over to the desk where the laptop was set up. The laptop had three different passcodes that needed to be entered in correct order plus two key fobs that generated random numbers. All very redundant, Tim thought, and it took almost five minutes to log into the server.

When Tim finally reached his email, he clicked on the very first one, which was from Bernard Haskell. Boy, it had not taken him long to get an account set up; unless, of course, Bernard had already had an account set up. Tim was still not clear whether Bernard had retired or was still working. The fact that Bob Fredericks was so willing to authorize a Navy Seal-led extraction from a domestic jail told Tim that Bernard still had some relevance at Langley. Bernard Haskell's email read:

Dear Tim,

Sorry for all of the mess in San Francisco but you have to believe that I was not directly involved in the murder of Carol Russo. I loved Carol as much as any other woman (with the exception of my dear wife) and had no cause to wish her any harm. Attached is the so-called "lost video" of someone entering Carol's condo after I left at around two AM. Although the figure appears to be a woman, I will not speculate as to who it might be.

Hope all is well and look forward to seeing you when you get back to DC. Please give my best to your lovely wife and tell her that I hold no hard feelings.

Best regards,
Bernard Haskell

"Gosh, I just can't wait to have Bernard over for dinner some night," Mary Ann replied rather sarcastically.

"Let's play the tape," Tim said as he downloaded the attachment.

As the video started, both Tim and Mary Ann saw that it would be far from clear. Instead, it was the usual grainy picture appearing to be composed of grain-like particles. In this case, the grain was more like white spots; however, it was clear that Bernard Haskell did walk out of the condominium, placed an object on the window sill, and was followed five minutes later by a hooded figure who picked up the object and used it to enter the condo. Two minutes later (according to the time clock running in the right-hand corner of the video) the hooded figure left the condo but did not leave the key. Tim and Mary Ann watched the video again, and again, and again, but came to the same conclusion. The video proved nothing whatsoever.

"It could all have been faked," Tim said.

"True, but someone who appeared to be a woman entered the condominium and it does give us something to work with. Here, let me show you something."

Mary Ann walked across the room and picked up her big bag of stuff, or at least that was what Tim called it. She rummaged through it for a minute until she produced a large notebook, which looked to Tim like something a high school student might have. The notebook contained the names and pictures of every employee at the San Francisco FBI office.

"Now, call Darrell and ask him to come up here. I have something I would like to try," Mary Ann said as she walked to the door and opened it. "Susan, will you come in? I want to try something."

"Sure, as long as you think it is OK to leave my post."

"I think it will be. Anyhow, I will tell Darrell. So, what I need you to do is sit here and watch the following video ten or eleven times and tell me when you are finished. Tim? You better go out and catch Darrell before he freaks out when he discovers that Susan is not there."

Tim stood out in the hallway waiting for Darrell while Susan started watching the video.

"Am I looking for anything in particular?" Susan asked.

"No," replied Mary Ann. "I'm hoping you'll get a visual picture of what this figure may look like. Afterward, I am go-

THE DECOYS

ing to show you a number of pictures and ask you to pick out three photographs of who you think the subject in the video might be. There are no wrong answers."

Darrell was now standing in the doorway.

"I not sure how good of a job we can do of protecting you if everyone is in here," Darrell said.

"Relax, Darrell, this will only take a minute," Mary Ann reassured him.

Susan had now finished viewing the video and was going through the photos. Each photograph had a number under it and Susan was instructed to just write the number down on a Post-it note. Darrell was soon finished and performed the same task.

"Don't we get to know who we picked out?" Darrell wanted to know as he handed his Post-it note to Mary Ann.

"Oh, we will tell you just as soon as Tim and I finish our analysis," Mary Ann said but doubted that Darrell actually cared.

After Darrell left the room, Mary Ann revealed the results.

"So, Susan picked numbers six, twelve, and twenty-one while Darrell picked two, twelve, and twenty-six."

"And the winner is?"

"The winner is number twelve: Special Agent Cindy Andrews."

"Somehow I am not surprised," Tim said, "but do you believe there is any real science behind your test?"

"Nothing that we could take to court, but it is interesting and something to go on. I think that we really need to bring her in for questioning. Plus, we should turn over the tape to the lab and let them analyze it."

Mary Ann picked up her cell phone and began to dial a number.

"Who are you calling?" Tim asked.

"Oh, my good friend Angela Rice," Mary Ann replied. "I just need to let her know that I am still actively involved in investigating the murder of Carol Russo."

Mary Ann called the FBI but it took her a couple of minutes to track down Angela Rice. Finally, she picked up.

"Angela? Mary Ann Hall here. Yes, we are still in town and yes we are still investigating the homicide of Carol Russo."

There was a long pause, during which Tim could hear Angela's voice providing some long explanation. Meanwhile, Mary Ann began to look as if she was losing patience. Finally, she interrupted Angela.

"Angela, just stop. Stop speaking right now. First of all, I am taking orders from the attorney general of the United States, not Agent in Charge Perez. Second, if I receive any more interference from you, I will send a planeload of federal agents and suspend and reassign every agent in that building."

Mary Ann's ultimatum seemed to have worked. Tim heard Angela's tone of voice change from one of defiance to one of reconciliation.

"OK, Angela, that is good to hear. No, I'm not mad at you. Angela, now listen. I need Cindy Andrews brought in for questioning. No, I don't care if she is out working a case. I want her back in the office and sitting in an interrogation room by the time I get in the office. I will be there in ninety minutes. OK, right, and thank you, Angela."

Mary Ann lay down on the bed with a look of exhaustion.

"I have never, ever, witnessed an outfit like the San Francisco office of the FBI. Angela tried to tell me that Agent in Charge Perez no longer saw a need to continue the investigation into Carol Russo's murder and that I was no longer authorized to access the San Francisco FBI office."

"Well, hopefully that will be rectified by the time you get down there," Tim said.

Tim's cell phone began to ring and he saw that Inspector Joanne Dombrowski was calling.

"Hi, Inspector Dombrowski," Tim said. "My wife is here so let me put you on speakerphone."

"Uh, hello?" The inspector's New York accent was loud and clear.

"We're here, Inspector. Do you have anything for us?"

"Well, we checked out the logbooks at the Northern Station for that evening and there was an attempt to serve a warrant on—guess who?"

"We have not got a clue," Mary Ann replied, trying not to laugh.

"There was a warrant on a Brent Wilkins—the real Brent Wilkins. The strange thing is that apparently Mr. Wilkins was apprehended by FBI Special Agent Cindy Andrews and transported to San Francisco FBI headquarters by one of our units. I spoke with the officer and he told me that he and his partner did transport Mr. Wilkins to the FBI office, where they turned him over to Special Agent Andrews. That was the last anyone heard or saw of the real Brent Wilkins until he was found in Bayview Park. Needless to say, the SFPD would very much like to speak with Special Agent Andrews."

"OK Inspector, do what you need to do on this. I am supposed to interview Ms. Andrews in an hour and I do plan on placing her under arrest. You are welcome to her after that, however, and this is important. Do not speak with any federal law enforcement officer with the exception of me. That goes for the US attorney too. Something is rotten here, Inspector Dombrowski—we just do not know what. Please feel free to call me anytime, and Dombrowski?"

"Yes, ma'am?"

"Please be careful. There are a lot of ruthless characters involved in this conspiracy."

"And I left Queens for this?" Dombrowski said as she hung up.

Chapter 32

"OK, Darrell is downstairs waiting for us. Do you have everything you need?"

"Oh, I guess so," Mary Ann replied but she seemed frustrated. "Tim, I guess that I'm not sure how to wrap this up. The best result is for Cindy to confess to everything. Then we just take that to Bob Declan and he makes the case."

"Yes, provided that she confesses. On the other hand, she could just deny everything that Dombrowski told us. She could say that Brent was just taken to one of the San Francisco jails. They have seven or eight of the damn things."

"But what do you think it is all about, Tim?"

"I think that Cindy, at some point, picked up Brent, most likely because he resembled her confederate, the phony Brent. Next, Cindy gets Brent into some kinky sex thing and ties him to the bed using scarfs. Except, the last time that they do it, she strangles the poor guy and dumps him out in Bayview Park."

"She has to get over to Carol Russo's condo and murder her," Mary Ann said. "Maybe she has already murdered Brent and has him in in the trunk of her FBI car or maybe he is still alive but, at some point, she has to do him in. We need to get over to the FBI office and check any CC tapes."

Mary Ann left the room with Tim following close behind. She ran to the elevator and impatiently waited for it to take her to the lobby. Mary Ann then ran to the garage where Darrell was waiting for her. Tim arrived a minute later.

"Is there any way to get over to the federal building more quickly, Darrell?" Mary Ann asked.

"I did install two sun visors with the blue lights and a siren, but I don't know if that will get us there any faster."

"Well, let's go for it, Darrell."

Tim could see how pumped up his wife was. He also expected that Mary Ann would ultimately be disappointed. He felt this way because he figured that Cindy Andrews had contacts and help within the San Francisco PD who had by now alerted her to the fact that Mary Ann was looking to arrest her.

That appeared to be exactly the case when they arrived at the federal building seven minutes later. Mary Ann was met by Angela Rice in the lobby.

"Do we have Special Agent Andrews Angela?" Mary Ann asked.

"Cindy signed out this morning and reported that she was working a case, Mary Ann."

"Case? What kind of case?" Mary Ann asked.

"Something to do with mail fraud. She has been working with some postal inspectors on it."

"Have you called her?" Mary Ann wanted to know.

"We have called her, we have paged her—she's not even answering the radio in the car, the one she signed out today. All our vehicles have GPS devices fitted and we are looking for hers now."

"We need to impound that vehicle and have forensics give it the once-over. We are looking for blood or anything else that may be suspicious. Do agents usually use the same vehicles?"

"Yes, most of the time. Sometimes, we don't have enough cars to go around."

Mary Ann motioned for Tim and Angela Rice to follow her into her office. Mary Ann sat down, as did Tim, but, when Angela Rice attempted to do same, Mary Ann told her to remain standing.

"OK, Angela, this is what I need you to do. We need to obtain a warrant for the arrest of Agent Cindy Andrews on the charge of murder of a federal law enforcement officer. She is considered armed and dangerous and supreme caution should be used in her apprehension. After you obtain the warrant, get every agent together and I will explain it to them. Is Agent Perez in the building?"

"Agent Perez has taken a few days of leave and is in the Los Angeles area."

"So who is in charge?"

"That would be me, Agent Hall," Angela Rice said.

"Good, that makes it easy then," Mary Ann replied, not seeming to care that, technically speaking, Angela Rice outranked her. Mary Ann was now reporting directly to the United States attorney general and, for all intents and purposes, she was in charge.

"Angela, you or I will also need to notify all of the resident agents across the Bay. I know that it is hard when we have to go after one of our own, but we have to take care of this as efficiently and as quietly as possible. Now, I have two more requests. I need to see any security video of Cindy on Tuesday, November nineteenth, and Wednesday, November twentieth, between ten PM and two AM. Anything at all. Second, is Matthew Boykins in the office?"

"Yes, he is working on some internet scam project."

"OK, tell him that we would like to see him—Tim and I, that is, but do not tell him why. Sit him down in the interrogation room. And Angela? Take his weapon."

Angela Rice continued writing in her notebook until she was finished. She showed no emotion whatsoever.

"Will there be anything else, Agent Hall?"

"No, Angela, just keep me updated, and thank you. You have been a big help."

Angela Rice just smiled, turned, and left the office.

"You can be a real ballbuster when you want to be, Mary Ann," Tim said as he leaned back.

"It comes with the territory, babe. You know, I was really hoping we could catch that bitch Cindy here at the office drinking a Starbucks, but it looks as though she was tipped off."

"Yeah, it was most likely caused by our new friend Joanne Dombrowski asking questions about last Tuesday night at the police station. Someone must have sent her a text or made a phone call. Cindy Andrews killing Carol Russo may be debatable, but the fact that she was the last person to see Brent Wilkins alive does not look very good."

"What I find strange, Tim, is how she expected to get away with killing the real Brent Wilkins."

"Maybe she did not murder the real Brent. Maybe someone else did while she was over in Carol Russo's condo killing her."

Mary Ann's office phone interrupted her and Tim's discussion.

"Mary Ann Hall," she said into the phone. Her next words were, "OK, we will be right there," and she hung up. "Matthew Boykins is waiting for us in Interrogation Room Number One."

"Do you think we should ask Darrell to come up here for the intimidation factor?"

"Sure, why not," Mary Ann replied. "Let's see if we can scare this kid into telling us something."

Darrell was waiting for them outside Interrogation Room Number One, looking rather unhappy.

"You know, I was hoping to catch up on some sleep in the SUV when you called."

"Darrell? We need you to provide some security because, quite frankly, we cannot trust anyone in this building," Mary Ann said.

"Well, as long as you put it that way; besides, I suppose you are overpaying me. What would you like me to do?"

"Just sit in the corner and look scary," Tim said.

"OK, I got it. Big black guy in the corner," Darrell replied as the three of them entered the interrogation room.

"Hi, Matthew. You remember us, don't you?" Mary Ann started out.

"Oh, sure. Special Agent Russo had me and Special Agent Andrews pick you up at the airport, but you did not want us to drive you."

"But you followed us anyhow. Why?" Tim asked.

"Cindy—I mean, Special Agent Andrews—called Special Agent Russo, who told us to follow you."

"And you did follow us, Matthew, until I tried to lose you by getting off on the Third Street exit."

"Yeah, that was kind of funny." Matthew laughed.

"What's so funny, Agent Boykins?" Mary Ann said, sounding serious.

"Oh, I'm sorry, ma'am. I did not mean to laugh on purpose. It is just that so many people try to lose us at that exit. You see, you can also pick up the subject you are following on Third Street."

"So you have spent a lot of time in and around Hunters Point?" Tim was again asking the questions.

"Too much time if you want to know the truth."

"Now that is what we are interested in, Matthew, the truth. What do you know about Bayview Park?"

"I would not want to be caught there after dark," Matthew replied. "As a matter of fact, I am not too happy there in the daytime."

"Why is that, Matthew?" This time it was Mary Ann asking.

"Well, for one thing, it is gang central, not to mention that over the years they have found a number of dead bodies out there.

"I heard that they found one just the other day, Matthew. Did you know that?"

"Yes, it was mentioned on the hot sheet."

"What's the hot sheet, Matthew?"

THE DECOYS

"It is just a list of crimes in and around San Francisco County."

"Do you think Bayview Park is a good place to dump a dead body? I mean, in a pinch."

"I'm not sure what you mean by a 'pinch,' Mr. Hall."

"What I mean, Matthew, is if you happened to have an unexpected dead body on your hands a little after midnight last Wednesday—one that your friend Cindy Andrews gave you and told you to get rid of."

"Cindy Andrews is not my friend," Matthew Boykins said sounding exasperated. "I don't like working with her that much, but we are two of the newer agents so they seem to pair us up a lot. We were on a special assignment for Special Agent Russo."

"Yes, Matthew, tell us all about that special assignment," Mary Ann said.

"Special Agent Russo told me and Special Agent Andrews that you—I mean, Special Agent Hall and Mr. Hall—were coming out to San Francisco in order to close the office."

"Close the San Francisco FBI office, Matthew? That is just absurd," said Mary Ann.

"Well, Special Agent Russo told us that we were going to combine with the resident agent office in Oakland and move to some new development at Naval Air Station Alameda."

"That is just silly, Matthew, and is totally untrue—but even if it was true, so what?"

"That is what I thought as well, but when we reported that you and Mr. Hall were not cooperating and were not staying in the hotel we had picked out for you, Special Agent Russo said we would have to go to plan B."

"And what was plan B, Matthew?"

"I never found out, Agent Hall. Special Agent Russo was dead on Wednesday morning."

"OK, Matthew. I need you to write a statement swearing that what you've told me and Mr. Hall is true. Now, just for your information, none of what Special Agent Russo told you was true. My husband and I were sent out here to investigate a number of things, but none of it had anything to do with relocating the San Francisco FBI office across the Bay to Oakland. However, since we have been here, at least two people have died, not to mention the poor man who died in the explosion that was most likely meant for my husband and me. Let me give you a piece of advice, Matthew: never let one of your supervisors talk you into performing something illegal. It never works out."

"Am I still an FBI special agent?" Matthew asked.

"Yes, for the time being, but get out of here and start writing up that statement before I change my mind."

Matthew Boykins picked up his notebook and hurried out of the room. Tim had to hold his breath until the young special agent left the room before he began to laugh.

"Get out of here before I change my mind. Which *Lethal Weapon* movie did you pick that line from?" Tim said.

"Well what did you want me to say, honey? You're a sweet kid but dumber than a bag of hammers?"

"By the way, it has not been lost on me that no one is calling me Agent or Deputy Marshal Hall," Tim complained.

THE DECOYS

"That because none of the FBI special agents buy into your special deputy act," replied Mary Ann.

"I *am* a special deputy," Tim said, defending himself.

"Only in relation to the safe house."

"Which this is related to."

"Will you two shut up?" Darrell said from the corner of the room. Tim and Mary Ann had forgotten that he was there. "Now, if it is all the same to you, can I go back to the SUV?"

"Yes, sure Darrell, Tim and I will be here for another hour or so."

With that, Darrell left the room without saying another word.

"Do you think he's mad?" Mary Ann asked.

"For what he is being paid, I don't care if he is mad," Tim replied. "So, what do you think?"

"About Matthew? I don't think he had anything to do with the murder of Brent Wilkins, but I do think Cindy did. I'm going to have to brief the agents about her and the warrant. You can't be in the room when I do that, but you can watch it on the closed-circuit TV."

"Speaking of that, I wonder if Angela has found anything from the other night."

"Maybe, let me find out."

While Mary Ann called Angela, Tim checked for any messages on his iPhone. There was a message from Inspector Dombrowski asking if he would give her a call. This was something Tim thought that he would do while Mary Ann gave her talk to the FBI agents. There was a knock on the door and Angela walked into the room.

"You have to see this," Angela said, sounding somewhat excited. She took her iPhone and placed it on the table, where both Mary Ann and Tim could see it.

"Now, this is behind the building, Tuesday evening, eleven-thirty PM."

The video showed an SFPD patrol car pull up to the building. Two cops got out and opened the back door of the car. One cop grabbed the arm of a man with both of his hands cuffed behind his back. Next, Cindy Andrews appeared, wearing a vest with *FBI* embossed on the front. Cindy and the two cops took the handcuffed man through the backdoor.

"Let me speed this up two minutes," Angela said.

Tim and Mary Ann next witnessed both of the SFPD cops leave.

"OK, so nothing really unusual. Cindy makes an arrest and they bring the suspect to our office, which is a little out of the ordinary since most of the time they would bring the suspect to the Hall of Justice holding cell, but this does happen. What happens next really does not."

Fifteen minutes later, Cindy and the suspect left through the same back door, except this time the suspect is no longer handcuffed. The suspect and Cindy next embrace and share what appears to be a passionate kiss that lasts for almost ten seconds. The pair then walk off-camera, but a car appears to leave the parking lot.

"Hey, that's one way to get a date," Tim joked, but both Angela and Mary Ann ignored him.

"What about the cameras in the building?" Mary Ann asked.

THE DECOYS

"Someone erased all the video from eleven PM until two AM. Whoever did that was unaware of the backdoor camera."

"OK, that tells us a little more about what Cindy was doing on Tuesday night and Wednesday morning, but not a whole lot. Angela? Is everyone assembled?"

"Yes, they are, Mary Ann. Ready and waiting."

"Tim, I won't be long."

"Sure honey, take your time."

Tim waited until Angela and Mary Ann had left the room before dialing Joanne's phone number. She picked up after one ring.

"Joanne? What's up?"

"We found a body at the landfill today but we figured it must have been dumped sometime the other day. Most likely was in a dumpster that one of the trucks picked up. You said that you were missing the guy who was driving for you? The reason I bring it up is that he resembled the stiff we found out at Bayview Park."

"Yeah, I bet you dollars to donuts that he is my guy. Do you have a cause of death?"

"Looks like a broken neck. The doc said it looks like someone just snapped it in two."

"Your pathologist really has a way with words. You may want to mention to your husband that your landfill body may have been involved in that hotel explosion last Monday, assuming your husband is working on that."

"Believe me, I have not seen the man since that explosion happened, not to say that there ain't dividends, if you know what I mean. Do you have any more?"

"Not yet, but you may start running some prints and even some DNA tests. Test his skin for any traces of explosives and—"

"OK, OK, OK, I'll tell him. You guys think you are the only cops in the room?"

"I'm not really a cop, Joanne. As a matter of fact, I'm not sure what I am right now."

"Well, if you just ID'd that bomber, you will be a big hero to my husband, Ed. Oh, and I see that your girlfriend Cindy Andrews is wanted for murder? I just received an all-points bulletin."

"Yeah, and be careful Joanne, she is probably desperate, which makes her a little dangerous."

"You and your wife are the two that are in danger, so be careful, my friend."

Tim could hear footsteps coming toward the door. "Got to go, Joanne, stay in touch."

"Who was that?" Mary Ann said as she walked into the room.

"My new girlfriend, Inspector Dombrowski. How did it go?"

"Oh, OK, I guess. I told them that, if Cindy tried to contract anyone, they should advise her to turn herself in. Oh, and also, I got a few questions about moving the office to Oakland. Let's just go home to the hotel."

Tim and Mary Ann were escorted back to their hotel room by Susan, who then placed herself in her usual spot outside their door.

"This is getting pretty old, Tim. How long do you think we are going to have to stay here?"

"I guess it depends on you, honey, but I think our work here is almost complete."

"Cindy Andrews must know by now that she is a fugitive from justice. I guess I should finish the job, but I want to go back to DC. I mean, here we are in one of the most romantic cities in the USA, and we are not getting our money's worth."

"Maybe we could have dinner in the room and see what happens then?"

"Sounds like a plan," Mary Ann said as she placed her arms around his neck. "Why don't you take a shower?"

Tim could use a nice hot shower and quickly got undressed. He looked at his wife as she began to get undressed herself. Despite their bickering about law enforcement techniques, Tim really considered himself a very lucky man.

The shower was just the right temperature and Tim began to enjoy the heat on his back. He was just about to relax when he heard a sound. Not a loud sound, but a sound none the less. The sound was like one or two people moving. He next heard a kind of popping sound. That was enough for Tim to reach up to the showerhead and find the Smith and Wesson 640 snub nose that he always brought with him to the shower. Tim sensed that things were moving fast and that there was no time to leave the bathtub, so he turned sideways and crouched down while pointing the pistol at a forty-five-degree angle.

The bathroom door burst open and the shower curtain was pulled back. The first thing Tim saw was a flash of red hair belonging to Cindy Andrews. She had Mary Ann by her hair and was pushing her forward with her left hand. Her right hand held the standard Glock 22 that all special agents carried. Cindy seemed confused when Tim wasn't standing there. By the time she looked down at Tim knelling, he had already fired the Smith and Wesson 640, striking Cindy in the middle of her chest. The Glock 22 fell out of her right hand and she let go of Mary Ann with her left. She clutched her chest with both hands and fell back onto the floor.

Mary Ann, who was dressed in only her underwear, was on top of Cindy right away, checking for wounds.

"She has a vest on Tim; the bullet does not appear to have penetrated."

Tim was now out of the tub and picking up Cindy's Glock 22 in order to secure it.

"Go check on Susan. She is in the bedroom," Mary Ann said.

Tim found Susan on her side. Her hands were tied behind her back with a zip tie and a piece of duct tape was over her mouth. Tim tried to be gentle pulling the tape off, but Susan still made a face—either from the pain or from the fact that Tim was naked.

"I'm so sorry, Mr. Hall. She was on me so quickly and—"

"It's OK, Susan. It's our fault for not letting you know that she was around."

"What happened? I heard a shot?"

"Yeah, that was from me, Susan. I shot her."

"Is she dead?"

"That remains to be seen," Tim said, but he now heard Mary Ann speaking with Cindy. He grabbed a bathrobe and put it on before reentering the bathroom.

Mary Ann had removed the vest and opened Cindy's shirt, revealing a bright red spot on her skin. Cindy was now semi-conscious and appeared to be going into shock.

"Susan? Call 911 and tell them we have a police shooting and a gunshot wound. Do you have paramedic training?"

"Yes, I do," she said as she got down on her knees.

"Well, the bullet did not appear to enter her chest," Tim said.

"I think I see it over there," Mary Ann said, now pointing to an object in the corner.

"Why did you shoot me?" Cindy murmured.

"Because you broke into our hotel room brandishing a firearm, Cindy," Mary Ann replied, flabbergasted that Cindy would ask such a question.

"But I just wanted to talk."

"With a gun?" Tim asked.

"I did not think that you would listen to me otherwise."

Tim and Mary both looked at each other, amazed at Cindy Andrew's explanation; however, Tim said later that perhaps she was in shock.

"Cindy, the bullet did not penetrate your vest. You may actually survive this and we have called the paramedics so, in the meantime, would you like to tell me if you killed Carol Russo?"

"No, I did not kill Carol. I don't know who killed Carol."

"What about Brent Wilkins? Did you murder Brent?" Tim asked.

"No, no, Brent was my boyfriend. I loved Brent but—"

Cindy appeared to pass out again. Meanwhile, Tim grabbed some clothes and his cellphone. He called Joanne

Dombrowski, who picked up after one ring. Tim could hear a siren and Joanne yelling at Tom Harvey to turn it off.

"This is Joanne."

"Joanne, this is Tim. I shot Cindy Andrews, but it appears that her vest stopped the bullet."

"Lucky girl. Just tell me, is the scene secure? Can I send the paramedics up to your room?"

"Yes, it is, but hurry," Tim replied.

"We are just pulling up now."

Tim looked over at Mary Ann, who was still in her bra and panties.

"You better put some clothes on, babe. We are about to have company."

Chapter 33

"I just can't seem to get rid of you two," Deputy Doris Hamlet said to Tim and Mary Ann as she opened the door to the San Francisco county jail ward. "I take it you are here to see Special Agent Cindy Andrews?"

"Yes, that's right, Doris. Can we go right in?" Mary Ann asked.

"Her doctor would like to speak with you first, so if you don't mind waiting in the interrogation room? You know where it is," Doris said sarcastically.

Tim looked at his watch and saw that it was already 9:30 PM. He began to wonder if this day would ever end.

Earlier, after calling and speaking with Joanne Dombrowski, Tim had next called Bob Fredericks to report what had happened. Although Bob was not happy that one of his agents had shot an FBI special agent, he did understand the circumstances and made the appropriate phone calls. By the time Inspectors Dombrowski and Harvey made it up to Tim and Mary Ann's hotel room, they had already received a phone call from their commander. The shooting of Special Agent Cindy Andrews would be handled internally by the FBI.

"Tim, you have to tell me where I can get a job that allows me to shoot an FBI special agent and not be questioned about it," Inspector Joanne Dombrowski had said.

"It's not that I won't be questioned," Tim had told her.

"Just not by the SFPD," Joanne said, finishing Tim's sentence.

"Don't take it personally, Joanne. This is very complicated and I have not put it together yet."

"Tell me, off the record and all, do you always keep a snub-nose magnum 640 in your shower?" Joanne asked.

"We have been lately, but that is also a long story."

Mary Ann had told the two police inspectors earlier that she thought there was a good chance that Tim would be armed, ready and waiting, in the shower.

"You two have to be the strangest couple of cops I have ever met."

"Well, Tim is not technically a law enforcement officer, and—"

"Mary Ann, please give it a rest. At least for the rest of the day," Tim begged.

Tim looked back at Inspectors Dombrowski and Harvey. They were both giving him and Mary Ann looks of disbelief.

As the paramedics had taken Cindy Andrews out of the room, Mary Ann had informed her that she was under arrest for murder but, at that point, Cindy Andrews no longer seemed to care.

There was quite a lot of activity out in the hallway of the jail ward. Deputy Doris Hamlet escorted a man who looked to be about thirty years old into the interrogation room. He was wearing a suit that made Tim think that he was a US attorney. He was soon proven correct.

"Hi, I'm Steward Granger, one of the US attorneys from the Northern California District."

"Steward Granger the actor?" Tim joked.

The US attorney gave Tim a confused look but then appeared to get the joke. "Oh yeah, there was some old actor by that name. I have been meaning to watch one of his movies."

Mary Ann gave Tim a look of disapproval and then turned her attention back to the US attorney.

"I'm Special Agent Mary Ann Hall and this is my husband Tim."

"Oh yes, the man who shot Special Agent Andrews," Steward Granger replied as he fumbled around in his briefcase. "I have a note here that says they plan to handle this shooting back in DC, where you two work. I am fine with that. For God's sakes, I have enough to do; however, would you like to tell me how it happened?"

"I heard a commotion in the hallway and next in our hotel room. Special Agent Andrews broke into the bathroom without identifying herself and she appeared, to me, to have taken my wife hostage. I then shot her."

Tim's rather short explanation did not appear to have any effect on the US attorney. He then looked at Mary Ann.

"And Agent Hall, can you support your husband's statement?"

"Yes, I can. The FBI had issued a warrant for the arrest of Special Agent Andrews on the charge of first-degree murder. That fact had been conveyed to Special Agent Andrews, and all agents in contact had advised her to turn herself in. Instead, she assaulted our personal bodyguard, broke into our hotel room, threatened me with her service weapon, and entered our bathroom without identifying herself. My husband was more than justified in firing his weapon since, by all appearances, Agent Andrews appeared to be intent on bodily harm, despite what she may state to the contrary."

"And what do you think that she may state, Agent Hall?"

"I think that she may contend that she simply wanted to interview me or my husband; but, if that was the case, she certainly used an unusual method."

"OK, I understand," Steward Granger said. "Agent Andrews has retained an attorney and my guess is that she will claim that she was simply trying to interview you and that your husband assaulted her. I also think that she will try to have your husband arrested for assault with a deadly weapon, but I can tell you right now that that's not going to happen. To me, the shooting was justifiable; however, I will not be making that call. As I said, that is being handled back in DC, thank God. What I am concerned about is the murder charge. I wish we had more to work with than a couple of videos."

"Well, that is why we want to interview her now opposed to a couple of days from now," Mary Ann said. "Let's go in. Tim, honey, you better stay here."

"Uh, a couple of things, Agent Hall. First, we need to meet with Agent Andrews' doctor and, in regards to your husband, the assistant attorney general in DC feels that it would be beneficial for your husband to sit in. Now, let me find this doctor."

Once Attorney Granger left the room, Tim shot Mary Ann a glance.

"What is the problem, Mary Ann? Bob Fredericks sent us out here together. I don't think he intended me to just sit on the bench."

"Oh, I just love sports analogies, Tim. No, the problem I have is that this is an FBI matter, not a CIA one. Seems like you told me that in Florida."

"And you are holding that against me? Sometimes you are incredible, Mary Ann."

Tim felt his iPhone vibrate. He pulled it out of his pocket and saw that it was a text from Joanne Dombrowski.

We have ID'd the John Doe. Name is Sam Applewood. LKA Milwaukee Wisconsin. More to come.

LKA, Tim knew, was shorthand for "last-known address."

"Who was that?" Mary Ann asked.

"Joanne Dombrowski," Tim said, still reading the text.

"I'm beginning to worry about you two."

"Oh please, Mary Ann, give it a break."

Tim had to lower his voice since Stewart Granger had returned with Cindy Andrews's doctor. The doctor, a woman named Lewis, explained to Tim and Mary Ann that Cindy Andrews had suffered the "worst contusion" she had ever witnessed. It was located in the area around her sternum. She would, however, make a full recovery. She only hoped that Tim, Mary Ann, and Steward Granger would not "stress her out" too much.

"The doctor would not want to know what I would like to do to Agent Andrews," Mary Ann said under her breath as Doctor Lewis left the room.

"They are ready for us now," Steward Granger told Tim and Mary Ann, who followed him as he left the room.

"We will continue this later," Tim said, referring to his and Mary Ann's disagreement.

The three navigated the jail ward until they found Cindy Andrews' room. Outside sat a female deputy sheriff who asked to see everyone's IDs. Tim showed his deputy United States marshal ID, which seemed to satisfy the deputy.

Cindy Andrews was sitting up in her hospital bed. A woman sitting beside her got out of her chair and introduced herself as Amanda Fisher, Cindy's lawyer.

"I just want to advise you that my client is on morphine and that I plan to contest any statement that she may give you."

"Does he have to be here? The guy who shot me? He is not a member of law enforcement; he's some kind of spy," Cindy said.

"Is that true, Mr. Hall?"

"I am a United States deputy marshal," Tim replied, showing his ID to Amanda Fisher.

"Yeah and I am the fucking queen of England," Cindy Andrews said.

"Well, the ID looks good to me," Amanda Fisher said to her client.

"Cindy? Why did you murder Brent Wilkins?" Mary Ann asked, getting straight to the point.

"I did not kill Brent."

THE DECOYS

"Really? Then who did? We have a video of you leaving the FBI office with Brent on Tuesday night."

Cindy hesitated for a moment.

"I did not kill Brent," she repeated.

"Are you into bondage, Cindy? Do you like to tie up guys in bed? It does give a girl an amount of control, doesn't it?" Mary asked.

Cindy remained silent and just seemed to stare out into space.

"Let me ask you this, Cindy. Why did you pretend to arrest Brent Wilkins on Tuesday evening in Haight-Asbury? And before you make up something lame, we have at least three SFPD officers who will testify that you had a warrant for his arrest for—" Tim saw that Mary Ann had stopped on purpose and was pretending to look for a piece of paper that did not exist. She produced a blank one and continued to question Cindy.

"A warrant as a material witness. That is fascinating, Cindy. What was Brent a witness to?"

"I don't know what you are talking about," Cindy replied.

"OK, let me explain it to you. There is this cab driver named Brent Wilkins—or, at least, that is the name he gives to me and my husband Tim. Now, he is driving us around and then, all of a sudden, there are police cars converging on this address in Haight-Asbury and guess what? We see you and we see you arresting some guy; a guy who turns out to be the real Brent Wilkins. So, who is this guy driving us around and why did he drive us past you making an arrest?"

"Lady, I have no clue who was driving you around and yes, I was making an arrest that night. After all, that is what I do."

"The name of the person driving us is Sam Applewood," Tim said. "We now have him in custody, Cindy. Turns out that he and Brent grew up in the same city in Wisconsin and went to high school together. Sam turned up about ten days ago, hooked up with Brent, and—"

"I told Brent it was a dumbass plan but I did not kill him, no matter what that asshole Sam says, and—"

"Cindy! Be quiet," Amanda yelled. "Steward? Can we take a break so I can confer with my client?"

"Sure, Amanda, but when we reconvene, we want a statement. A true statement and no more BS about your client not knowing anything."

Tim, Mary Ann, and Steward Granger walked out of Cindy's room and made sure that they were well out of earshot before anyone spoke.

"Tim? Who in the hell is Sam Applewood?" Mary Ann asked, not trying to hide her anger.

"Sam Applewood was the real name of the man that was driving us around last week. I just received that information ten minutes ago."

"Well we need to speak with him and find out everything he knows. This is the big break we needed," Steward Granger exclaimed.

"Yes, I agree, but the trouble is that Sam Applewood is dead. He was found in the landfill yesterday. Inspector Dombrowski thinks that he must have ended up in a dumpster somewhere downtown, which is how he ended up in the landfill."

"So, we don't have him," Mary Ann said. "Great work, Tim."

"No, this is not a bad thing," Steward Granger said. "Tim never said whether this Sam Applewood character was dead or alive, just that we had him in custody, which we do. So, there is no judicial malfeasance on our part. It appears that Sam Applewood shows up and pays Brent to drive his cab and pretend he is Brent. It is possible that Brent did not know why. Let's see what Cindy says in her statement. I need to get a stenographer up here," Steward said and began making calls on his iPhone.

Tim suddenly felt a pain in his back and realized that Mary Ann had just slugged him. Because of his rib injury, he doubled over.

"Oh my God, I forgot about your rib injury. I'm really sorry," Mary Ann said, sounding sincere. "I was just fooling around and—"

"What is your problem with me working the case, Mary Ann?"

"It is only because you seem to be better at it than me, and that makes me angry."

"Why does everything have to be a contest with you?"

"I wish I knew, Tim, I really do."

Chapter 34

Tim, Mary Ann, US Attorney Steward Granger, and a stenographer named Michelle returned to Cindy Andrew's hospital room.

"My client is ready to make a statement pertaining to the murder of Brent Wilkins," Amanda Fisher said as everyone found a seat.

"We will decide what it pertains to," Mary Ann said. "Go ahead Cindy, what do you have to say for yourself?"

"Brent Wilkins was my boyfriend and we have been seeing one another for over six months. I met him at a singles night thing. You know, the ones they do at bars where guys have sixty seconds to tell girls about themselves?"

"Wow, can you actually meet people that way?" Tim asked.

"Well, it is one way. I mean, it is hard to find guys when you are a woman cop. Just ask your wife."

"Tim, be quiet. Go ahead, Cindy," Mary Ann said, sounding very annoyed at her husband.

"So, we start dating and he tells me about being in the Navy and about how he is going to school. He plays guitar and has his own place, so I could have done worse. Anyway, we start having sex and he tells me that getting tied up by a woman turns him on. At first, I say no way but, after I think about it for a while, it is kind of a turn-on, so we start doing that."

"Doing what, exactly?" Mary Ann asked.

"We start tying each other up during sex, but Brent seems to like being tied up more than me, so we start doing it on a regular basis."

"OK, I think we have heard enough about your sex life, Cindy, but how did Brent die?" Mary Ann said.

"Well, this guy Sam Applewood shows up about a week, maybe eleven days ago and he tells Brent that he wants to use his cab. He tells us that he is a freelance writer and is working on some kind of story. He offers Brent one thousand dollars to let him drive his cab and pretend to be Brent. I tell Brent that it all sounds nuts to me, but I figure that it's his business."

"All of this is fascinating, Cindy, but we are here to find out how Brent Wilkins died."

"Yes, I know, but it is all a little complicated. Brent and I have, or had, these sexual fantasy games. One of the games was that I arrest him, take him back to my office, tie him up and, well, have sex with him."

"And that is what you were doing on Tuesday night and Wednesday morning? Can you explain how Tim and I just happened to witness you in your little sex game?"

"No. All I can think is that Brent must have told Sam about it and Sam drove by to watch."

"With Tim and I there? Sounds very convenient, Cindy, but we still have not reached the point of Brent Wilkins' murder."

"Brent and I returned to his apartment for the night but then I get a text message from Carol Russo saying she needed to see me right away. I tried to call her but she did not pick up so I had to drive over to fucking Berkeley. While I was getting dressed, Brent asked me if I would tie him up and gag him. I told him that I would be gone for a couple of hours but he did not care; he told me it even turned him on more. I then drove over to Berkeley to Carol's condo. It must have been three-thirty AM by the time I got there. I pound on the door but she does not answer. I turn around and leave and drive back to the city. I go into the bedroom and Brent has been strangled by the scarf I used to gag him. It is tied around his neck. Someone strangled him while I was over in Berkeley. Can I have a glass of water?"

Cindy seemed to be hyperventilating and Amanda Fisher pressed a button that rang for the nurse.

"I think everyone needs to leave for a while. I need to have Doctor Lewis examine the patient," the nurse said.

Tim, Mary Ann, and Steward Granger returned to the interrogation room.

"We still don't know how Brent Wilkins made it from his apartment to Bayview Park. I can't tell if Cindy was generally upset or just faking it. What do you think, Tim?"

"You're asking me, Mary Ann? I thought this was an FBI matter."

"You know, you two are the talk of the Bay Area legal community, and now I understand why," Steward Granger said. "You come to this city and push everyone around with no regard for the rules, and yet the only result has been a kinky murder involving an FBI agent—and, by the way, it's not the first time that has happened here."

"Steward, I apologize for my behavior and for my wife's, but you will have to take our word that there is more going on here than just some sexual misadventure. That said, I promise that we will behave," Tim said as he looked to Mary Ann for agreement.

"Yes Steward, I also apologize," Mary Ann said.

"OK then, so here are the ground rules for when we go back in the room. Mary Ann, you lead, but Tim may also ask any pertinent questions—but Tim, no more bombshell announcements. You just revealed the name of Sam Applewood without discussing it with me or Mary Ann first. You know, my wife is also a lawyer—a trial lawyer—but we never, ever get involved in the same cases. We wouldn't last a minute," Steward Granger said.

When the three reentered Cindy Andrew's hospital room, Cindy appeared to have composed herself.

"Michelle? Can you read where we left off?" Steward asked the stenographer.

"Yes. Before requesting a glass of water, Agent Andrews said, 'Someone strangled him while I was over in Berkeley.'"

"OK, Cindy, that is a good place to pick up. Who strangled Brent Wilkins?"

"I don't know. First, I checked to see if he, Brent, was really dead, but he was so I just sat there with him until daylight, which is when Sam came home. He walked in and freaked out and began to call 911, but I stopped him."

"How did you stop him, Cindy?"

"I pointed my Glock at him. I know that sounds bad, but I just needed him to listen to me for a minute. After I told him everything, he put down the phone and I put away the Glock. Sam and I talked about what the best thing to do was, but then I decided that I needed to report it to the police after all, and this time Sam talked me out of it. He asked how many of my friends knew about my relationship with Brent and the answer was none. I mean, I'd never mentioned him to anybody at work and I really don't have any friends here in the city. So Sam suggested that we should just take Brent's body somewhere. I asked about his cab and he said that he would just park it someplace. Sam was planning on leaving town anyhow, so it would just seem like any other random murder. We both waited until night and I helped Sam take Brent's body down and placed him in the trunk of his taxi cab. Sam then left and I have not seen him since. Meanwhile, I gathered all of my personal belongings from Brent's apartment and took them back to my place. I have not been back there since."

"I think my client has said enough for the night. It is, after all after, midnight," said Amanda Fisher.

"Yes, I agree, Ms. Fisher. It is time we call it a night, but we will be in touch," replied Steward Granger.

As Tim was leaving the room, he caught Mary Ann and Cindy Andrews giving one another looks. Looks that could kill.

"So, what do you think, Mary Ann?" Steward asked.

"I think that she is lying about a lot of things, but I do get the feeling that she may be telling us the truth about Brent Wilkins. I do not believe she murdered Brent Wilkins."

"Well, if nothing else, we can get an indictment for accessory after the fact," Steward said.

"Just as long as her career as a special agent with the FBI is over."

"I can almost guarantee that," Steward replied.

"Well, I'm glad we got something accomplished tonight," Tim said sarcastically as he headed for the door.

Chapter 35

The next morning, Tim was drinking a cup of coffee in the lobby of the Fairmount Hotel. Mary Ann was still asleep and Tim had not bothered to wake her. He'd instead left a Post-it note on the mirror letting her know where he was. Tim had set up a meeting with Darrell Murphy in regards to his bodyguard, Susan Leak. It was Tim's understanding that Susan had quit and was about to fly back east.

"So, Darrell? What is going on with Susan?"

"She is just upset and feels that she let the team down and that she was overpowered by someone who was smaller than her."

"Cindy Andrews could have overpowered me."

"Yeah, but you are an old guy," Darrell laughed.

"Thanks, pal, just what I wanted to hear this morning. Anyway, I do not want Susan going anywhere at least for the time being and no, Mary Ann and I have not lost confidence in her ability. We should have informed her that Cindy Andrews was wanted in connection to Brent Wilkins' murder, but the last thing I expected was Cindy Andrews coming for us."

"In my experience, Tim, it is always the last thing you expect that happens. What do you think she planned to do?"

"She either wanted to sit Mary Ann and me down so she could explain her side of the story or kill the three of us. My thinking is the latter, since that would have solved a lot of her problems and possibly allowed her to collect from whoever has a bounty on us."

"You two are certainly not popular here in the City by the Bay, are you, Tim?"

"Darrell, I was more popular in Colombia, where I shut down half of the nation's drug production. Just send Susan up this evening—Mary Ann or I will speak with her."

Tim's iPhone rang. He saw it was from Inspector Joanne Dombrowski.

"Yes, ma'am," Tim answered.

"Are you going to give me a crack at Special Agent Andrews, oh great one from Washington, DC?" Joanne asked.

"You know you are really a wise-ass, Joanne, which is what I like about you. Yes, it is OK with me, as long as it is OK with US Attorney Steward Granger."

"Our district attorney is making the call now. As usual, there will be some negotiation on who prosecutes the case."

"Just as long as we get Special Agent Andrews disarmed and off the streets. Please let us know if you get anywhere with her. You do know that Sam Applewood moved Brent's body from his apartment to Bayview Park?"

"Yes, the US attorney transmitted Cindy Andrew's statement to us this morning. She sounds like quite a gal, Tim."

"Yeah, a true femme fatale."

"A true nut is what you mean. She reminds me of my sister-in-law. She is a cop too, and you should see the kinds of boyfriends she brings here for Thanksgiving. By the way, my husband Ed is very excited about this Sam Applewood. Apparently, Sam has some background with US Army Special Forces, but everything is classified."

"Figures. Let me work on that for a while and see if we can't get that unclassified."

"Well, if you can't do that, my husband will."

"Let's just leave that there for now," Tim laughed. "I will speak with you later."

A text message popped up on Tim's iPhone from Mary Ann's daughter Molly, the one he did not like.

Are you and my mom breaking up? was the message. Tim decided that this was worth a phone call. Molly picked up right away.

"I knew that would get you to call me," Molly laughed.

"So why do you think your mother and I are splitting up?"

"She sent me a text saying that you were driving her crazy."

"We drive each other crazy, Molly. Most married couples do. That is why it is so fun being married," Tim lied.

"OK, I just wanted to make sure."

"Not a problem, Molly, glad that you are concerned."

"I just wanted to know if Amy and I are still coming for Christmas. Katie says that she is coming."

Katie McNamara was a former US deputy marshal, now a CIA agent working somewhere in South America. Tim knew that if he did not solve this, whatever this was, then Mary Ann and he would still be in San Francisco over the holidays.

"Sure, you and Amy are still coming and, as far as I know, so is Katie. Molly, your mom is very competitive, even with me, and sometimes we disagree."

"Yeah, I know. She was very competitive with my dad, which I think is why they broke up."

"Why do you think that is, Molly?"

"My granddad says it is because of her brother Mac, who was killed before I was born. He was a detective in Cleveland and granddad says Mom is still competing with a ghost. No one talks about it much."

"I can understand why. Anyhow, everything is set for Christmas and I look forward to seeing you."

"Oh, I bet," Molly said and hung up.

Tim had had no clue that Mary Ann had a brother. That would have to be added to the list of things he'd not known about his wife. He considered calling Mary Ann's father to ask him about his late son, but decided against it, since he had recently discovered that Mary Ann's father was stealing from her. Tim had recently opened a checking account for Mary Ann and her paycheck was now deposited in her new account, but he had not bothered to mention this to her father. That was most likely the reason he had been calling her, but Mary Ann had not been picking up. After all, she and Tim had other things to worry about.

Back in the room, Tim found Mary Ann awake and eating an All-American Breakfast.

"Good morning, darling, what have you been up to today?"

"Speaking with your child Molly," Tim replied.

Mary Ann did not seem particularly surprised; she was well aware how Tim felt about her oldest child.

"And what is Molly up to?"

"Well, she was curious about whether you and I are breaking up. I am not aware if we are but, as you know, I am not aware of everything."

"Oh, she is just worried because I texted her that you were driving me crazy—which, by the way, you were—and I want to apologize, especially for hitting you on the back—I really did forget about the rib injury."

"I don't care about the hit, Mary Ann, but I do care about your anger issues. You never told me that you had a brother. What is that all about?"

Mary Ann continued to eat her breakfast and seemed to be pretending that she had not heard Tim's question. He was getting ready to ask her once again when she responded.

"My child should learn to keep her mouth shut."

"It not her fault, Mary Ann. She is just concerned and, quite frankly, so am I."

"It is really not that big a deal, Tim. I had a brother named Mac who was a Cleveland, Ohio police detective. He was shot and killed on the line of duty. April twenty-fifth, 1995. Mac was my father's pride and joy while I was just in the background. There was nothing I could do right to make my father love me. I have been over and over this, Tim. The FBI even made me go to therapy—all of this was discussed."

"Do you mean they made you go into therapy because of your undercover work with Toby?"

"No, way before all of that. I had just started with the bureau and I was sent out with an older guy. His name was Pete, Pete Siskins, and he was not far from retirement. We were walking up to someone's house for an interview—I don't even remember for what. All I remember is that this guy steps out of his house and shoots Pete and I just stand there. The shooter looks at me for a second and then just runs back into the house. Pete is bleeding out but this is before we carried portable radios, so I have to run back to the car and radio that we have an agent down. The dispatcher actually radios back and asks me to repeat myself but I just sit there. I had already been a cop for five years before I joined the FBI and I should have known what to do—but I just went blank. It did not matter, though—a million cops showed up and arrested the guy. The dumb thing, Tim, was that we had the wrong house. Pete had transposed the numbers. The guy who shot Pete thought that we were bill collectors there to take his TV. Isn't that a bitch?"

Mary Ann looked back down at her All-American Breakfast and continued eating. Tim walked over and lay down next to her.

"Do you want some of this, honey?" Mary Ann asked him.

"No, babe, I just want to lie here with you for a few minutes, if that is OK?"

"Sure, honey, lie here as long as you like."

Chapter 36

When Tim and Mary Ann woke up, it was almost 2 PM.

"Shit, we have things to do, don't we?" Mary Ann asked.

"I understand that the San Francisco cops are interviewing Cindy Andrews right now."

"You mean your new friends? Wonder who gave them permission?"

"US Attorney Steward Granger, along with the local DA, is working on some sort of deal. The San Francisco cops have a legitimate interest in this case, Mary Ann, and you yourself don't like her for the murder."

"Then who did murder Brent Wilkins?"

"I think that is fairly obvious, Mary Ann. Sam Applewood killed Brent while Brent was tied up. It was just too good an opportunity not to take advantage of, and who knows what kind of dumb thing Brent may have done—perhaps he blackmailed Sam. Brent was the one connection who could tie Sam back to himself—not to make a pun."

"And a bad pun it was, Tim. So, have we found out anything more about Sam Applewood?"

"I need to check our laptop first, Mary Ann," Tim said as he picked the computer up. "Yes, here's something from our friend Bernard." Tim opened the email and read it out loud. "Tim, checked out Sam Applewood. Yes, he was an explosives and detonation expert with the United States Army and would certainly have been capable of planting an explosive device in a hotel room. Applewood has used the following aliases: John Smith, John Nelson, Captain Anderson, JC Tanning, and Brent Wilkins. He has used that last one in several places besides San Francisco. Sam Applewood has worked for a number of contractors, including my favorite, B&K. Hope you intend on returning home. Icebox is running low on food. Best regards, Bernard. PS, I am working hard on removing you from the grid."

"He is staying at our house. God damn him," said Mary Ann.

"Look, it is a small price to pay if he can get us off this hit list."

"OK, back to Cindy for a minute. Don't you think that she may have suspected Sam Applewood as Brent's murderer?"

"It probably did cross her mind, but remember, she was looking out for herself."

"So what about Sam Applewood as the hotel bomber? What are you planning to do with that information?"

"I am forwarding that over to Ed Dombrowski of the ATF. That will give Cindy Andrews another interrogation to worry about."

"OK, so we end up with Sam as our driver; but what did he plan on doing with us?"

"Sam Applewood planned on blowing us up, not killing us face to face. He was not that kind. He liked to kill from a safe distance. For instance, he somehow hired the woman who tried to push me into oncoming traffic. When that did not work, he really was backed into a corner. With Darrell and his crew around, there was no way to plant any more bombs—I think he got scared and, as Darrell said, beat feet. Sam, however, knew way too much, and someone that Sam was working for decided that he had to go."

"And who do you think that could be?" Mary Ann asked.

"Have we considered Angela? Angela Rice?"

"Angela Rice?" Miss FBI 2019? You must be insane, Tim. How do you figure?"

"Well, first of all, both her guys, meaning Bob Declan and Perez, have left town. That tells me that they are running away from something; plus, no one made any noise when we extracted their main suspect in the case, Bernard Haskell. That makes me believe than even they did not believe he was guilty of Carol's murder; they were just hoping that he would take the rap for it. No, the only one left with any connections to this is Special Agent Rice."

"We still have to prove it, Tim."

Mary Ann was interrupted by a knock on the door. Mary Ann signaled to Tim that she would answer, but wanted Tim to stand behind her.

"Who is it?" Mary Ann calmly asked.

"It is me, Agent Hall, Bobby. Susan Leak is here and said that you and Mr. Hall wanted to speak with her?"

Tim suddenly recalled that he had told Darrell to send Susan up to the room.

"Mary Ann, Susan feels terrible about letting us down and I told Darrell that you would speak to her about it. You see, she is about to head back east, and I not sure if that is a good thing."

"Why is it not a good thing, Tim?"

"Because I am not convinced that she was overpowered by Cindy Andrews. I think it was all an act."

"You know, the same thing occurred to me. You and I are either very paranoid or we are thinking on the same wavelength."

"I think both—so, if you do not mind, would you speak with her?"

Tim opened the door for Susan while Mary Ann stepped into the bathroom to change into a pair of blue jeans and a t-shirt. In the corner of the hotel suite were three chairs and a small table, which were intended for impromptu meetings. Tim offered Susan a seat and observed that she appeared nervous. Mary Ann appeared from the bathroom and sat in the opposite chair. Tim remained standing. The bulge of her holstered Glock was not lost on him.

"So, how it going, Susan?" Mary Ann asked.

"I have been better, Agent Hall, and, if it is all the same to you, I would like to go home."

"Where do you live?" Tim asked.

"I live in Bowie, Maryland. Do you know where Bowie is?"

"Yep, sure do," Tim replied. "It's off of US 50, heading over to the Bay Bridge. Nice little town."

"Yeah, I guess," Susan replied while looking down at the floor.

"Tell us how it happened, Susan. How did Cindy Andrews take you out?" Mary Ann asked.

"I was at my post and I heard the elevator open. It opens a hundred times a day and when it opens I stand up. A woman about five-foot-six comes walking toward me, walking like a cop would walk. About ten feet from me, she shows an identification card and tells me she is FBI. At five feet, she produces a weapon and rushes me. She turns me around and zip ties my hands. She tapes my mouth, takes my keys, and opens the door. You know the rest, Agent Hall."

"Yes, I do Susan. The back of my head still hurts from where she was pulling my hair. So you did not see that she was wearing a vest?"

"No, it was not apparent to me."

"You are what? Five-foot-ten?"

"Almost five-eleven."

"And you were not able to break her hold?"

"She had a gun in my back, Agent Hall."

"How did she get your hands behind your back?"

"She told me to put them behind my back."

"You did not tell me that before, Susan. Did Cindy tell you to put your hands behind your back or did you just do it?"

"I'm not sure. All I know is that they ended up back there."

"I noticed that Cindy did not disarm you, Susan. What I mean is, you still had your weapon holstered. I noticed that when she pulled me off the bed. The only reason I mention it is, at the academy, they teach you to always disarm a suspect in custody since, well, since you just never know. However, Cindy did not take your Glock as she knew that you were on her side. Is that what happened, Susan?"

"No, you have it all wrong. I had no knowledge that anything like this would happen."

"Agent Angela Rice used to work out of the resident agents' office in Rockville and used to live in Bowie. Doesn't the FBI in Rockville handle PG County?" Tim asked.

"Sure, I'd seen her around, but so what? I was a cop for ten years before I—"

"Before you fucked up," Mary Ann said. "Susan, you are under arrest in connection to the murder of Brent Wilkins."

Susan Leak stood up and appeared to reach for her weapon.

"Don't even think about it, Susan. It will just make matters worse," Tim said.

Susan looked at Tim and saw that he was holding his magnum snub-nose 640 by his side.

"Turn around, Susan, and Susan? Place both hands behind your back," Mary Ann said as she placed a pair of handcuffs on each one of Susan's wrists.

"You better call your friend Dombrowski and tell her that we have another one for her to question."

Mary Ann removed Susan's Glock from the holster on her waist and was a little surprised to find a second gun strapped to her ankle.

"What is this for, Susie?" Mary Ann said as the placed the small .38 caliber pistol on the table. She next began to read Susan her Miranda rights.

Meanwhile, Tim stepped out onto the balcony to call Inspector Dombrowski. He felt sorry for Susan. Even though he had suspected that she'd probably let Cindy Andrews in the room, he'd still considered letting her go and fly back to

DC. The problem with that, however, was that Susan probably had pertinent information about Angela Rice that could lead back to the murder of Carol Russo. Then, Tim and Mary Ann could finally get out of San Francisco.

Tim's iPhone rang. It was Dombrowski.

"Tim Hall," Tim said into the phone.

"Oh great one from Washington, DC. I come bearing gifts," Joanne Dombrowski said.

"I have one for you too, though you may not want her. You go first."

"Our doctor discovered that Mr. Applewood has a bite mark on his wrist. He apologized for not finding it before now, but it's a bite mark all right—a bite mark that matches the teeth of a male subject and I am willing to bet my paycheck that male subject is Brent Wilkins!"

"Oh my God, you're kidding me?" Tim asked.

"Nope, saw it myself—so, now we have some DNA, although the bite mark does it for me."

"Not for nothing, Joanne, but does using one dead man to solve another dead man's murder seem kind of a hollow victory to you?"

"Gosh, Tim, you are beginning to sound like a real cop now, but hey, a case closed is a case closed! And who is the number-one closer in the Bay Area? Why it's me! All hail Joanne!"

"You better calm down, Inspector," Tim said, laughing.

"You better calm down Inspector Sergeant you mean, because I will be one once we wrap this up. So, who do you have for me?"

"I have an ex-bodyguard and ex-cop named Susan Leak who appears to have let former Special Agent Andrews into our hotel room."

"You mean that pretty blonde that Cindy overpowered?"

"Yeah, well, it turns out that she did not exactly overpower her. She kind of pretended to let her."

"Where was she an ex-cop?"

"Prince George's County, Maryland."

"You know, I have a cousin who goes down to a town named Brandenburg and volunteers for the fire department. He says he gets more calls in one weekend there than in a month in the Nassau County department where he usually works. Could that be true?"

"Believe or not, it probably is—but anyway, someone paid Susan and we are interested in who and how much."

"And you have her in custody?"

"My wife arrested her and we're hoping you and someone else could come and book her?"

"We can but your wife would be the one to make it a federal rap."

"That does not bother me, just so long as we get rid of her. By the way, did you get anything more out of Cindy?"

"Just that she is so, so sorry about covering up Brent's murder. She is probably only looking at five years, which means eighteen months in this state. Maybe even less than that."

"If we can tie her to the Russo murder somehow then maybe the US attorney will be more excited about pursuing something a little more serious."

"Well, maybe you and the missus would like to take a crack at her. She is still at the jail ward. In the meantime, I will have a unit come over and pick up your gal—but, just so you know, unless she confesses to taking part in your assault, we are going to have to let her go."

Ten minutes later, two San Francisco police officers came and picked up Susan Leak. Tim asked if they knew where to take her and they assured him that they did. They would transport her to SFPD HQ, where she would be questioned by Inspectors Dombrowski and Harvey.

"Joanne asked me if we would like to take another crack at questioning Cindy Andrews."

"So it's Joanne now?"

"Will you please give it a rest, Mary Ann. She has been the best friend we have made out here so far."

"Timmy, I am just busting your balls. Yes, you are right, she has been a good friend. I only wish that you and I could work that well together."

"It is different because Joanne and I are not married. Married couples never work well together; at least, not in my experience. So, do we question Cindy one more time before she makes some kind of deal with the US Attorney or city DA?"

"Yes, we do. Just let me make a phone call first to Steward Granger."

"Good. I'll meet you in the lobby," Tim said as he kissed Mary Ann. Tim's hands began to move down her side until she slapped them away.

"Later. We have to go."

THE DECOYS

When Tim emerged from the elevator, he found Darrell waiting for him in the lobby.

"So, you had Susan arrested?" Darrell said, but Tim could not tell if his bodyguard was angry or not.

"I really did not want to, Darrell, but Mary Ann found too many holes in her explanation. She thinks that Angela Rice paid her off. Did you know that Special Agent Rice worked out of the resident agents' office in Rockville?"

"As a matter of fact, I did know that, Tim. FBI special agents move around a lot and it is not unusual to run into them, especially if you were a cop yourself."

"So, you don't think Susan is rotten?"

"I would not give you anyone rotten, Tim; at least, not to guard you and your wife. Look, I get that you want to figure out whatever you are trying to figure out so you can go home, but I would appreciate it if you do not throw my people under the bus. At least, not without speaking with me first."

"Point taken, Darrell. Would you like me to call Dombrowski and have her released?"

"No, she can endure a little bit of questioning. I'm not happy that she let Cindy Andrews take her out so we can consider this her punishment."

Mary Ann appeared behind Tim, who nodded to her.

"So where are we headed now?" Darrell asked.

"Back to the jail ward. Our second home," Mary Ann replied, and it was not too far from the truth.

Chapter 37

As Tim and Mary Ann rode the elevator to the jail ward, they discussed their strategy.

"This will probably be our last shot at Cindy," Mary Ann said, "so I think we need to tell her that Susan has told us something that will implicate her in Carol Russo's murder."

"And what would that be?" Tim wanted to know.

"I'm not sure. I think I am going to have to make it up as I go along."

"I don't know if that is wise Mary Ann. I think we need to drop the Susan angle and work on why Cindy is lying about entering Carol's condo. There has to be a reason."

Mary Ann squeezed Tim's hand as they approached the large double-pane glass window and the heavy metal door that separated the jail ward from the rest of the hospital. They were a little disappointed not to find Deputy Doris Hamlet on duty. Instead, there was a large man with a shaved head controlling the door. Since the new deputy did not know Mary Ann and Tim by sight, it took the two a little longer than usual to get through. Once in, they made it to Cindy Andrew's room with no delay. They were greeted by the same female deputy guarding the hospital room door. Cindy was sitting up in her bed. In addition, her lawyer

THE DECOYS

Amanda Fisher was in the room. Tim wondered if she was sleeping there.

"Agent Andrews has finished giving her statement and we are presently working on a plea deal with the San Francisco district attorney," Amanda Fisher stated.

"Yeah, I hear you worked out a nice little deal, although if I were you, Cindy, I would have worked with the US attorney. Federal prisons are much nicer than the California woman's prison in Chino, or so I am told," Mary Ann said.

Cindy just sat in her hospital bed, not saying a word—most likely on the advice of her lawyer.

"Look, Cindy," Mary Ann continued, "I really don't think that you killed your boyfriend Brent, and I believe that you found him dead when you returned to his apartment."

"I'm glad to hear that because that is what happened," Cindy said.

"But what I am having a hard time believing is that you drove all the way over to Berkeley just to turn around and drive all the way back to the city. It is hard for me to think that you were not concerned about Carol's safety."

"Well, it is a dangerous world, Agent Hall."

"Yes, it sure is, Cindy, and sometimes knowing too much about—well, about *anything*—can get you in trouble. Such as, for example, a plan to relocate the San Francisco homeless population over to some abandoned US Navy airfield across the Bay."

"Campers," Cindy replied. "Carol liked to refer to the homeless as the campers since, in her mind, that was all they were doing. Carol did not think there was anything wrong with it."

Tim noticed that Cindy had pressed the button on her pain medication machine during Mary Ann's question and was receiving a new dose of morphine.

"Are you still in a lot of pain, Cindy?" Tim asked.

"What do you think, asshole? You shot me."

"Yeah, I know, Cindy, and I'm sorry that I had to do that, but I get a little upset when someone is holding a gun to my wife's head."

"I don't think we need to revisit that at this time," Amanda Fisher said.

"Yes, I agree," Mary Ann replied, although she recognized that the effects of the morphine would possibly encourage Cindy Andrews to expound more on the city's homeless problem.

"So, Carol Russo was an advocate for the homeless—or 'campers' as you called them?"

"Carol was convinced that there was a plot to move all of the homeless out of the city and that it was a human rights issue. She tried to start a federal investigation but that was stonewalled by Agent in Charge Perez and United States Attorney Robert Declan, but you know all of that. What maybe you don't know is that Carol had something else on Perez and Angela. Something big. Carol even told me a week ago that it was something that might even take down the President. That was a week before you two showed up. Carol was very worried about you."

"Yeah, I heard that," Mary Ann said, trying to sound sincere.

"Well that was why Bernard Haskell and Carol were secretly working together. Bernard was supplying information from someone who was making Perez and Declan very uncomfortable, but I did not want anything to do with it. *Any* of it."

Cindy Andrews was beginning to sound and act intoxicated, which appeared to concern Amanda Fisher.

"Cindy? I think that is enough for now."

"Amanda, this is not the first time I have interviewed a suspect who was in the hospital under the influence of some pain medication, and I certainly do not feel it is affecting Special Agent Andrews' statement."

"It's fine, Amanda. I am in control."

That was exactly what Tim and Mary Ann wanted to hear.

"Cindy, we have a video that shows you entering Carol's condo the morning she was murdered," Mary Ann said, which was a lie; she and Tim only suspected that Cindy was the woman in the video.

"Now, I do not think you murdered Carol, but I have to be sure; so, please tell me again. Did you enter Carol's condo?"

"I just opened the door to see that Carol was OK, but she was dead."

"So why didn't you call it in?"

"Because I knew it was a setup. I knew the plan was to implicate me and I was not going to let the bastards do that. Sometimes, I am not sure if we are FBI agents or the army of the resistance. Look, I am not political and maybe I don't say the right things during meetings, but I was not going to let those bastards railroad me for something I did not do."

"Cindy, as your attorney, I have to advise you to shut up. You are not doing yourself any favors here."

"I disagree, Ms. Fisher," Mary Ann said. "We have a senior special FBI agent murdered while investigating a civil rights complaint. Agent Andrews has an obligation to tell us everything that she may know about this crime."

Mary Ann turned her attention back to Cindy.

"Cindy, who sent you the text requesting you to go to Berkeley?"

"Agent Angela Rice texted me at around one AM. She said that she was concerned about Carol and asked me to check on her."

"And you did. You found her dead but you did not call it in. Why?"

"That is how they work. Perez and Angela, I mean. I call it into the local cops but, before you know it, they accuse me of the murder. Meanwhile, all of the text messages, meeting notes and any other communications between me and Angela suddenly disappear."

"So is that when you decided to implicate Bernard Haskell?" Tim asked.

"Someone left what appeared to be the murder weapon: a Glock 22. I picked it up and placed it in my jacket pocket. I carefully backed out of Carol's place and drove over to Bernard's camper. I placed the Glock under the rear bumper. There is a space where it fits under the bumper pretty well. I thought that the Berkeley cops would have an easy time finding it, which they did. You see, I figured you two would protect Bernard while taking all of the heat off of me."

THE DECOYS

"Cindy, I have to hand it to you, you are a piece of work. So, you get back to Brent's apartment and find him dead. Didn't that make you suspicious?" Tim asked.

"Yes, goddamn it, yes." Cindy began to cry. "That's why I did not suspect Sam Applewood. I figured Angela must have done it while I was across the Bay. I think they were hoping that I would freak out and commit suicide; that would have solved all of their problems. You may want to check for Angela's DNA."

It seemed to Tim and Mary Ann that Cindy was beginning to ramble, which risked making some of her new statement inadmissible in court. They decided that they'd better call it a day.

"We may indeed check Angela's DNA, Cindy. Where does Angela live?"

"She lives in Mill Valley. Has a very nice place that makes you wonder how she can afford it all."

"That is interesting, but Cindy, you may want to consider speaking with your lawyer here about cutting a new deal with the United States attorney general. We can get you out of here and out of the state. We can also perhaps recommend you for witness protection, which means you might not have to serve any time, but that is something we will have to discuss. It's just that I don't know how long you will last at the women's prison in Chino. Anyway, we will be in touch," Mary Ann said as she and Tim gathered up their belongings and left the hospital room. Cindy meanwhile lay back in bed, enjoying her high. This was not lost on Attorney Fisher.

"Mr. and Ms. Hall, my client appears to be high and somehow I feel that Mr. Hall has something to do with that."

Amanda Fisher said as she followed Tim and Mary Ann out to the hallway.

Tim turned and held up his hands in a mock surrender and then followed Mary Ann in to the elevator.

"I think Cindy is feeling no pain," Tim remarked.

"Cindy was a lot more forthcoming than I'd expected. Tell me, how did you get the hospital to increase her dose of morphine?"

"I made a phone call while I was waiting for you. They doubled the dose about an hour before we arrived. They should change it back; or, at least, I hope that they do. We would not want her to overdose."

"No, we certainly would not," Mary Ann agreed as she took Tim's arm.

"So, what next?"

"Next we speak with Special Agent Angela Rice, wrap this up, and go home."

"That is the best idea I have heard all day," Tim said.

Chapter 38

Back at the hotel, Tim called Bob Fredericks to report the days events. Bob appeared extremely interested about Mary Ann's suspicions of Special Agent Angela Rice. When Tim mentioned that Mary Ann intended to interview Angela the next day, he asked Tim to sit tight and wait for him to call back.

One hour later, Bob called back.

"Tim, put Mary Ann on speaker so I can read this to both of you"

Tim waved Mary Ann over and motioned that she sit on the bed. Tim next activated the speaker feature on his IPhone.

"OK Bob, Mary Ann is here."

"What I am about to read is also being transmitted to all FBI offices in the United States. The United States Attorney General has ordered that the San Francisco and Bay Area offices of the FBI stand down. This order is effective immediately. All FBI Special Agents assigned to these offices are suspended with pay until further notice. All FBI Special Agents assigned to the San Francisco and Bay Area Offices will report to their assigned duty station on December 12th, 2019 at 09:00 for further instructions.

Tim and Mary Ann both sat in a stunned silence. Neither had never recalled an office of the FBI ordered to stand down. Bob Fredericks continued.

"So that is the official announcement. Now here is what will happen next. Senior Supervising Agent James Hickey and his team are currently en route to San Francisco. Agent Hickey will contact you as soon as he arrives. He will be leading the investigation and it is very important that you two do nothing to tip off anyone in any of the Bay Area FBI Offices. In the meantime Mary Ann, as the only active FBI Special Agent in San Francisco, you should continue to go to the office and maintain your cover. Special Agent Hickey will be there soon to relieve you".

"So Bob, I am supposed to just sit on my hands until someone from DC shows up? Tim and I are very close to breaking this case wide open."

"Mary Ann, over the last year and a half I have become very fond of you and my wife just loves you to death but if you want to continue as an FBI Agent, then I suggest you follow orders. I really hope I have made myself clear." Bob said as he hung up the phone.

Tim or Mary Ann had ever heard Bob Fredericks speak to them in such a way.

"Do you know this guy? Hickey?" Tim asked.

"Yes, and he is a real prick," Mary Ann replied. "He will get here and run roughshod over everything we've accomplished."

"I am really trying to figure out what exactly we have accomplished, Mary Ann."

"Tim, the FBI is meant to uphold the Constitution, and civil rights are a big part of that—or, at least, it is to me. The homeless, these campers, all have a right to due process, which they will not receive if they are rounded up and shipped across the Bay. This country is one step away from becoming another Nazi Germany."

Tim Hall did not believe that the United States was anywhere close to becoming another Nazi Germany; however, many people did believe this to be true and said as much each day on TV and social media.

"Mary Ann, I don't really believe that this is all about the homeless. What I mean is that it may have started out as an issue of moving the homeless across the Bay to Oakland but this has now become something much bigger. I mean my god, they have deactivated over one thousand FBI Special Agents. No it has to be something else.

"We have to interview Angela Rice before Jim Hickey gets to her," Mary Ann said. "Otherwise Albert Perez will make Angela disappear, just like he made Bob Declan disappear." Mary Ann said appearing to have heard nothing that her husband just stated.

"Well why don't we just sleep on it, honey, You can go in to the office and interview Angela in the morning."

"If I show up at the office in the morning, I will be swamped by FBI Agents demanding to know why they have all been suspended plus my guess is that Angela will stay at home. No, there has to be another way."

Mary Ann almost seemed resigned to waiting until she suddenly sat up in bed. She remembered Matthew Boykins.

She picked up her iPhone and found his number. Matthew picked up after one ring.

"Matthew? Hi, Mary Ann Hall here. Matthew? Would you come by and pick me up in the morning?" Tim watched Mary Ann as she listened to Matthew Boykins. After about a minute, Mary Ann said, yes I know but I'm still an active agent Matthew and between us, this action by the AG is just an administrative one. All the suspended special agents will be reinstated by the end of the day".

"Yes, that would be great, Matthew, see you then."

"What was that all about?" Tim wanted to know.

"I want to get up to see Angela before she gets to work. Matthew has been her driver since she has been working for Perez and he knows where she lives. He also told me that she is alone, Tim. I am going to interview her before she gets into the office and speaks with Hickey."

"I really don't think that is such a good idea, especially after what Bob Fredericks told us."

"I don't work for Bob Fredericks, Tim, and he cannot tell me who I can speak with and who I cannot."

Tim was too tired to continue, especially as he knew it was an argument that he would never win. His wife was obviously intent on reaching the bottom of the investigation before all of the bigshots from DC arrived.

Mary Ann undressed and climbed into bed naked. Tim joined her and the two soon began to make love. Tim marveled over how Mary Ann never seemed to let the arguments she and Tim had about work get in the way of having sex. Their sex lives were completely separate. One benefit of daily sex was the sleep it seemed to produce afterward, and both Tim and Mary Ann were soon out for the night.

Mary Ann was dressed and ready to go when Tim opened his eyes the next day.

"So, where are you off to?" Tim asked, still half asleep.

"Matthew Boykins—you know, the other special agent we met at the airport? He is taking me up to get Angela Rice in Mill Valley. Do you know where Mill Valley is?"

"It is on the other side of the Golden Gate Bridge in Marin County, I think. At least you will get the chance to go across the Golden Gate. Everyone should."

"You are such a romantic, Tim, you really are," Mary Ann said as she bent over to kiss him.

"What about this Special Agent Hickey guy?"

"I will meet him after I arrest Angela," Mary Ann said.

Now Tim was sitting up. He had not understood from the previous evening's discussion that his wife planned to actually arrest the senior agent.

"Do you have enough to arrest her?"

"I will by the time I get back to the city. What are your plans today?"

"My orders are to stay put, but I have no intention of going over to the FBI office without you. I don't think they like me very much."

Mary Ann was now fully dressed in her black pants, pink satin blouse, and linen jacket. Tim certainly though she looked sexy in a cop kind of way. Mary Ann gave Tim one more kiss and left the room. Tim heard her say good morning to Bobby the bodyguard as she made her way to the elevators.

Tim's iPhone rang and buzzed, which was a special sound Tim set had up for when Bob Fredericks called.

"Good morning, sir," Tim answered.

"Good morning, Tim, has the gang arrived?"

By "gang," Bob was referring to the new special agent in charge of God knows what.

"I have not seen hide nor hair of anyone, but my wife is on her way to the office," Tim said, leaving out the part about Mary Ann arresting Angela on her way to work.

"Tim, I expect that Agent Hickey will want to meet with you and your wife first so he can get the story firsthand."

"Well, he will have to come here because I have had enough of the FBI."

"Great news, so I don't need to worry about you jumping ship and working for them?" Bob said jokingly.

"I have been pretending to be a cop for the last ten days and the short answer is no. I will not be leaving my job as an international spy."

"We don't like calling ourselves spies"

"Really? Then why do we have an entire museum that uses exactly that term?

"PR, son. PR."

"Excuse me, Bob, the house phone is ringing."

Tim walked over and picked up the phone.

"Tim Hall."

"Mr. Hall? This is the front desk calling. There is an FBI agent by the name of James Hickey here to see you."

"Tell him that I will meet him in five minutes."

Tim got back on the iPhone and told Bob Fredericks that the FBI agent from DC had arrived. Tim next called

Darrell to make sure that there really was an FBI agent waiting to see him and not some kind of assassin. Darrell was in the lobby and had already scoped out the agent. Tim then asked Darrell if he would stay close by; he suddenly had a feeling that something was not right.

Tim quickly dressed and headed to the lobby. As he walked out of the elevator, he saw two men who could only be senior agents with the Federal Bureau of Investigation. The older of the two had to be Hickey, whereas the younger one was most likely his number-one something or other.

"If you are Agent James Hickey then I am Tim Hall," Tim said from across the room.

"You can call me Jim," Agent Hickey said and suddenly seemed to be much nicer than Tim had anticipated.

"Let's sit in these seats over here," Tim said, pointing to some chairs.

"This is Special Agent John Watson and yes, he has heard all of the Doctor Watson jokes."

Everyone had a good phony laugh about the younger agent's name.

"So, your wife will not be joining us?" Jim Hickey asked.

"I'm afraid that she has already gone to the office and is waiting for you to arrive. She wanted to speak with Angela Rice before you came in today and—"

"We would also like to speak with Agent Rice but we have not been able to contact her. Angela has been very critical to our investigation into the San Francisco office."

"Really? My wife seems to feel that Agent Rice is somehow involved in, well, whatever is going on."

"Mr. Hall, what has been going on at the San Francisco FBI office covers everything from extortion to misappropriation of government funds and even mail fraud. Angela Rice was working undercover."

"Then maybe you can tell me why in the hell my wife and I were sent out here?"

"Mr. Hall, there are people, some very bad people, who had become very suspicious of Albert Perez and Angela Rice. You and your wife were sent out here as decoys, so to speak, intended to take the heat off of them."

Tim took a very deep breath. He had been used as a decoy before, but had been informed of his role beforehand. This was the first time he had been kept in the dark. Tim, however, decided that he needed to keep his cool.

"OK, so we were decoys, but why not tell Mary Ann and me? I feel like I have been running around in circles for the last ten days."

"Yes, I know, Mr. Hall, and once again, I apologize. However, you and your wife's implication of Agent Rice as a suspect in the murder of Carol Russo has, well, has helped. Helped immensely."

"I'm afraid that my wife may continue to help. You see, she told me this morning that she intended to arrest Ms. Rice this morning."

Both Agents Hickey and Watson laughed.

"Well, that is something I would like to see. Two female FBI special agents trying to arrest each other. So, taking that into consideration, we'd better get going. We have a lot to finish up."

"I guess the three attempts on our lives have not been part of your deception?" Tim wanted to know.

"Unfortunately no, Mr. Hall. Those are for real."

Tim tried to call Mary Ann in order to warn her of the impending embarrassment. He could only imagine each agent trying to arrest the other until Mary Ann was confronted with the truth. She would then be humiliated in front of everyone and Tim knew that that would kill her. He tried to call her once again but the phone went to voicemail. *Strange*, Tim thought.

Tim got up from his seat and began to walk toward Darrell when his phone rang. Expecting it to be Mary Ann, he was disappointed to see that it was Inspector Joanne Dombrowski.

"Hey Joanne," Tim said.

"The bite mark we found on Sam Applewood does not match Brent Wilkins' teeth, so now I've had to rule him out as a suspect," Joanne said, sounding disappointed. The ME does however feel that the bite marks do belong to a man."

"I have bigger problems. My wife drove off this morning with an FBI agent by the name of Matthew Boykins and I have not heard back from either of them."

"Why don't you just call the FBI and ask for his address?"

"Mary Ann works for the FBI, I do not; they won't tell me anything."

"Hold on, I actually think I know where he lives," Joanne said. Tim could hear her flipping through the pages of her notebook.

"He lives on Key Avenue."

"How do you know that and why does that street sound familiar?"

"Key Avenue is that little street that runs off of Third Street and leads to Bayview Park. We were canvassing the neighborhood and that is how we found out. It's an unusual place for an FBI agent to live, but—"

"Do you have a number?

"Yes, two-three-four-five. Apartment three."

"It is possible that my wife may be there."

"Now, why would you think that, Tim? What is going on?"

"Like I said, my wife went out this morning to arrest somebody but I have not heard from her since and this Special Agent Matthew Boykins was supposed to give her a ride."

"OK, so why don't we both drive over to his apartment and see if he is home."

"I am on my way, Joanne," Tim said as he hung up.

Chapter 40

Darrell drove the SUV, its blue lights flashing and sirens blaring, south on Third Street. Tim's imagination was beginning to run wild. If Mary Ann had driven up to Angela's house and Angela had shot her, Angela could probably get away with it as she was working undercover. Tim next got mad at Bob Fredericks. How dare he use him and Mary Ann as decoys?

"Tim, would you like to tell me what is going on?" Darrell asked.

"This entire trip has been BS, Darrell. Mary Ann and I were sent out here just to take attention off of Angela Rice. We were sent out here just to bumble around and piss people off so the real investigators could maintain their covers. Apparently, that is all I am good for these days: getting in the way."

Darrell made the left-hand turn off Third Street on to Key Avenue. He parked behind the two police cars and Joanne's unmarked Ford. Joanne was standing at the entrance to Matthew's building. She waved Tim over as soon as she saw him.

"No one is answering the door, Tim, and we don't have probable cause for a warrant and—"

Joanne suddenly noticed that Darrell had a crowbar and Tim held a baseball bat. The front door opened easily enough, but gaining entrance to Matthew's apartment was a little harder. Darrell left and returned with an ax. The door was soon in splinters.

Tim led the way with his magnum snub-nose 640, while Joanne followed with Inspector Harvey and two uniformed officers. At first, the apartment appeared empty, but Joanne heard a faint noise coming from the bedroom closet. Tim opened the closet door but it appeared empty. He picked up his baseball bat and called for Mary Ann. A muffled sound came back from behind the wall. *A fake wall.*

"Officer, knock it down," Tim yelled and two SFPD cops started working on the false wall. After the plywood that made the false wall was removed, they found a woman, but it was not Mary Ann. As they pulled her from the enclosed space, Tim saw the tattoo on the woman's wrist. It was Special Agent Angela Rice. Tim pulled the duct tape off of her mouth.

"Angela? Where is Mary Ann? Where is my wife Mary Ann?"

"Tim, give her a minute. She has been badly beaten and god knows how long she has been in there," Joanne said. "Guys? Get her on the bed while I call for assistance."

While Joanne was speaking into her portable radio, it suddenly dawned on Tim that Matthew Boykins had been behind everything all along. He was the main person, the main subject at the center of all this. Tim and Mary Ann had chased so many false leads that they had overlooked the one person no one had paid any attention to: Matthew Boykins. And now he had Mary Ann.

The reality of the situation began to sink in. That little creep Matthew had Mary Ann somewhere and Tim could not think what to do. As soon as the FBI found out that their undercover agent, the one they'd been trying so hard to protect, was critically injured, they would descend on Matthew Boykins' apartment like only the FBI can, and they would be mad, very mad. They'd be looking for someone to blame, Tim knew, and that someone would be Tim Hall. Meanwhile, Tim's wife's whereabouts would be lost in the shuffle until she turned up dead someplace. It was all a bad dream come true.

Angela Rice was now semi-conscious. She just kept repeating, "Matthew Boykins," "Matthew Boykins," over and over.

"Tim, I'm no doctor, but I can see that she is dehydrated and traumatized. Angela is not going to be able to tell you anything for God only knows how long, but at least we found her alive," Joanne said.

"Yeah, I guess," Tim replied, but his thoughts were interrupted by his iPhone ringing.

He looked down and saw it was an unknown number. He stepped outside to take the call.

"Dude, I got your old lady."

It was Matthew Boykins, except he no longer sounded like the scared and nervous young FBI agent. Now he sounded like a real asshole.

"Matthew, where is Mary Ann?"

"Oh, she is right here. Say hi, Mary Ann."

"Tim, don't—" Mary Ann said in the background but Matthew cut her off.

"That will be enough, Mary Ann," Matthew said. "Now Tim, I know that all the bigshots are at the San Francisco FBI office, but so far they are not looking for me, are they?"

"No, not as far as I know, Matthew."

"Good. Now, I know from listening to my police radio that Inspectors Dombrowski and Harvey are over at my apartment. Is that correct?"

"Yep, right so far, Matthew."

"And you are with them? Have you found Angela yet? Is she dead? I'm afraid that I had to beat her very badly last night."

"They are just bringing her out, Matthew, but they are not aware who she is," Tim lied.

"Oh, that is good news, Tim. Let's keep it like that for now."

"Sure, Matthew, not a problem."

"I like you, Tim, and I have seen how your wife pushes you around. Tim, it's just wrong, and is not how God intended men and women to live. The Bible says so you know."

Oh hell, Tim thought. *Matthew Boykins is one of those types of guys. The ones who believe God has special roles for men and women.* Tim knew that guys like Matthew could be extremely dangerous and very unpredictable.

"We need to keep Angela's identity a secret. At least long enough for you, me, and Mary Ann to get out of town—just like you got Mr. Haskell out of town," Matthew said.

"Sure, Matthew, I think we can do that. Where are you right now?"

"Not far from the Golden Gate, Tim. Just start heading this way and I will call you. But Tim? Lose the big black guy. We will not be needing him."

Tim hung up the iPhone and walked back to Joanne.

"It is Matthew Boykins and it has always been Matthew Boykins and I totally fucking missed it."

Tim was mad now; mad enough to hit anyone who got in his way. Joanne saw this and tried to calm her new friend.

"Tim, sit down and take some deep breaths. Then tell me what is going on."

"Matthew Boykins has my wife Mary Ann and is somewhere around the Golden Gate Bridge. Do you have any clue where 'somewhere' might be?"

"Sure: Fort Point. That is where you can watch other people jump off the bridge. I mean, if you want to do that kind of thing. There are also a bunch of fortifications still there. It is possible that that's where they are hiding."

A fire engine and ambulance pulled up in front of Matthew's house along with two more police cars. The crews from the fire department headed into the house.

"The victim is on the bed, guys," Joanne said to no one in particular. Instead, she was focused on a uniformed police officer approaching.

"Shit, Tim, that is the shift officer and she is going to ask a bunch of questions, like who the victim is. What do you want me to tell her?"

"Tell her that we don't really know yet, Joanne, which is close to the truth. After all, there is no ID and the only way I know it is Angela is because of the tattoo."

"But Tim, racing off to save your wife without a plan is not a good idea."

"Joanne, I have spent the majority of my career out of the country and not playing by the rules. I'm afraid that I would not last five minutes as a real cop. Now, I know how to bring Matthew Boykins out because he needs me, but I only have one chance. Matthew Boykins really wants to kill my wife, Joanne, and I can't let that happen—even if I die trying."

"Inspector Dombrowski? May I have a word?" The shift supervisor was now approaching them.

"Tim, I owe you one. Actually, I owe you a couple favors, so let me do one for you. I can hold off for an hour or so from letting anyone know that this is Angela Rice. Also, the SFPD usually has a guy running surveillance at and around Fort Point. Let me at least call him and see if he has seen anyone hanging around."

"Yes, please do that, Joanne. Meanwhile, let me speak with my bodyguard."

Tim walked back to the SUV to find Darrell standing out front.

"Darrell, Matthew Boykins has grabbed Mary Ann and he is somewhere around the Golden Gate Bridge. He wants me to come and pick them up by myself."

"And you think that is wise?"

"No, I don't think it is wise, but I am also not sure what this guy is capable of doing. So far, he has convinced me and Mary Ann that he is some kind of Casper Milquetoast guy, but now I am not so sure."

"Who in the fuck is Casper Milquetoast? Is he like Casper the Friendly Ghost?" Darrell asked.

"Yeah, kind of," Tim responded, not wanting to take the time to go into the full explanation.

"OK, but that doesn't mean that he is invincible."

"You're right, Darrell, it doesn't. Now look, Darrell, if you know anything about me, it's that I take the direct approach to solving problems. In other words, I am not planning to make any deals or play any games with this asshole. Mary Ann knows that about me as well. What I am trying to say is that I plan on killing this guy the first chance I get."

"Tim?" It was Joanne calling to him. "Tim, my guy running the stakeout under the bridge said that he saw a couple: a young guy and a middle-aged woman. Said that they looked like they were walking the bridge. Lots of people do that, but he said that it did not appear that he was forcing her anyplace and, as a matter of fact, they were holding hands."

"OK, Darrell and I are heading over now."

"Tim, you are going to need some backup," Joanne said.

"What about the shift supervisor?"

"Oh, she is so excited that they have a victim," Joanne said as she looked over at the woman, who was now speaking on the phone. "Anyway, she won't bother us."

"OK, just give me a thirty-minute head start, Joanne. You can call the FBI and tell them that you may have found Angela Rice and that she is on her way to the ER. Don't mention me unless you have to," Tim said as Darrell started the SUV and drove off.

Tim's iPhone rang as soon as Darrell and he were on California 101. He looked at the caller ID: *Unknown*.

"Tim Hall."

"Tim? Are you on your way?" It was Matthew Boykins.

"Yes, Matthew, I am."

"Great, now please do what I tell you. If you do then Mary Ann and you will be able to return home and have Christmas with the kids, Molly and Amy."

Tim had no clue how Matthew had been able to get the names of Mary Ann's children, but there was no time to think about that.

"Sure, Matthew, just tell me what you want me to do."

"Do you know where Fort Point is, Tim?"

"Sure do."

"Good, just drive to Fort Point and find a place to park and I will call you back."

"How will you know when I park, Matthew?" Tim asked.

"Oh, well I can see you, Tim. So just find a place to park."

Matthew hung up the phone.

"It sounds like Matthew will have eyes on us, Darrell, which tells me he must have a high vantage point."

"He could be in that fort or whatever it is," Darrell replied, referring to the old fortifications at the park, "unless he is up on the bridge somewhere."

"That occurred to me as well, so let's take a drive over the bridge, Darrell, and see where they might be hiding."

Darrell continued on California 101 as they passed Fort Point. Tim wondered whether Matthew and Mary Ann were someplace in or around the park, but couldn't shake the hunch that they were on the bridge.

As they started to cross, Tim saw that the huge cables extended from the towers to large cement structures on either side and at both ends of the bridge. Tim also saw that there

THE DECOYS

were doors to the cement structures as well as to the gigantic towers. It was certainly possible that the two were someplace in one of the four towers, but Tim felt that it was more likely that they were someplace in or around the cement structures—most likely the first one on the right as they drove north. Darrell and Tim reached the other side of the Golden Gate Bridge and entered Marin County.

"Darrell, turn around and let me out before you reach the toll plaza. I am going to check out that first large concrete bunker. Go ahead and park at the fort and meet me back up here. I am probably going to need you."

"That is your plan?" Darrell asked in a tone of disbelief.

"Yep, that is the plan."

Darrell slowed at the toll plaza and let Tim out. Tim then began to walk on to the westernmost walkway over the bridge. At about fifty yards from the cement structure, Tim saw them. Matthew and Mary Ann were standing at the railing. Matthew appeared to be using a gun sight as a kind of telescope. He was looking in the direction of the Fort Point parking lot. Matthew was holding Mary Ann's left hand, but Tim guessed that they were handcuffed or tied somehow together.

Tim pulled out his snub-nose magnum 640 and began to cross the road. Cars from either direction sounded their horns in protest, but he remained focused on Matthew and Mary Ann.

Matthew turned around to see what the cars were honking at and spotted Tim. He placed his gunsight back in his pocket and produced a Glock 22.

"It's over, Matthew," Tim yelled over the sound of blaring horns, but Matthew pointed his Glock as Tim approached and fired two shots. The bullets struck a box truck that was crossing the bridge. The truck swerved, struck a car, and they both came to a stop. This gave Tim some much-needed cover.

"Federal agent, stay in your vehicle!" Tim yelled but he suddenly recalled that was almost exactly what his late wife Pam had said before she died. On a bridge, no less.

Tim walked to one side of the box truck as Matthew began to run north across the bridge with Mary Ann in tow. Matthew turned back toward Tim but stopped when he ran into a crowd of sightseers. Matthew pointed his Glock at the tourists, who began to scream and run out onto the road. He next turned around and aimed his Glock back at Tim, but Mary Ann took her free hand and slammed it into Matthew's face. Mary Ann was now wrestling with Matthew and Tim no longer had a clear shot. Mary Ann grabbed Matthew's gun but their momentum took the two toward and over the railing of the bridge.

Tim ran and grabbed Mary Ann's arm with one hand but she was in a very awkward position. Her free arm was wrapped around the railing but Matthew was still handcuffed to her other hand. He was swinging from side to side below her but was also pulling her down. Tim could see her right arm beginning to slide off the railing. Darrell had now come to Tim's aid and he gabbed Mary Ann's right arm with both of his hands but it was no use. Matthew was just too heavy and both men were beginning to lose their grips.

"Hold on to her, Darrell!" Tim said as he leaned over the railing and fired the magnum 640 at the handcuffs that attached Mary Ann to Matthew. The first shot missed but the second did not. Tim watched as Matthew Boykins disappeared into the waters below.

Chapter 41

Tim did not recall the scream Matthew Boykins made as he fell the 220 feet from the bridge to the mouth of the San Francisco Bay, but others said it was horrifying. All Tim really remembered was the flying metal from the handcuffs attached to his wife's hand. As soon as Matthew became unattached, Mary Ann came flying back onto the bridge, or so it seemed. Tim and Darrell had been pulling her so hard that she seemed to fly up and over their heads. The entire event happened so quickly that it took some time to explain it all to the cops. In this instance, it was the California Highway Patrol, who had jurisdiction over the bridge.

Mary Ann had identified herself as a special agent with the FBI and told the Highway Patrol officers that Tim was a special agent with the United States Department of Justice. Tim also informed the CHP officers that he was a special agent with the Department of Justice, but neither seemed to believe him or his US deputy marshal badge. Fortunately, Joanne Dombrowski had made it to the scene, but Tim felt that it was a better idea for her to take care of Mary Ann. His wife's left arm, hand, and wrist were badly injured, and Tim had overheard one of the paramedics mention that she might need surgery in order to save it.

THE DECOYS

Tim was relieved to see Joanne climb into the back of the ambulance while he was handcuffed and placed in the back of a CHP patrol car. Tim heard Mary Ann scream his name as the police car made a U-turn in the middle of the bridge, but he knew she would be OK with Joanne. Tim also saw Darrell Murphy standing in the crowd, watching. *No reason for him to get involved*, Tim thought. *He would have a hard time explaining himself.*

Tim was transported to the CHP station on Eighth Street in the city. "Usually we take guys like you to the city jail intake unit, but I got a message here that you are something special. Did you see he was packing a snub-nose magnum 640? Who are you, pal? Dirty Harry?"

Tim ignored the jabbering of the two Highway Patrol officers. All he could think of was the theme song from the very, very old TV show of the same name.

They pulled into the parking lot of the CHP station, and Tim was surprised by how few police cars there were. The place actually looked deserted. Maybe this was it; maybe the California Highway Patrol was going to kill Tim and collect the bounty.

One of the cops opened the back door and pulled Tim out before shoving him toward the back door.

"Foley!" someone yelled. "Take those handcuffs off now or your next assignment will be running radar on I-5," a man said to the CHP officer, referring to Interstate 5.

"Oh shit, it's Colonel Maclin. You did not say Colonel Mac was here!" one of the CHP cops said to the other.

"Hey, man, they just said bring the guy here; they did not say what for."

"Mr. Hall, I'm Colonel Douglas Maclin of the California Highway Patrol and I have been sent to escort you to the FBI office. If you would follow me, please."

"Sure, but can I retrieve my weapon first?"

"Why did you remove this agent's weapon, Foley?"

"Well, sir, we—"

"Foley, when you are in a hole, quit digging."

CHP Patrolman Foley scurried over and handed Tim his snub-nose magnum 640. Tim placed it in his shoulder holster.

"So, you are old school, I see. I have the same weapon but I use it for hunting," Colonel Douglas Maclin said.

"This is not my primary weapon, Colonel. I carry a Glock 22 like almost everyone else, but today it certainly came in handy."

"I'm told that was one hell of a shot you took, Agent Hall."

"I had no choice, Colonel, the suspect had my wife. If she went over, I would have followed."

Tim's statement seemed to bring an emotional reaction out of Colonel Macklin, but Tim was completely serious. He would have gone after Mary Ann. As he'd climbed over the railing, his first thought had been to try to grab Mary Ann by her belt, but he'd not been able to reach. He'd then saw that the cuff on Mary Ann's hand was close to coming off but that she was slipping. He'd fired the gun out of sheer desperation. Although it had paid off, Tim couldn't help but ask himself the same question over and over: *what if it had not?*

THE DECOYS

Colonel Macklin continued to go on about how they no longer had cops like Tim, and Tim did not have the heart to tell the colonel that he really was not a cop, just a spy on loan.

"These FBI officials are going to want to congratulate you, Tim," Colonel Macklin told Tim as they pulled up in front of the Federal Building.

"I don't know about that, Colonel. We almost got their undercover agent killed and I am not too sure if she is going to make it. Seems like the only thing we did was bust some kinky FBI agent for accidentally killing her boyfriend."

"Oh, you mean the gal who tied up her boyfriend and came back to find him dead?"

"Yeah, the very same."

"Do you think she will do any time?" the colonel said, sounding interested.

"I would not be surprised if she is back on the streets by April 2020," Tim laughed.

"Well, if you see her again, give her my card."

Tim looked at the man's business card and placed it in his wallet. *Stranger things had happened*, he thought to himself.

Tim walked up the steps to the Federal Building but was met by Special Agent James Hickey of the FBI and his boss, Bob Fredericks. Tim start to explain.

"Look, I'm sorry," Tim said, "but I had no clue Angela Rice was working undercover and you, Bob, next time you want me to be a decoy, at least tell me."

"Cool down, Tim. The operation was a success. Angela Rice is doing fine and now that creep Matthew Boykins is dead, she can go back undercover," Jim Hickey said.

"Huh?" was all Tim Hall could say.

"Yes, Matthew Boykins was the only person who knew Angela Rice was working undercover, or at least that is what our intelligence says. Now that he's gone out to sea, well, we feel that there is no reason Angela cannot continue her work."

"Tim, I'm afraid Matthew Boykins was just your run-of-the-mill psychopath. He disliked women, felt rejected by women, and therefore needed to get even with women. You see, men have three dominating motivators in life. Those are to provide, protect, and prove their power. Matthew Boykins was lacking in all three. This was a prescription for violence. He murdered Carol Russo and, if not for you, he would have also murdered Angela Rice. He planned to murder Cindy Andrews but murdered Brent Wilkins instead, probably as some sort of punishment for allowing her to dominate him. He probably would have killed your wife Mary Ann too. He certainly came close to murdering Angela, and would have if you had not found her this morning."

"OK, Jim, then tell me about Sam Applewood."

"I'm afraid Mr. Applewood followed you and your wife to San Francisco to kill you. He had nothing to do with Angela or Carol. However, when you and Mary Ann changed hotels at the last minute, well, that bomb he attached to the room thermostat proved a wasted effort."

"Except for the poor guy who ended up taking our hotel reservation," Tim said, but his comment was met with silence.

"When the assassination attempt failed, Tim, Applewood gave Brent Wilkins money to impersonate him in order to get close to you. He might have succeeded if you had not brought out Darrell Murphy."

"So who killed Applewood?"

"We suspect he was murdered by the same people who tried to have you run over, Tim. Applewood tried twice and failed, so he became a liability to whoever he was working for. Plus, we think the presence of Darrell and his security team made him nervous. Someone killed him and threw him in a dumpster. We can't tie Cindy Andrews to it, so that is the theory we are working with."

"What about Susan Leak?"

Both Bob Fredericks and Jim Hickey gave Tim a quizzical look until Bob seemed to remember.

"Oh, the woman working with Darrell. She was clean and was released. Darrell sent her back east."

"OK, and Cindy Andrews? What happens to her?"

"Well, first and foremost Cindy Andrews is no longer a special agent with the FBI. That was the first thing I took care of," Jim Hickey said.

"How about an accessory after the fact for the murder of the real Brent Wilkins?" Tim asked.

"Tim, that would mean an indictment and a trial and it could compromise Angela's investigation, since she might have to be called as a witness. No, Cindy has been fired although the reasons will have to be classified. She will probably end up refinancing mortgages for a living." Jim Hickey laughed.

"Yeah, or something," Tim said. "Look, if you see Cindy, this guy wanted her to have his business card."

Jim Hickey looked at Macklin's business card and chuckled.

"On the other hand Cindy Andrew's may cut a nice figure in a CHP uniform. I will be sure she gets it,"

"So look, I need to take a leak. Can I use the facilities before I go?" Tim asked.

"Tim, we don't think that would be a good idea. As a matter of fact, you probably should not go back into the Federal Building while you are still here in San Francisco. See, we are working on a cover story to explain your and your wife's presence out here, and we don't need any embarrassing questions from any of our special agents. You see when we closed down this office yesterday, many jumped to the conclusion that you and your wife were behind it so you can understand that many are somewhat angry. Bob and I feel that it would be better if you just disappeared."

"No, I would not want to embarrass anyone,"

"Tim, Mary Ann is very anxious to see you and I promised that I would bring you over to the hospital as soon as you were debriefed. You do know that she needed surgery on her wrist?" Bob said.

"So is that what we have been doing here on the steps of the Federal Building? My official debriefing, Bob?"

"Tim, you have accomplished what we sent you and your wife out here to do. That is your job for which you get paid. If you no longer like it then—"

"Cool down, Bob. You and I don't have a problem."

"Bob, I got to go," Jim Hickey said as he turned and headed back inside. "I will see you back in DC, and Tim? Thanks again for everything. Be sure to tell your wife hello."

"Yeah, and FU," Tim said, but Jim Hickey had already gone.

"Tim, you know what kind of business we are in. Sometimes I just don't get you. I mean, what did you want for all of your work? A parade?"

"That's the thing, Bob. I'm just no longer sure what I want."

Chapter 42

Tim had spent so much of the last week in the hospital jail ward that it almost seemed strange walking through the regular hospital. Mary Ann was somewhere in the orthopedic section, and when Tim began to see patients using walkers while trying out their hip replacements, he figured that he was in the right area. However, he was still unable to find his wife.

"Mary Ann?" he finally said in a louder-than-normal voice.

"I'm in here, Tim," came the reply. Tim had walked right past her room.

"Here she is, Tim," said the voice of Inspector Joanne Dombrowski.

"Where is Bobby?" Tim asked, referring to the bodyguard.

"I sent him to get me a Pepsi," Mary Ann said. "I thought I would be safe with Joanne."

"Good, and hi, Joanne, I'm glad that you two have had the opportunity to bond."

"So, Mary Ann was just telling me that this is how you two met: in a hospital room? Really?"

"That is almost true. I did meet the real Mary Ann Wilson while she was recovering in a Virginia hospital, but I had met the undercover Mary Ann some months before."

Joanne gave Tim a confused look but decided to move on. "I don't want you two to take this the wrong way but I have been told in no uncertain terms by my boss that I am no longer allowed to play with you two. Now, I have always had a difficult time doing what I have been told, but the bosses seemed pretty serious about it. Do you want to tell me what it is all about?"

"I haven't a clue," Mary Ann said.

"I think I know, Joanne, but what I have to tell you is completely off the record. My wife and I were sent out to San Francisco to investigate possible malfeasance at the San Francisco FBI office but, in reality, we were in fact decoys, intended to provide cover for the real agent working undercover and—"

"Maybe that is all I need to know, Tim," Joanne said, now seeming to be in a hurry. "Just tell me if Matthew Boykins really did murder Carol Russo."

"Yes, he did," Tim replied.

"So who killed Brent Wilkins while he was tied to the bed?"

"That was also Matthew" Mary Ann said. He confessed to me yesterday that he'd planned to kill Cindy Andrews but, when he found Brent bound and gagged, well, that was just too good of an opportunity to pass up."

"And there is no suspect for the murder of Sam Applewood?"

"Not that I am aware of, Joanne." Tim replied.

"Great that is all I really need to know," Joanne said as she started for the door. She stopped and turned back to Tim and Mary Ann. "Look, you two seem like very nice people and I'm sure that in another time or place we would get along great, but I need my job and so does my husband. We have two teenage boys and, to be honest, we can barely afford to live out here, not to mention that Ed and I never even see each other these days. I was told before I came here today not to associate with either of you. My boss told me that you two did something very bad, but that was all he would say. Like I said, I feel you two needed to at least know why I am ghosting you."

With that, Joanne Dombrowski left the room.

"Ghosting?" Tim asked.

"Ghosting is when a friend cuts off all contact with you on social media without explanation. Ghosting is a very big issue with Molly and Amy," Mary Ann said, referring to her children.

Tim walked over and gave Mary Ann a kiss.

"I'm sorry that I did not do that first, but I did not expect Joanne to be here."

"She is the only one who has been here except for Bobby the bodyguard."

"You mean no FBI, no Bob Fredericks, and no San Fran cops?"

"Nope, just doctors and nurses who, by the way, keep asking me if I was really swinging off the Golden Gate. They might still need to operate on my wrist, which is why they have it in this contraption."

Mary Ann motioned to the right side of the bed.

"Come and lie down next to me and tell me what is going on."

Tim kicked off his shoes and climbed into the hospital bed with his wife. Tim lay on his side facing Mary Ann.

"Why did you fight with Boykins, Mary Ann? I had a clear shot at him."

"And he had a clear shot at you, Tim. What would have happened if Boykins killed you? What would have happened to me?"

"Darrell would have taken him out."

"I don't love Darrell; I love you."

"You know, if you had fallen, I would have come after you."

"I knew that was not going to happen. I was just lucky I was able to grab the railing."

"Can anyone join this party?"

Tim turned to see a smiling Bob Fredericks standing in the doorway of the hospital room.

"Here is the man who will explain to you why we will be sneaking out of San Francisco," Tim said.

"Actually, Tim, I have someone who would like to thank both of you," Bob said as he motioned to someone in the hallway. A nurse pushed a wheelchair into the room that contained a woman wearing a veil. After the nurse left, the woman removed her disguise to reveal herself: Angela Rice. She certainly looked much better than she had earlier that day.

"Tim, Mary Ann. I felt that you were owed an explanation that only I could provide," Angela said in a raspy voice. "You'll have to excuse my voice. You see, Matthew was torturing me for much of last night. If you had not called when you did, Mary Ann, I think he would have killed me."

"Angela, you don't have to do this now. Wait until you are feeling better," Mary Ann said.

"No, I will be leaving here today to return to my assignment. Albert is waiting for me in Los Angeles and, from there, we will be going to Mexico."

"Is Albert Perez a good or bad guy?" Tim asked.

"Albert is a very good and very brave man, Tim. We were both in danger of being discovered by the drug cartels. They believe that both Albert and I are corrupt agents and, if they find out we are double agents, they'll kill us. Now, with your help and, ironically, the help of Matthew Boykins, there is no longer any suspicion."

"Besides discovering that Matthew Boykins was a creep, I'm still not sure how we helped you, Angela," Tim said.

"Let's just say that you and Mary Ann created a lot of suspicion that Angela, Bob Declan, and Albert Perez were on the take," Bob said. "The cartels now believe more than ever that both Albert and Angela are the corrupt FBI agents that they pretend to be. You see organized crime cannot succeed without corrupt officials."

"Mary Ann? I'm sorry that we tricked you into believing we were corrupt but Albert, Bob , and I were being watched at all times. That is why we pretended to recruit you in the private room of the restaurant. Their eyes were on us and you were excellent." Angela said.

"Well you had me convinced to the point of coming to arrest you this morning." Mary Ann replied as everyone pretended to laugh.

THE DECOYS

"Angela? I want to give you a hug but, as you can see, they have placed my arm in this contraption."

Bob helped Angela from the chair and over to Mary Ann, who used her free hand to hold Angela's.

"I just wanted to wish you good luck. I know what you are going through."

"Yes, Bob told me that you were undercover for two years. Maybe you and I can have a drink back in DC when all of this is over."

"Angela, we have to go," Bob said.

Angela Rice got back into her wheelchair and placed the veil over her head. She then turned to address Tim.

"Tim, when I first met you, I have to confess that I did not like you very much. Now, though"—Angela paused for a second—"now I think you are a pretty good guy."

"You are going to give him a big head, Angela, you better leave while you can," Mary Ann laughed.

After Bob and Angela had left the room, Tim turned to Mary Ann.

"You know, I hear that a lot."

"Hear what, honey?"

"It seems like people are always telling me that they did not like me at first but then come around."

"I didn't like you at first either, Tim, but now I cannot imagine my life without you."

"I guess I am just that sort of guy."

"Gosh, we sure had Angela figured wrong," Mary Ann said.

"Maybe, but maybe not. I have still not made up my mind about her or Albert or Declan for that matter."

"What do you mean by that, Tim?"

"I was struck by Bob's comment how organized crime cannot succeed without corrupt officials. If that is the case then how do we know who is honest?"

"I imagine that you just have to learn how to trust people before you try and figure them out"

"Said the policewoman who trusts no one" Tim laughed. "You know in this business, Mary Ann, you never really figure out anyone. At least, not completely. Some people are good, other people are bad, but most have a little bit of both."

"That is certainly profound, Timmy. I will have to think about that."

"Yeah, do that, Mary Ann," Tim said as he lay back down beside her. "And if you do figure it out, please let me know." With that, Tim fell asleep.

Chapter 43

Tim was awoken by Mary Ann's nurse and the doctor. He was not sure how long he had been asleep, but the light outside told him that it was late afternoon. The doctor held a pile of scans, and explained the damage to Mary Ann's wrist did not require surgery after all; at least, not at this time. He recommended that she check with an orthopedic doctor back in DC. It was also decided that Mary Ann would be kept overnight for observation. Tim meanwhile decided to take a walk and check his messages on his iPhone. He saw three from Bernard Haskell. He decided that he'd better call him back while Mary Ann was still signing forms and listening to her physician.

"Hi, Bernard, what's up?"

"It's over, buddy," Bernard exclaimed.

"Yes, I know, Bernard. I just found out the real reason my wife and I were sent here. A true wild goose chase."

"I'm not talking about that, Tim; I am referring to the contract that was placed on your life. It has been canceled! It is finished! It no longer exists! Uncle Bernard has taken care of everything."

"But I thought people were trying to kill me because they thought that I was some kind of international drug dealer?"

"The Department of Agriculture had set up a program with Colombia—the country, not DC—and there was a clause about the establishment of the security forces needed to enforce to transition from coca leaf farming to the farming of legitimate crops. With that came a list of individuals who the government felt might threaten the transition—and your name, my friend, was on top."

"My name? You have to be kidding."

"I wish I was, but I can only think that it was a holdover to when you were known as '*El Muy Malvado.*'"

"That was over twenty years ago and I was working undercover!"

"You don't have to convince me, Tim, you just need to speak with the ten or so hit men and women out to kill you; however, they should all be getting messages now stating that you no longer have a price on your head and, since the United States government will no longer pay anyone to kill you, the assassination attempts should stop. At least, theoretically."

It took Tim a few seconds to take in what Bernard had just told him. For over two weeks, Tim had been expecting to die, and he'd become resigned to that expectation. He had only hoped Mary Ann would be spared. Tim had seen too many people murdered and wondered if his desensitized attitude to death had damaged him over the years. Post-traumatic stress disorder was recognized as a disorder these days, but even that was still a recent medical development. Tim wondered if perhaps he suffered from it.

"Tim? Are you still with me?" Bernard asked.

THE DECOYS

"Yeah, Bernard. I was just thinking. So, you think it is safe for Mary Ann and me to return to our normal lives?"

"Well, I would be careful for a couple of days, Tim, just to be sure that everyone has received the news, but I'm guessing that text messages have already been sent out to the world of hired killers."

"Bernard, I don't know what to say. I guess I owe you, man."

"I'm the one who owes you, Tim. If not for you and Mary Ann, that little pick Boykins would have had me stitched up for a murder that I did not commit; the murder of a woman I really loved."

"That's OK, Bernard. By the way, are you still living at my safe house?"

"Yep! I think the two marshals taking care of your house are getting a little tired of me. Rest assured, I will be moving on very soon."

"Bernard, if it was up to me, you could become a permanent house guest; however, we are expecting company for the holidays and we—"

"I have already purchased a condo in McLean, old buddy, and will be moving in at the end of the week. That said, I certainly would not mind an invite for Christmas..."

"Consider it done, my friend," Tim replied and hung up the phone.

"So Tonto, our work here is finished?" Bob Fredericks said as he walked up behind Tim.

"Bob, I have never witnessed the agency be in such a hurry to remove personnel at the end of a mission—that is, assuming that this actually *was* a mission."

"Oh, it was a mission all right, Tim, a very important mission, and you don't know how close it came to blowing up in our faces. If Carol had—" Bob Fredericks stopped speaking, but not before Tim had heard him mention Carol Russo's name.

"If Carol had done what, Bob?" Tim asked, but he was afraid that he already knew the answer.

"Bob? Was Carol Russo blackmailing Albert Perez and Angela Rice? Was Carol threatening to reveal the fact that Perez and Angela were working undercover? Was that what this was really about?"

Bob gave Tim a very serious look; one that Tim had never witnessed before.

"Tim, the CIA does not deal with blackmailers. I hope that answers your question."

"Yes, Bob, it does," Tim replied and Bob's face returned to its normal smiley self.

"So, you have heard from Bernard about the unfortunate mix-up with the Department of Agriculture?"

"Yes, I have, Bob. So, is it safe to go back outside?"

"Yes, I think it is," Bob said as he reached into his jacket pocket and produced an envelope, which he handed to Tim. Tim opened it to see that it contained two first-class United Airlines tickets to Washington Dulles International Airport, in addition to ten thousand dollars.

"Of course, you two are welcome to fly back with me."

Although Tim did trust Bob Fredericks, he had heard too many stories of poor slobs accepting agency plane rides only to somehow make an exit at ten thousand feet without a parachute. Perhaps these were only myths, but flying commercial suited Tim just fine.

"What's with the ten Gs?" Tim asked.

"Actually, nine thousand and ninety-nine dollars. The banks have to report anything over ten. Just a little thank you gift from some very grateful San Francisco citizens," Bob said.

"And what about Mary Ann? What is her future?"

"It goes without saying, Tim, that the CIA would love for Mary Ann to come and work for us fulltime. As a matter of fact, I think the FBI would support that move."

"Are you saying that the FBI no longer wants my wife?"

"I simply feel that the FBI now thinks that we are a better fit for Mary Ann right now."

"You do know that Mary Ann likes being a cop, Bob; she really does not consider the CIA to be law enforcement."

"Which is correct, Tim, and you know that. Law enforcement organizations have to exist within the framework of federal and state laws. We, on the other hand, are not required to operate in that manner. Look, all cops and lawyers are in the revenge business. They catch and punish people who commit crimes, whereas we are just trying to make the world a better place."

Tim was not entirely sure whether the mission of the CIA was to try to make the world a better and safer place; sometimes it seemed to exist just to create chaos and confusion.

"Tim, perhaps I am not getting my point across. The FBI no longer wants your wife, Tim. They no longer trust her."

"I don't see why, Bob; besides, how can they fire Mary Ann? Especially with her record."

"Tim, if Mary Ann stays with the FBI, her next assignment will be managing a unit at the fingerprint warehouse in Clarksburg, West Virginia. That's it. Now, I can tell her or she can let the FBI tell her, but she is going to have to make a choice."

"OK, Bob, I'm sorry. Look, I do appreciate everything you have done for us."

"Tim, I need you and I need your wife. You make a good pair and, now that it looks like you may live past 2020, I have some big plans for both of you. By the way, Shelia is expecting you, Mary Ann, and the girls over on Christmas Eve. Are the girls coming in from Ohio?"

"Molly and Amy can't wait, Bob."

"Great. Now, let's get out of here."

"Just have one more thing to do, Bob, but, after that, Mary Ann and I will be on the redeye tomorrow night."

Chapter 44

It was early when Tim and Mary Ann arrived back at the Fairmount Hotel in a taxi. Tim stopped by the front desk to inform management that they would be checking out that evening. He then looked across the vast lobby and saw Darrell Murphy sitting at the same table he usually occupied. Like many others in the room, Darrell was focused on his iPhone, but Tim was sure that Darrell was aware that both he and Mary Ann had entered the room. Still, Darrell did not bother to look up when Tim approached and sat down opposite him. It was as Tim expected.

"So, tell me, Darrell, when were you planning on killing me and Mary Ann?"

"Tonight," Darrell said without looking up. "I was planning on killing you and Mrs. Hall at around nine PM."

"And how were you planning on doing that?"

"I was planning on shooting both of you in the head and then leaving the hotel. I was going to knock on your door and shoot both you and Mrs. Hall."

Darrell was now staring directly at Tim but not in an aggressive manner. Tim was impressed by how nonchalant their conversation had been so far.

"So why kill Mary Ann? She was not on any hit list, Darrell."

"Your wife would have hunted me down until she had exacted her revenge, Tim. I certainly did not want to be looking over my shoulder for the rest of my life."

"Yes, I'm afraid you are right about that, Darrell," Mary Ann said. She had approached Darrell from the rear and was holding her Glock 22 low and out of sight, keeping it aimed at Darrell's back.

"Mrs. Hall, that really is not necessary. Your husband no longer has a contract on his life. If I were to kill him, I would not be paid."

"Darrell does have a point, honey," Tim said but Mary Ann continued to aim the weapon at Darrell.

"So, Tim, how long have you known I was planning on killing you?"

"I was pretty sure of your intentions the day Brent—or I should say Sam Applewood—disappeared. I knew that he did not, as you put it, 'beat feet.'"

Darrell laughed.

"I was sure the day that nutty woman tried to push you into oncoming traffic that Brent was a phony. You should have seen him, sweating bullets as he watched you cross the street. Then he really freaked out when the woman got it instead of you. He really thought you were going to find out."

"Well, in Sam Applewood's defense, he was a bomb guy and not a professional killer. That's why I'm surprised that he did not try to blow us up again."

"Oh, believe me, Tim. He really wanted to make another bomb and that is when he tried to recruit me. The day you were extracting Bernard Haskell from the hospital, he said that he would go fifty-fifty with me. Can you believe that?

I broke the little asshole's neck then and there. I then drove him around the corner and threw him in a dumpster. I really thought that you would have figured out that I killed Brent, or whatever his name was."

"Tim, if you knew Darrell was here to kill us then why did you keep him around?" Mary Ann asked.

"Because I knew we were paying enough for him to protect us from the other hit men, Mary Ann. Darrell would have plenty of time to kill us later, once our job here was finished."

"Yes, Tim is right, Mrs. Hall. Perhaps if I had done it last night I could have collected, but *c'est la vie*," Darrell said as he stood up from the table.

"Tim, I don't expect you and I will be seeing each other again, but I did want to tell you that my intention to kill you was nothing personal. It was just business."

And with that, Darrell Murphy walked out of the San Francisco Fairmount Hotel.

"That's it?" Mary Ann said. "He just walks out of here?"

"So, you're the cop, honey. What are we supposed to do? Arrest the guy because he was thinking about murdering the two of us?"

"Well, it seems like we should do something about him."

"Sometimes problems take care of themselves, Mary Ann.

Tim and Mary Ann returned to their room and ordered lunch. They have a few hours to kill but neither felt the desire for sightseeing. They both felt that they had seen enough.

"Tim, Bob spoke with me about coming to work for the Agency fulltime."

"And what do you think about that?"

"I think I would rather be a spy than the manager of fingerprints," Mary Ann said "But I am a little sad that the FBI no longer seems to want me."

I'm afraid that FBI management feels that you have become a liability. That is how I read the situation.

"A liability? Why would they think that?"

"I am probably to blame Mary Ann. After the accident on the bridge, the FBI advised you to stay away from me but you did not. So that is one strike. Next you take an assignment in Florida with one of their golden boy senior agents who turns out to be corrupt. That is strike two. Then you come out to San Francisco to simply assist in an investigation which results in the entire Bay Area FBI office ordered to stand down by the United States Attorney General. I believe that is a first".

"OK, OK, enough. I get it but none of that was personally my fault".

"The bottom line Mary Ann is that the FBI likes agents that are team players. A good agent would not have tried to arrest Angela Rice after being told to back off.

"Yeah, I guess I see what you mean"

"Mary Ann, over the years it seems like I have met only two types of FBI agents. They are either young and dumb or old and cynical."

"Really? And which category would I fall in to?"

"Well there is a third type that falls in between young and dumb and old and cynical. I think that is where you were when I met you." Tim laughed trying to avoid a fight with

THE DECOYS

his wife. "I am just hoping you don't fall in with the old and cynical.

"I think I get what you are saying honey but who is to say I will not become the same person with the CIA?"

"You may but I'm hoping that together, you and I will make sure that does not happen to either of us.

Mary Ann turned and faced Tim. She gave him a kiss and placed her head on his shoulder.

"Darling, if you think this is the right move then count me in but I hope that Bob and you don't expect me to change."

I can't speak for Bob but I don't want you any other way."

"Tim, do you think we did anything good while we were here in San Francisco?"

"We did our jobs, Mary Ann."

"Yes, but did we do any good?"

"Let me ask you something. Do you ever think of the Kennedy assassinations?"

"I was not born when that happened," Mary Ann laughed.

"I think John and Robert Kennedy were a couple of guys whose father was a gangster. Perhaps a high end gangster but a gagster none the less. I think that their father used his influence and power to get his son John elected president. He used his mob connections to swing the union vote. After John was elected, John appoints his brother Robert attorney general and Roberts goes after organized crime like no one had ever done before—he even targeted the same people who'd helped get his brother get elected. The strange thing at least to me is that by 1968, both John and his brother Robert are murdered and someone made sure that their old man was alive to see it."

"And you are telling me that was all the Kennedy assassination were about? Some old mob guys seeking vengeance because they were double crossed?"

"Yep, that is what I think. You know, it is a little like finding out how a magician does a magic trick. At the end, when you find out that the trick was not very complicated, you are disappointed."

"If you ask me, Tim, the Kennedy assassination was a lot more complicated than that. I mean, you had the failure of the Bay of Pigs invasion, you had the Cuban Missile Crisis, you had the Cold War, you had the Civil Rights Movement and the death of Martin Luther King—"

"Yes, Mary Ann, someone did a good job of confusing everything, and we will probably never know what really happened."

Mary Ann stood and looked at her husband. He had turned around and was now staring at the San Francisco skyline. She walked up and gave him a hug. He turned and kissed her.

"How is your hand?" he asked her.

"Fine," she replied.

"Good, then let's go to the airport."

Tim decided to leave the SUV at the hotel and arranged for Hertz to come and pick it up. Tim billed the car and the hotel to the agency. The total bill was a little less than ten thousand dollars, not including the protection provided by Darrell Murphy. Tim never did find out the price on his head, but he really did not want to know. He was afraid that he might not be worth as much as he thought.

As Tim and Mary Ann made their way through the lobby, they were stopped by the hotel manager, who thanked them for their stay and hoped that they would stay again. Tim apologized for the incident involving Cindy Andrews, but the manager pretended he did not know what Tim was referring to. Tim knew there and then that Bob Fredericks had paid off the hotel.

The traffic on the 101 out to San Francisco International Airport was heavy, but Tim and Mary Ann were in no hurry. As a matter of fact, they were both exhausted and found themselves falling asleep. They were at the airport before they knew it.

"Mr. and Mrs. Hall," a voice called to them as they stepped out of the SUV, "I am Special Agent Russel Simmons and I am here to make sure you catch your flight this evening."

Agent Simmons showed his ID to both Mary Ann and Tim and they examined it carefully. Even though Tim was no longer on the hit list, it was not lost on either of them that someone could still have not received the news. Satisfied that Agent Simmons was indeed who he claimed to be, Tim and Mary Ann followed him through a series of special doors and down secret hallways. They soon found themselves at the United Airlines Priority Lounge, a room that neither Tim nor Mary Ann had ever occupied before. There were big comfy chairs and sofas, beverages, and food, and it was all for free—or, at least, someone else was paying.

"Well, this is the life," Tim remarked.

"This is the life for someone, but certainly not for us. Why are they treating us so well, honey?"

"I think someone feels bad for the trashing we're receiving back at the San Francisco FBI office, Mary Ann. They are telling everyone how we screwed up the internal investigation—the one we were pretending to do."

"Meanwhile, my reputation is being trashed back in DC."

"Mary Ann, you and I are making a difference. We came here and prevented two undercover agents from being exposed. We got a sex-crazed murderer off the streets. We saved a man from being falsely accused of a murder and removed a nutty FBI special agent."

"On the other hand, Tim, if we had not come out here, Carol Russo may still be alive, a man would not have been mistakenly killed by a bomb that was meant for us, and an FBI special agent just might have had a successful, if kinky, relationship with a cab driver."

"Now you are overthinking everything," Tim said as he leaned in to kiss Mary Ann.

"Err, excuse me?" said Special Agent Simmons. "We are pre-boarding, so if you would step this way."

Agent Simmons led Tim and Mary Ann through a long hallway and out through one of those mysterious doors one sees at airports.

"This is how we pre-board celebrities on airplanes, just in case you are wondering," Agent Simmons said as he directed Tim and Mary Ann to the Jetway.

"Here are your boarding passes. Have a safe flight," Agent Simmons said as he turned and disappeared through the same secret door.

As Tim and Mary Ann headed for the plane, Tim's iPhone rang. He saw it was Joanne Dombrowski. Mary Ann continued ahead as Tim stopped in the Jetway and answered his phone.

"I thought that we were no longer friends, Joanne."

"Tim, Tom Harvey and I are both here at Bayview Park and I got another John Doe. This time it is a large African-American male who has been shot in his face. It is hard to see, but to me he looks an awful lot like that bodyguard driver you have been with for the last several days. Can you tell me anything?"

"I'm sorry, Joanne, but I was also told by my boss to no longer exchange information with you or anyone with the SFPD. You are welcome to speak with your local FBI office. I am sure they will be happy to help you," Tim said and hung up the phone.

He continued down the Jetway and found his wife in the second row window seat drinking a glass of champagne.

"Who was that, Tim?"

"It was no one, Mary Ann. It was nothing personal. Just business. Business as usual."

Made in the USA
Coppell, TX
22 October 2021